D1568940

A
GALAXY
OF
STRANGERS

Books by Lloyd Biggle, Jr.

A GALAXY OF STRANGERS
THIS DARKENING UNIVERSE
MONUMENT
THE METALLIC MUSE
THE LIGHT THAT NEVER WAS
THE WORLD MENDERS
THE STILL, SMALL VOICE OF TRUMPETS
THE RULE OF THE DOOR, AND OTHER FANCIFUL REGULATIONS
WATCHERS OF THE DARK
THE FURY OUT OF TIME
ALL THE COLORS OF DARKNESS
THE ANGRY ESPERS

Edited by Lloyd Biggle, Jr.

NEBULA AWARD STORIES SEVEN

A
GALAXY
OF
STRANGERS

LLOYD BIGGLE, JR.

DOUBLEDAY & COMPANY, INC.
GARDEN CITY, NEW YORK, 1976

ACKNOWLEDGMENTS

And Madly Teach: first published in *The Magazine of Fantasy and Science Fiction*, May 1966. Included in *The Best from Fantasy and Science Fiction*, Sixteenth Series, edited by Edward L. Ferman (Doubleday & Company, 1967). Copyright © 1966 by Mercury Press, Inc.

The Double-Edged Rope: first published in *Analog*, June 1967. Copyright © 1967 by the Condé Nast Publications, Inc.

Eye for an Eye: first published in *The Far Side of Time*, a Science Fiction Anthology edited by Roger Elwood (Dodd, Mead & Company, 1974). Copyright © 1974 by Roger Elwood.

First Love: first published in *Amazing Science Fiction Stories*, September 1959. Copyright © 1959 by Ziff-Davis Publishing Company.

Who's on First?: first published in *If Worlds of Science Fiction*, August 1958. Included in *The Third Fireside Book of Baseball*, edited by Charles Einstein (Simon and Schuster, 1968). Copyright 1958 by Quinn Publishing Co., Inc.

Round Trip to Esidarap: first published in *If Worlds of Science Fiction*, November 1960, as *Esidarap ot pirt Dnuor*. Included in *Out of This World 3*, An Anthology of Science Fiction edited by Amabel Williams-Ellis and Mably Owen (Blackie & Son Ltd., 1962). Copyright 1960 by Digest Productions Corporation.

No Biz like Show Biz: first published in *Analog*, May 1974. Copyright © 1974 by the Condé Nast Publications, Inc.

What Hath God Wrought!: first published in *Strange Gods*, edited by Roger Elwood (Pocket Books, 1974). Copyright © 1974 by Roger Elwood.

Library of Congress Cataloging in Publication Data

Biggle, Lloyd, 1923-
    A galaxy of strangers.

    CONTENTS: Introduction.—And madly teach.—The double-edged rope. [etc.]
    1. Science fiction, American. I. Title.
PZ4.B593Gal [PS3552.I43]   813'.5'4
ISBN 0-385-12246-2
Library of Congress Catalog Card Number 76-2992

For The Workshoppers

Kathy Albaugh
Peter Hubbard
Ted Reynolds
Sally A. Sellers
Lawrence Tucker

Contents

Introduction

DOOMSDAY, ANYONE?

As long ago as the 1930s, Bernard DeVoto was grumbling about science fiction stories "which deal with both the World and the Universe of To-morrow and . . . take no great pleasure in either." "Prognosticators of doom" is one of the milder captions applied to those of us who have the temerity to set our stories in the future. Our defenders—outside the boundaries of science fiction—have been few, and the kindest excuse they've been able to offer for what even they consider our excessive morbidity has been to point out diffidently that, well, a future where everything is sweetness and light and milk and honey would make for rather insipid stories, wouldn't it?

To any impartial arbiter, the looming catastrophes to which science fiction condemns an ill-starred humanity must seem grossly overdone. A cross section of science fiction concerned with tomorrow and the year or two after would offer horrific subject matter dealing with crime in the streets; with cities so unsafe after dark that one walks a dog or strolls to the neighborhood drugstore at the risk of one's life; with a tragic disparity of wealth; with the failure of our educational system; with the diminution of personal liberties; with our esteemed democratic processes perverted by unscrupulous or corrupt politicians; with an advertising industry blatantly and dishonestly attempting to manipulate human values; with Earth's beauty and bounty laid waste by the greed of large corporations; with the very air we breathe imperiled by pollution; with life prolonged meaninglessly if not tragically by medical science; with the elderly in dire want, their savings and pensions eroded by inflation, living on into old, old age in stark misery; with automated factories pouring out luxury goods that huge numbers of citizens can't buy because they're unemployed; with the decline of the work ethic and the appeasement of the idle masses with prime-time gladiator shows; with craftsmanship so deteriorated that nothing can be purchased with any assurance that it will function; with repair services blunderingly incompetent and exorbitantly expensive—this is no more than the beginning of a list.

It does indeed sound like a morbid prognostication of doom. Unfortunately, it is not. Neither is it science fiction. This is the present, as delineated by your daily newspaper.

More than one science fiction writer has said this: "We are not predicting; we are writing to keep these things from happening." Obviously we have failed. Today we are living yesterday's science fiction —its glowing predictions of technological marvels and its gloomy prognostications of social catastrophe. Both have come true.

Consider these few examples:

• The failure of our educational system. When I was a high school student in Waterloo, Iowa, more years ago than either I or my classmates care to count, a teacher startled my social studies class with the question, "Do we graduate morons from East High?" The answer was yes—but at that time the moron was considered the exceptional case. Today's schools must cope with another dimension of moronism, the functional moron whose retardation is educational rather than mental. As a result, the moron with a high school or even a college diploma is not uncommon. Tomorrow he will be in the majority. U. S. Office of Education statistics: Twenty per cent of adult Americans are so sketchily educated that they are unable to cope with such routine activities as shopping or getting a driver's license. Another thirty-four per cent barely gets by. This adds up to more than half, and the deficiency trend is upward, at an alarming rate. Achievement tests given regularly throughout our school systems continue to show this deterioration at every age level. The future described in C. M. Kornbluth's *The Marching Morons* is not yet upon us, but we are advancing toward it at an accelerating pace.

Are educators to blame for the decline? They have the onerous task of educating our first television generation—the generation of children raised on TV from babyhood—as well as coping with extremely difficult and changing social conditions. High school teachers tell me that their students will not do homework—"When they walk out the door, that's it!" Discipline among our young people has so deteriorated that too frequently teachers' lives are in danger in their own classrooms—yesterday's prognostication of doom; today's reality. Many students have jobs, feel affluent, and regard the time spent in school as wasted.

As evidence of how reading and writing skills have deteriorated, one teacher of high school literature told me that stories formerly assigned for reading at home or during study periods now must be read aloud to the students. The story *And Madly Teach* was first written in 1957. The resultant of the educational system it describes is already with us; the cause may follow.

• Our esteemed democratic processes perverted. The entire, reeking, convoluted mess that we now label Watergate is sheer science fiction. A standard science fictional technique consists of taking certain trends and projecting them into the future, in effect saying, "If this goes on, here is what might happen." For example, if population growth continues at the present rate, this is what life on Earth might be like in the year 2076. Notice the "if" and the "might." These are not predictions. By focusing public attention on genuine dangers, we wistfully hope to make our minute contribution toward preventing the catastrophes we describe.

All of the various trends of Watergate—corruption in campaign management and contributions, abuses of governmental power, the permissible lie in politics, bribery, influence peddling, and so on—all of these things had been increasingly present in our government for years, and it would have been possible, say, in 1970, for a science fiction writer to put them together and project them to describe a fictitious Watergate happening about the year 2020. But in 1970 it would have been extremely difficult to make this fictitious Watergate convincing, and the result probably would have been a rather inept science fiction novel.

Then chance brought together the right men at the right time, or the wrong men at the wrong time, and what occurred was nothing less than a mutation in morality and ethics at the highest level of our government. The unbelievable science fiction tale of the future suddenly became a terrifying true adventure of the present.

• In 1975, the state of Michigan added a new dimension to its state lottery: the instant winner. You rub your ticket with a coin and read off your winnings (if any). With the smaller prizes, a winning ticket can be cashed at once, with the merchant who sold it.

The instant-winner lottery already has spawned a new psychosis: lottery addiction. Recently I watched an elderly couple eagerly buy five tickets. Without leaving the counter they rubbed the numbers into view and found they'd beaten the odds by having two two-dollar prizes. They cashed the tickets and used the money to buy four more tickets, which won them another two dollars. They bought two more tickets, both of them nonwinners, and sadly went their way—having had five minutes of entertainment that cost them a mere dollar a minute. A recent newspaper story described the experience of a man who went that same route—but with five hundred dollars, not five dollars—and the current jokes about parlaying a two-hundred-dollar paycheck into three hundred worthless lottery tickets merely underscore the close relationship between comedy and tragedy.

There is hoopla enough with a state lottery, including million-dollar winners, but eventually it dawns on most people that their chances of winning anything substantial are dim indeed. (State lotteries are in fact ripoffs in the form of voluntary taxation—one can get better gambling odds at Vegas.) More hoopla is required to restimulate interest—a new kind of prize, or, as with Michigan's instant winning tickets, a new kind of game. When the National Lottery finally arrives—and don't think our national legislators will ignore forever the enormous profits to state treasuries produced by the local lotteries—there will be a veritable end all hoopla. People will be gambling for a zillion, or the moon, or a brief reign as God. You read it here first.

Down through the centuries, few human activities have been more universally condemned than gambling, for sound reasons. Now governments are following the lead of churches not merely in condoning gambling but also in encouraging it—as long as they can turn a profit on it. And if a government promotes gambling for its own profit, what won't it do for profit?

I remember a discussion of D. H. Lawrence in a college lit class, when a student said to the professor, "He was such a nice little old man—how could he have such thoughts?"

Science fiction writers, too, number many eminently respectable—even nice—individuals in their ranks. Where do they get those horrific thoughts that make them prognosticators of doom?

Arthur C. Clarke once remarked that most other literature isn't concerned with reality. Look around you. Science fiction authors are realists.

Ypsilanti, Michigan
December 1975

A
GALAXY
OF
STRANGERS

AND MADLY TEACH

Miss Mildred Boltz clasped her hands and exclaimed, "What a lovely school!"

It shimmered delightfully in the bright morning sunlight, a pale, delicate blue-white oasis of color that lay gemlike amidst the nondescript towers and domes and spires of the sprawling metropolitan complex.

But even as she spoke, she qualified her opinion. The building's form was boxlike, utilitarian, ugly. Only its color made it beautiful.

The aircab driver had been muttering to himself because he'd drifted into a wrong lane and missed his turn. He looked at her quickly. "I beg your pardon?"

"The school," Miss Boltz said. "It has a lovely color."

They threaded their way through an interchange, circled, and maneuvered into the proper lane. Then the driver turned to her again. "I've heard of schools. They used to have some out West. But that isn't a school."

Miss Boltz met his serious gaze confusedly and hoped she wasn't blushing. It wasn't proper for a woman of her age to blush. She said, "I must have misunderstood you. I thought that was—"

"Yes, ma'am. That's the address you gave me."

"Then—of course it's a school! I'm a teacher. I'm going to teach there."

He shook his head. "No, ma'am. We don't have any schools."

The descent was so unsettlingly abrupt that Miss Boltz had to swallow her protests and clutch at her safety belt. Then they were in the ground-level parking area, and he had the door open. She stepped out with the dignity demanded of a middle-aged schoolteacher, paid him, and turned toward the building. She would have liked to investigate this queer notion of his about schools, but she didn't want to be late for her appointment. And anyway—the idea! If it wasn't a school, what was it?

In the maze of lettered and double-lettered corridors, each turning she took seemed to be the wrong one. She was breathing heavily and fighting off a mild seizure of panic when she finally reached her destination. A receptionist took her name and said severely, "Mr. Wilbings is expecting you. Go right in."

The office door bore a bristling label: ROGER A. WILBINGS. DEPUTY SUPERINTENDENT OF EDUCATION (SECONDARY). NORTHEASTERN UNITED STATES SCHOOL DISTRICT. PRIVATE. Miss Boltz hesitated, and the receptionist said again, "Go right in."

"Thank you," Miss Boltz said. With fumbling fingers, she managed to open the door.

The gentleman behind the desk at the distant center of the room seemed to have adopted a fiercely blank expression for her. She moved forward timorously, and the expression resolved itself into the hair-framed oval of a bald head. She blinked her eyes, wishing she'd worn her contact lenses. Mr. Wilbings's attention was fixed upon the papers that littered the top of his desk, and he indicated a chair for her without bothering to look up. She approached the desk tightrope-fashion and seated herself.

"One moment, please," he said.

She ordered herself to relax. She was not a recent college graduate, hoping desperately for a first job. She had a contract and twenty-five years of tenure, and she was merely reporting for reassignment.

Her nerves disregarded the order.

Mr. Wilbings gathered up his papers, tapped them together, and returned them to a folder. "Miss—ah—Boltz," he said. His curiously affected appearance fascinated her. He was wearing spectacles, a contrivance that she hadn't seen for years; and he had a trim little patch of hair on his upper lip, the like of which she had never seen outside of films and theatricals. He held his head thrust forward and tilted back, and he sighted at her distastefully along the high arc of his nose.

He nodded suddenly and turned back to his desk. "I've gone through your file, Miss—ah—Boltz." He pushed the folder aside impatiently. "My recommendation is that you retire. My secretary will give you the necessary papers to fill out. Good morning."

The suddenness of the attack startled her out of her nervousness. She said calmly, "I appreciate your interest, Mr. Wilbings, but I have no intention of retiring. Now—about my new assignment."

"My dear Miss Boltz!" He had decided to be nice to her. His expression altered perceptibly and hovered midway between a smile and a sneer. "It is your own welfare that concerns me. I understand that your retirement might occasion some financial sacrifice, and under the circumstances I feel that we could obtain an appropriate adjustment in your pension. It would leave you secure and free to do what you like, and I can assure you that you are not—" He paused and tapped his desk with one finger. "—*not* suited for teaching. Painful as the idea may be for you, it is the blunt truth, and the sooner you realize that—"

For one helpless moment she could not control her laughter. He broke off angrily and stared at her.

"I'm sorry," she said, dabbing at her eyes. "I've been a teacher for twenty-five years—a good teacher, as you know if you've checked over my efficiency reports. Teaching is my whole life, and I love it, and it's a little late to be telling me that I'm not suited for it."

"Teaching is a young people's profession, and you are nearly fifty. And then—we must consider your health."

"Which is perfectly good," she said. "Of course I had cancer of the lung. It's common on Mars. It's caused by the dust, you know, and it's easily cured."

"You had it four times, according to your records."

"I had it four times, and I was cured four times. I returned to Earth only because the doctors felt that I was unusually susceptible to Martian cancer."

"Teaching on Mars—" He gestured disdainfully. "You've never taught anywhere else, and at the time you were in training your college was specializing in training teachers for Mars. There's been a revolution in education, Miss Boltz, and it has completely passed you by." He tapped his desk again, sternly. "You are not suited for teaching. Certainly not in this district."

She said stubbornly, "Will you honor my contract, or do I have to resort to legal action?"

He shrugged and picked up her file. "Written and spoken English. Tenth grade. I assume you think you can handle that."

"I can handle it."

"Your class meets from ten-fifteen to eleven-fifteen, Monday through Friday."

"I'm not interested in part-time teaching," she said.

"This is a full-time assignment."

"Five hours a week?"

"The position assumes forty hours of class preparation. You'll probably need much more than that."

"I see," she said. She never had felt more bewildered.

"Classes begin next Monday. I'll assign you to a studio and arrange an engineering conference for you immediately."

"A—*studio?*"

"Studio." There was a note of malicious satisfaction in his voice. "You will have approximately forty thousand students."

From a drawer he took two books, one a ponderous volume entitled *Techniques and Procedures in TV Teaching*, and the other, mecha-typed and bound with a plastic spiral, a course outline of tenth-grade English, Northeastern United States School District. "These should contain all the information you'll need," he said.

Miss Boltz said falteringly, "TV teaching? Then—my students will attend class by television?"

"Certainly."

"Then I'll never see them."

"They will see you, Miss Boltz. That is quite sufficient."

"I suppose the examinations will be machine graded, but what about papers? I couldn't get through one assignment in an entire semester."

He scowled at her. "There are no assignments. There are no examinations, either. I suppose the educational system on Mars still uses examinations and assignments to coerce its students into learning, but we have progressed beyond those dark ages of education. If you have some idea of bludgeoning your material into your students with examinations and papers and the like, forget it. Those things are symptomatic of bad teaching, and we would not permit them even if it were possible, which it isn't."

"If there are no examinations or papers, and if I never see my students, how can I evaluate the results of my teaching?"

"We have our own method for that. You receive a Trendex rating every two weeks. Is there anything else?"

"Just one thing." She smiled faintly. "Would you mind telling me why you so obviously resent my presence here?"

"I wouldn't mind," he answered indifferently. "You have an obsolete contract that we have to honor, but we know that you will not last out the term. When you leave we will have the problem of finding a midyear replacement for you, and forty thousand students will have been subjected to several weeks of bad instruction. You can hardly blame us for taking the position that it would be better for you to retire now. If you change your mind before Monday, I'll guarantee full retirement benefits for you. If not, remember this. The courts have upheld our right to retire a teacher for incompetence, regardless of tenure."

Mr. Wilbings's secretary gave her a room number. "This will be your office," she said. "Wait there, and I'll send someone."

It was a small room with a desk, book shelves, a filing cabinet, a book-film cabinet, and a film reader. A narrow window looked out onto long rows of narrow windows. On the wall opposite the desk was a four-foot TV screen. It was the first office Miss Boltz had ever had, and she sat at her desk with the drab brown walls frowning down at her and felt lonely, and humble, and not a little frightened.

The telephone rang. After a frantic search she located it under a panel in the desktop, but by then it had stopped ringing. She examined the desk further and found another panel that concealed the TV controls. There were four dials, each with numbers zero through nine. With a minimum of calculating she deduced the possible number of channels as 9,999. She tried various numbers and got a blank screen except for channel 0001, on which a printed announcement was displayed: CLASSES BEGIN MONDAY, SEPTEMBER 9. REGISTRATION IS NOW IN PROGRESS. YOU MUST BE REGISTERED TO RECEIVE GRADUATION CREDITS.

A knock sounded on her door. It was a kindly looking, graying man of fifty plus, who introduced himself as Jim Pargrin, chief engineer. He seated himself on the edge of her desk and grinned down at her. "I was afraid you'd lost yourself. I telephoned, and no one answered."

"By the time I found the telephone, you'd hung up," Miss Boltz said.

He chuckled, and then he spoke seriously. "So you're the Martian. Do you know what you're getting into?"

"Did they send you up here to frighten me?"

"I don't frighten anyone but the new engineers. I just wondered— but never mind. Come over to your studio, and I'll explain the setup."

They turned a corner and quickly left the rows of offices behind them. Now each room they passed featured an enormous glass window facing on the corridor. Miss Boltz was reminded of the aquarium on Mars, where she sometimes took her students to show them the strange marine life of Earth.

Pargrin unlocked a door and handed her the key. "Six-four-three-nine. A long way from your office, but at least it's on the same floor."

A hideous black desk with stubby metal legs squatted in front of a narrow blackboard. The camera stared down from the opposite wall, and beside it was a pilot screen. Pargrin unlocked a control box, touched a switch, and abruptly the lights blinded her.

"Because you're an English teacher, they figure you don't need any special equipment," he said. "See these buttons on the desk? Number one gives you a shot of the desk and the blackboard and just about the space enclosed by those lines on the floor. Number two is a closeup of the desk. Number three is a closeup of the blackboard. Ready to try it out?"

"I don't understand."

He touched another switch. "There."

The pilot screen flickered to life. Miss Boltz faced it—faced the dumpy looking, middle-aged woman who stared back at her—and thought she looked cruelly old. The dress she had purchased with such care and for too much money the day before was a blur of repulsive colors. Her face was shockingly pale. She told herself sadly that she really should have spent more time on the sun deck, coming back from Mars.

"Try number two," Pargrin suggested.

She seated herself at the desk and pressed button number two. The camera twitched, and she contemplated the closeup of herself and shuddered. Number three, with herself at the blackboard, was equally bad.

Pargrin switched off the camera and closed the control box. "Here by the door is where you check in," he said. "If you haven't pressed this button by ten-fifteen, your class is automatically canceled. And you must leave immediately when your class is over at eleven-fifteen, so the next teacher can get ready for the eleven-thirty class. Except that it's considered good manners to clean the blackboard and tidy things up. The stuff is in the desk. Everything clear?"

"I suppose," she said. "Unless you can tell me how I'm to teach written and spoken English without ever hearing my students speak or reading anything that they write."

He walked by her side in silence until they reached the door of her office. She opened it and turned to face him.

"I know what you mean," he said. "Things were different when we were kids. TV was something you watched when your folks let you, and you went to school with all the other kids. But it's changed, now, and it seems to work well this way. At least, the big shots say it does. Anyway—the best of luck to you."

She returned to her desk and thoughtfully opened *Techniques and Procedures in TV Teaching.*

At five minutes after ten o'clock on the following Monday morning, Miss Boltz reached her studio and pressed the button to check in. She was rewarded with a white light over the pilot screen. She seated herself at the desk, and after pressing button number two, she folded her hands and waited.

At precisely ten-fifteen the white light changed to red, the camera lights blazed, and from the pilot screen her own image looked down on her disapprovingly. "Good morning," she said. "This is tenth-grade English. I am Miss Boltz."

She had decided to devote that first class period to introducing herself. Although she couldn't become acquainted with her thousands of students, she felt that they should know something about her. She owed them that much.

She talked about her years of teaching on Mars—how the students attended school together, how there were only twenty or twenty-five students in one room instead of forty thousand attending class by way of as many TV sets. She described the recess period, when the students who went outside the dome to play had to wear air masks in order to breathe. She told them about the field trips, when the class, or perhaps the entire school, went outside the dome to study Martian plant life or rocks and soil formations. She told them some of the questions her Martian students liked to ask about Earth.

The minutes dragged tediously. She felt imprisoned under the unblinking eye of the camera, and her image on the pilot screen began to look haggard and frightened. The steady warmth of the lights soon had her perspiring. She had not realized that teaching could be such a strain.

The end of the hour came as a death throes. She smiled weakly, and from the pilot screen a hideous caricature of a smile grimaced back at her. "I'll be seeing you tomorrow," she said. "Good morning."

The red light changed to white. Miss Boltz took a last, shuddering look at the camera and fled.

She was seated at her desk, forlornly fighting to hold back her tears, when Jim Pargrin looked in on her.

"What's the matter?" he asked.

"Just wishing I'd stayed on Mars."

"Why would you be wishing that? You got off to a very good start."

"I didn't think so."

"I did." He smiled at her. "We took a sample Trendex on you this morning, during the last ten minutes. We sometimes do that with a new teacher. Most students will start off with their assigned classes, but if the teacher isn't good they switch to something else in a hurry. So we check at the end of the first hour to see how a new teacher is doing. Wilbings asked for a Trendex on you, and he came down to watch us take it. I think he was disappointed." He chuckled slyly. "It was just a fraction under one hundred, which is practically perfect."

He departed before she could thank him. She turned to her desk again, her gloom dispelled as if by magic. Cheerfully she plunged into the task of rewriting the outline of tenth-grade English.

She had no objection to the basic plan, which was comprehensive and well constructed and at times almost logical. But the examples, the meager list of stories and novels and dramas supplied for study and supplemental reading—these were unbelievable. Just unbelievable.

"Recommended drama," the outline said. "*You Can't Marry an Elephant,* by H. N. Varga. This delightful farce—"

She crossed it out with firm strokes of her pen and wrote in the margin, "W. Shakespeare, *The Merchant of Venice.*" She substituted Dickens's *A Tale of Two Cities* for *Saddle Blankets and Six Guns,* a thrilling novel of the Old West, by Percivale Oliver. She found no unit at all that concerned itself with poetry, so she created one. Her pen slashed its way relentlessly through the outline, and her conscience troubled her not at all. Didn't the manual say that originality was encouraged in teachers?

The next morning, when she started down the corridor toward her studio, she was no longer nervous.

The vast unfriendliness of the building and the drab solitude of her office so depressed her that she decided to prepare her classes in her apartment. Not until the middle of the third week did she find her way to the tenth floor, where, according to her manual, there was a cafeteria. As she awaited her turn at the vending machines, the young teachers who silently surrounded her made her feel positively prehistoric.

A hand waved at her when she turned toward the tables. Jim Pargrin bounded to his feet and took her tray. A younger man helped her with her chair. After so many hours of solitude, the sudden attention left her breathless.

"My nephew," Pargrin said. "Lyle Stewart. Miss Boltz. She's the teacher from Mars. Lyle teaches physics."

He was a dark-complexioned, good-looking young man with a ready smile. She said she was pleased to meet him and meant it. "Why, you're the first teacher I've spoken to!" she exclaimed.

"Mostly we ignore each other," Stewart agreed. "It's strictly a survival-of-the-fittest occupation."

"But I'd think that some kind of co-operation—"

Stewart shook his head. "Supposing you come up with something that clicks. You have a high Trendex, and the other teachers notice.

So they watch your class, and if they can steal your stuff they will. Then you watch them, to see if they have something you can steal, and you see them using your technique. Naturally you don't like it. We've had teachers involved in assault cases, and lawsuits, and varying degrees of malicious mischief. At best, we just don't speak to each other."

"How do you like it here?" Pargrin asked her.

"I miss the students," Miss Boltz said. "It worries me, not being able to know them or check on their progress."

"Let's not be dragging in abstractions like *progress*," Stewart said bitterly. "The New Education looks at it this way: We expose the child to the proper subject matter. The exposure takes place in his own home, which is the most natural environment for him. He will absorb whatever his individual capacity permits, and more than that we have no right to expect."

"The child has no sense of accomplishment—no incentive to learn," she protested.

"More irrelevant abstractions. What the New Education strives for is the technique that has made advertising such an important factor in our economy. Hold the people's attention, make them buy in spite of themselves. Or hold the student's attention and make him learn whether he wants to or not."

"But the student learns no social values!"

Stewart shrugged. "On the other hand, the school has no discipline problems. No extracurricular activities to supervise. No problem of transporting children to school and home again. You aren't convinced?"

"Certainly not!"

"Keep it to yourself. And just between us, I'll tell you the most potent factor in this philosophy of the New Education. It's money. Instead of a fortune invested in buildings and real estate, with thousands of schools to maintain, we have one TV studio. We save another fortune in teachers' salaries by having one teacher for a good many thousands of students instead of one for maybe twenty or thirty. The bright kids will learn no matter how badly they're taught, and that's all our civilization needs—a few bright people to build a lot of bright machines. And the school tax rate is the lowest it's been in the last century and a half." He pushed back his chair. "Nice to meet you, Miss Boltz. Maybe we can be friends. Since you're an English teacher, and I teach physics, we aren't likely to steal from each other. Now I have to go think up some new tricks. My Trendex is way down."

She watched thoughtfully as he walked away. "He looks as if he's been working too hard," she announced.

"Most teachers don't have contracts like yours," Pargrin said. "They can be dismissed at any time. Lyle wants to go into industry after this year, and he'll have a tough time finding a job if he's fired."

"He's leaving teaching? That's a shame!"

"There's no future in it."

"There's always a future for a good teacher."

Pargrin shook his head. "Look around you. The teachers are all young. They hang on as long as they can, because the pay is very good, but there comes a time when security means more than money. Anyway, in the not too distant future there won't be any teachers. Central District is experimenting now with filmed classes. Take a good teacher, film a year of his work, and you don't need the teacher any longer. You just run the films. No, there's very little future in teaching. Did you get your copy of the Trendex ratings?"

"Why, no. Should I have gotten one?"

"They come out every two weeks. They were distributed yesterday."

"I didn't get one."

He swore under his breath, and then he looked at her apologetically. "Wilbings can be downright deceitful when he wants to. He probably thinks he'll take you by surprise."

"I'm afraid I don't understand these ratings."

"There's nothing complicated about them. Over a two-week period we'll take a thousand samples of a teacher's students. If all of them are watching their assigned class, as they should be, the teacher's Trendex is one hundred. If only half are watching, then the Trendex is fifty. A good teacher will have about a fifty Trendex. If a teacher's Trendex falls below twenty, he's dismissed. Incompetence."

"Then the children don't have to watch their classes unless they want to?"

"The parents have to provide the TV sets," Pargrin said. "They have to see that their children are present during their assigned class hours—'in attendance,' it's called—but they aren't responsible for making them watch any particular class. They'd have to supervise them every minute if that were so, and the courts have held that this would be unreasonable. It also would be unreasonable to require sets that worked only on assigned channels, and even if that were done the students still could watch classes on the channels they're supposed to use at another time. So the students are there, and their sets are on, but if they don't like your class they can watch something else. So it's extremely important for the teacher to make the classes interesting."

"I understand. What was my Trendex?"

He looked away. "Zero."

"You mean—*no one* is watching me? I thought I was doing well."

"You must have done something that interested them that first day. Perhaps they just got tired of it. That happens. Have you watched any of the other teachers?"

"Goodness, no! I've been so busy I just never thought of it."

"Lyle may have some ideas for you. I'll ask him to meet us at your office for the two-o'clock class. And then—well, we'll see."

Lyle Stewart spread some papers on the desk in front of her and bent over them. "These are the Trendex ratings," he said. "You were supposed to get a copy."

She glanced down the list of names and picked out hers. Boltz, Mildred. English, tenth grade. Time, 10:15. Channel 6439. Zero. Year's average, zero.

"The subject has something to do with the tricks you can use," Stewart said. "Here's a Marjorie McMillan at two o'clock. She teaches eleventh-grade English, and her Trendex is sixty-four. That's very high. Let's see how she does it." He set the dials.

At precisely two o'clock Marjorie McMillan appeared, and Miss Boltz's first horrified impression was that she was disrobing. Her shoes and stockings were piled neatly on the floor. She was in the act of unbuttoning her blouse. She glanced up at the camera and recoiled in mock fright.

"What are you cats and toms doing in here?" she cooed. "I thought I was alone."

She was a trim blonde, with a flashy, brazen kind of prettiness. Her profile displayed sensational curves. She smiled, tossed her head, and started to tiptoe away.

"Oh, well, as long as I'm among friends—"

The blouse came off. So did the skirt. She stood before them in an alluringly brief costume that consisted exclusively of shorts and a halter. The camera recorded its scarlet and gold colors brilliantly. She pranced about in a shuffling dance step, flicking the switch for a closeup of the blackboard as she danced past her desk.

"Time to go to work, all you cats and toms," she said. "This is called a sentence." She read aloud as she wrote on the blackboard. "The—man—ran—down—the—street. 'Ran down the street' is what the man did. We call that the predicate. Funny word, isn't it? Are you with me?"

Miss Boltz uttered a bewildered protest. "*Eleventh*-grade English?"

"Yesterday we talked about verbs," Marjorie McMillan said. "Do you remember? I'll bet you weren't paying attention. I'll bet you aren't even paying attention now."

Miss Boltz gasped. The halter suddenly came unfastened. Its ends flapped loosely, and Miss McMillan snatched at it as it started to fall. "Nearly lost it that time," she said. "Maybe I will lose it, one of these days. And you wouldn't want to miss that, would you? Better pay attention. Now let's take another look at that nasty old predicate."

Miss Boltz said quietly, "A little out of the question for me, isn't it?"

Stewart darkened the screen. "Her high rating won't last," he said. "As soon as her students decide she's really not going to lose that thing—but let's look at this one. Tenth-grade English. A male teacher. Trendex is forty-five."

He was young, reasonably good-looking, and clever. He balanced chalk on his nose. He juggled erasers. He did imitations. He took up the reading of that modern classic, *Saddle Blankets and Six Guns*, and he read very well, acting out parts of it, creeping behind his desk to point an imaginary six-gun at the camera. It was quite realistic.

"The kids will like him," Stewart said. "He'll probably last pretty well. Now let's see if there's anyone else."

There was a history teacher, a sedate-looking young woman with a brilliant artistic talent. She drew sketches and caricatures with amazing ease and pieced them together with sprightly conversation. There was an economics teacher who performed startling magic tricks with cards and money. There were two young women whose routines approximated that of Marjorie McMillan, though in a more subdued manner. Their ratings also were much lower.

"That's enough to give you an idea of what you're up against," Stewart said.

"A teacher who can't do anything but teach is frightfully handicapped," Miss Boltz said thoughtfully. "These teachers are just performers. They aren't teaching their students—they're entertaining them."

"They have to cover the subject matter of their courses. If the students watch, they can't help learning *something*."

Jim Pargrin had remained silent while they switched from channel to channel. Now he stood up and shook his graying head solemnly. "I'll check engineering. Perhaps we could show some films for you.

Normally that's frowned upon, because we haven't the staff or the facilities to do it for everyone, but I think I could manage it."

"Thank you," she said. "That's very kind of you. And thank you, Lyle, for helping out with a lost cause."

"The cause is never lost while you're still working," he said.

They left together. Long after the door closed after them, Miss Boltz sat looking at the blank TV screen and wondering how long she would be working.

For twenty-five years on barren, inhospitable Mars she had dreamed of Earth. She had dreamed of walking barefoot on the green grass, with green trees and shrubs around her; and over her head, instead of the blurring transparency of an atmosphere dome, the endless expanse of blue sky. She had stood in the bleak Martian deserts and dreamed of high-tossing ocean waves racing toward a watery horizon.

Now she was back on Earth, living in the unending city complex of Eastern United States. Streets and buildings impinged upon its tiny parks. The blue sky was almost obscured by air traffic. She had glimpsed the ocean once, from an aircab.

But they were there for the taking, the green fields and the lakes and rivers and ocean. She had only to go to them. Instead, she had worked. She had slaved over her class materials. She had spent hours writing and revising and gathering her examples, and more hours rehearsing herself meticulously, practicing over and over her single hour of teaching before she exposed it to the devouring eye of the camera.

And no one had been watching. During those first two weeks her students had turned from her by the tens and hundreds and thousands, until she had lost them all.

She shrugged off her humiliation and took up the teaching of *The Merchant of Venice*. Jim Pargrin helped out personally, and she was able to run excellent films of background material and scenes from the play.

She said sadly, "Isn't it a shame to show these wonderful things when no one is watching?"

"*I'm* watching," Pargrin said. "I enjoy them."

His kindly eyes made her wistful for something she remembered from long ago—the handsome young man who had seen her off to Mars and looked at her in very much the same way as he promised to join her when he completed his engineering studies. He'd kissed her good-bye, and the next thing she heard he'd been killed in a freak accident. There were long years between affectionate glances for Miss Mildred Boltz, but she'd never thought of them as empty years. She had never thought of teaching as an unrewarding occupation until she found herself in a small room with only a camera looking on.

Pargrin called her when the next Trendex ratings came out. "Did you get a copy?"

"No," she said.

"I'll find an extra one and send it up."

He did, but she knew without looking that the rating of Boltz, Mildred, English, tenth grade, and so on, was still zero.

She searched the libraries for books on the technique of TV teaching. They were replete with examples concerning those subjects that lent themselves readily to visual presentation, but they offered very little assistance in the teaching of tenth-grade English.

She turned to the education journals and probed the mysteries of the New Education. She read about the sanctity of the individual and the right of the student to an education in his own home, undisturbed by social distractions. She read about the psychological dangers of competition in learning and the evils of artificial standards; about the dangers of old-fashioned group teaching and its sinister contribution to delinquency.

Pargrin brought in another Trendex rating. She forced herself to smile. "Zero again?"

"Well—not exactly."

She stared at the paper, blinked, and stared again. Her rating was .1—one tenth of one per cent. Breathlessly she performed some mental arithmetic. She had one student! At that moment she would have waived all of her retirement benefits for the privilege of meeting that one loyal youngster.

"What do you suppose they'll do?" she asked.

"That contract of yours isn't anything to trifle with. Wilbings won't take any action until he's certain he has a good case."

"It's nice to know that I have a student," she said and added wistfully, "Do you suppose there are any more?"

"Why don't you ask them to write to you? If you got a lot of letters, you could use them for evidence."

"I'm not concerned about evidence," she said, "but I will ask them to write. Thank you."

"Miss—ah—Mildred—"

"Yes?"

"Nothing. I mean, would you like to have dinner with me tonight?"

"I'd love to."

A week went by before she finally asked her students to write. She knew only too well why she hesitated. She was afraid there would be no response.

But the morning came when she finished her class material with a minute to spare, and she folded her hands and forced a smile at the camera. "I'd like to ask you a favor. I want each of you to write me a letter. Tell me about yourself. Tell me how you like the things we've been studying. You know all about me, and I don't know anything about you. Please write to me."

She received eleven letters. She handled them reverently, and read them lovingly, and she began her teaching of A *Tale of Two Cities* with renewed confidence.

She took the letters to Jim Pargrin, and when he'd finished reading them she said, "There must be thousands like them—bright, eager children who would love to learn if they weren't drugged into a kind of passive indifference by all this entertainment."

"Have you heard anything from Wilbings?"

"Not a thing."

"He asked me to base your next Trendex on two thousand samples. I told him I'd need a special order from the board. I doubt if he'll bother."

"He must be getting ready to do something about me."

"I'm afraid so," Pargrin said. "We really should start thinking of some line of defense for you. You'll need a lawyer."

"I don't know if I'll offer any defense. I've been wondering if I shouldn't try to set myself up as a private teacher."

Pargrin shook his head. "There are private schools, you know. Those that could afford it would send their children there. Those that couldn't wouldn't be able to pay you, either."

"Just the same, when I have some time I'm going to call on the children who wrote to me."

"The next Trendex is due Monday," Pargrin said. "You'll probably hear from Wilbings then."

Wilbings sent for her on Monday morning. She had not seen him since that first day, but his absurd appearance and testy mannerisms had impressed themselves firmly upon her memory. "Are you familiar with the Trendex ratings?" he asked her.

Because she knew that he had deliberately attempted to keep her in ignorance, she shook her head innocently. Her conscience did not protest.

He patiently explained the technique and its purpose.

"If the Trendex is as valuable as you say it is," she said, "why don't you let the teachers know what their ratings are?"

"But they do know. They receive a copy of every rating."

"I received none."

"Probably an oversight, since this is your first term. However, I have all of them except today's, and that one will be sent down as soon as it's ready. You're welcome to see them."

He went over each report in turn, ceremoniously pointing out her zeros. When he reached the rating of .1, he paused. "You see, Miss Boltz, out of the thousands of samples taken, we have found only one student who was watching you. This is by far the worst record we have ever had. I must ask you to retire voluntarily, and if you refuse, then I have no alternative—"

He broke off as his secretary tiptoed in with the new Trendex. "Yes. Thank you. Here we are. Boltz, Mildred—"

His finger wavered comically. Paralysis seemed to have clogged his power of speech. Miss Boltz found her name and followed the line across the page to her rating.

It was twenty-seven.

"Evidently I've improved," she heard herself say. "Is there anything else?"

His voice, when he finally was able to speak, had risen perceptibly in pitch. "No. Nothing else."

As she went through the outer office she heard his voice again, still high-pitched, squawking angrily from his secretary's communicator. "Pargrin. I want Pargrin down here immediately."

He was waiting for her in the cafeteria. "It went all right, I suppose," he said, with studied casualness.

"It went too well."

He took a large bite of sandwich and chewed solemnly.

"Jim, why did you do it?" she demanded.

He blushed. "Do what?"

"Arrange my Trendex that way."

"Nobody *arranges* a Trendex. It isn't possible. Even Wilbings will tell you that." He added softly, "How did you know?"

"It's the only possible explanation, and you shouldn't have done it. You might get into trouble, and you're only postponing the inevitable. I'll be at zero again on the next rating."

"That doesn't matter. Wilbings will take action eventually, but now he won't be impulsive about it."

They ate in silence until the cafeteria manager came in with an urgent message for Mr. Pargrin from Mr. Wilbings. Pargrin winked at her. "I think I'm going to enjoy this. Will you be in your office this afternoon?"

She shook her head. "I'm going to visit my students."

"I'll see you tomorrow, then."

She looked after him thoughtfully. She sincerely hoped that he hadn't gotten himself in trouble.

On the rooftop landing area she asked the manager to call an air-cab for her. While she waited, she took a letter from her purse and reread it.

My name is Darrel Wilson. I'm sixteen years old, and I have to stay in my room most of the time because I had Redger disease and part of me is paralyzed. I like your class, and please, could we have some more Shakespeare?

"Here's your cab, ma'am."

"Thank you," Miss Boltz said. She returned the letter to her purse and stepped briskly up the cab ramp.

Jim Pargrin ruffled his hair and stared at her. "Whoa, now. What was that again? *Class*room?"

"I have nine students who are coming here every day to go to school. I'll need some place to teach them."

Pargrin clucked his tongue softly. "Wilbings would have a hemorrhage!"

"My TV class takes only five hours a week, and I have the entire year's work planned. Why should anyone object to my holding classes for a selected group of students on my own time?" She added softly, "These students *need* it!"

They were wonderful children, brilliant children, but they needed to be able to ask questions, to articulate their thoughts and feelings, to have their individual problems dealt with sympathetically. They desperately needed each other. Tens of thousands, hundreds of thousands of gifted children were being intellectually and emotionally stifled in the barren solitude of their TV classes. It was stark tragedy.

"What Wilbings doesn't know won't hurt him," Pargrin said. "At least, I hope it won't. But—a classroom? There isn't anything remotely resembling one in the building. Could you use a large studio? We could hang a curtain over the glass so you wouldn't be disturbed. What hours would your class meet?"

"All day. Nine to three. They'll bring their lunches."

"Whoa, now. Don't forget your TV class. Even if no one is watching—"

"I'm not forgetting it. My students will use that hour for a study period. Unless—could you arrange for me to hold my TV class in this larger studio?"

"Yes. I can do that."

"Wonderful! I can't thank you enough."

He shrugged his shoulders and shyly looked away.

"Did you have any trouble with Mr. Wilbings?" she asked.

"Not much. He thought your Trendex was a mistake. Since I don't take the ratings personally, the best I could do was refer him to the Trendex engineer."

"Then I'm safe for a little while. I'll start my class tomorrow."

Three of the students arrived in power chairs. Ella was a lovely, sensitive girl who had been born without legs, and though science had provided her with a pair, she did not like to use them. Darrel and Charles were victims of Redger disease. Sharon was blind. The TV entertainers failed to reach her with their tricks, but she listened to Miss Boltz's every word with a rapt expression on her face.

Their intelligence level exceeded by far that of any other class in Miss Boltz's experience. She felt humble, and not a little apprehensive; but her apprehension vanished as she looked at their shining faces that first morning and welcomed them to her venture into the Old Education.

She had two fellow conspirators. Jim Pargrin personally took charge of the technical aspects of her hour on TV and gleefully put the entire class on camera. Lyle Stewart, who found the opportunity to work with real students too appealing to resist, came in the afternoon to teach two hours of science and mathematics. Miss Boltz laid out her own study units firmly. History, English, literature, and social studies. Later, if the class continued, she would try to work in a unit on a foreign language. That Wednesday was her happiest day since she returned to Earth.

On Thursday morning a special messenger brought in an official-looking envelope. It contained her dismissal notice.

"I already heard about it," Jim Pargrin said when she telephoned him. "When is the hearing?"

"Next Tuesday."

"It figures. Wilbings got board permission for a special Trendex. He even brought in an outside engineer to look after it, and just to be doubly sure, they used two thousand samples. You'll need an attorney. Know any?"

"No. I know hardly anyone on Earth." She sighed. She'd been so uplifted by her first day of actual teaching that this abrupt encounter with reality stunned her. "I'm afraid an attorney would cost a lot of money, and I'm going to need what money I have."

"A little thing like a Board of Education hearing shouldn't cost much. Just you leave it to me—I'll find an attorney for you."

She wanted to object, but there was no time. Her students were waiting for her.

On Saturday she had lunch with Bernard Wallace, the attorney Jim Pargrin recommended. He was a small, elderly man with sharp gray eyes that stabbed at her fleetingly from behind drooping eyelids. He questioned her casually during lunch, and when they had pushed aside their dessert dishes he leaned back and twirled a key ring on one finger and grinned at her.

"Some of the nicest people I ever knew were my teachers," he said. "I thought they didn't make that kind any more. I don't suppose you realize that your breed is almost extinct."

"There are lots of fine teachers on Mars," she said.

"Sure. Colonies look at education differently. They'd be committing suicide if they just went through the motions. I kind of think maybe we're committing suicide here on Earth. This New Education thing has some resultants you may not know about. The worst one is that the kids aren't getting educated. Businessmen have to train their new employees from primary-grade level. It's had an impact on government, too. An election campaign is about what you'd expect with a good part of the electorate trained to receive its information in very weak doses with a sickening amount of sugar coating. So I'm kind of glad to be able to work on this case. You're not to worry about the expense. There won't be any."

"That's very kind of you," she murmured. "But helping one worn-out teacher won't improve conditions very much."

"I'm not promising to win this for you," Wallace said soberly. "Wilbings has all the good cards. He can lay them right out on the table, and you have to keep yours hidden because your best defense would be to show them what a mess of arrant nonsense this New Education is, and you can't do that. We don't dare attack the New Education. That's the board's baby, and they've already defended it successfully in court, a lot of times. If we win, we'll have to win on their terms."

"That makes it rather hopeless, doesn't it?"

"Frankly, it'll be tough." He pulled out an antique gold watch and squinted at it. "Frankly, I don't see how I'm going to bring it off. Like I said, Wilbings has the cards, and anything I lead is likely to be trumped. But I'll give it some thought, and maybe I can come up with a surprise or two. You just concentrate on your teaching and leave the worrying to me."

After he left she ordered another cup of coffee, and sipped it slowly, and worried.

On Monday morning she received a surprise of her own in the form of three boys and four girls who presented themselves at her office and asked permission to join her class. They had seen it on TV, they told her, and it looked like fun. She was pleased but doubtful. Only one of them was officially a student of hers. She took the names of the others and sent them home. The one who was properly her student she permitted to remain.

He was a gangling boy of fifteen, and though he seemed bright enough, there was a certain withdrawn sullenness about him that made her uneasy. His name was Randy Stump—"A dumb name, but I'm stuck with it," he mumbled. She quoted him Shakespeare on the subject of names, and he gaped at her bewilderedly.

Her impulse was to send him home with the others. Such a misfit might disrupt her class. What stopped her was the thought that the suave TV teacher, the brilliant exponent of the New Education, would do just that. Send him home. Have him watch the class on TV in the sanctity of his own natural environment, where he couldn't get into trouble, and just incidentally where he never would learn to get along with people.

She told herself, "I'm a poor excuse for a teacher if I can't handle a little problem in discipline."

He shifted his feet uneasily as she studied him. He was a foot taller than she, and he looked past her and seemed to find a blank wall intensely interesting.

He slouched along at her side as she led him down the corridor to the classroom, where he seated himself at the most remote table and instantly lapsed into a silent immobility that seemed to verge on hypnosis. The others attempted to draw him into their discussions, but he ignored them. Whenever Miss Boltz looked up, she found his eyes fixed upon her intently. Eventually she understood: He was attending class, but he was still watching it on TV.

Her television hour went well. It was a group discussion on *A Tale of Two Cities*, and the youthful sagacity of her class delighted her. The red light faded at eleven-fifteen. Jim Pargrin waved his farewell, and she waved back at him and turned to her unit on history. She was searching her mind for something that would draw Randy Stump from his TV-inflicted shell.

When she glanced up from her notes, she found her students staring at a silently opening door. A dry voice said, "What *is* going on here?"

It was Roger Wilbings.

He removed his spectacles and replaced them. "Well!" he exclaimed. His mustache twitched nervously. "Well! May I ask the meaning of this?"

No one spoke. Miss Boltz had carefully rehearsed her explanation in the event that she should be called to account for this unauthorized teaching, but such an unexpected confrontation left her momentarily speechless.

"Miss Boltz!" Wilbings's mouth opened and closed several times as he groped for words. "I have seen many teachers do many idiotic things, but I have never seen anything quite as idiotic as this. I am happy to have this further confirmation of your incompetence. Not only are you a disgustingly inept teacher, but obviously you suffer from mental derangement. No rational adult would bring these— these—"

He paused. Randy Stump had emerged from his hypnosis with a snap. He leaped forward, planted himself firmly in front of Wilbings, and snarled down at him. "You take that back!"

Wilbings eyed him coldly. "Go home. Immediately." His gaze swept the room. "All of you. Go home. Immediately."

"You can't make us," Randy said.

Wilbings poised himself on the high pinnacle of his authority. "No young criminal—"

Randy seized his shoulders and shook vigorously. Wilbings's spectacles flew in a long arc and shattered. He wrenched himself free and struck out weakly, and Randy's return blow landed with a shattering thud. The Deputy Superintendent reeled backward into the curtain and then slid gently to the floor as glass crashed into the corridor beyond.

Miss Boltz bent over him. Randy hovered nearby, frightened and contrite. "I'm sorry, Miss Boltz," he stammered.

"I'm sure you are," she said. "But for now—I think you had better go home."

Eventually Wilbings was assisted away. To Miss Boltz's intense surprise, he said nothing more; but the look he flashed in her direction as he left the room made further conversation unnecessary.

Jim Pargrin brought a man to replace the glass. "Too bad," he observed. "He can't have it in for you any more than he already had, but now he'll try to make something of this class of yours at the hearing."

"Should I send them all home?" she asked anxiously.

"Well, now. That would be quitting, wouldn't it? You just carry on—we can fix this without disturbing you."

She returned to her desk and opened her notebook. "Yesterday we were talking about Alexander the Great—"

The fifteen members of the Board of Education occupied one side of a long, narrow table. They were business and professional men, most of them elderly, all solemn, some obviously impatient.

On the opposite side of the table, Miss Boltz sat at one end with Bernard Wallace. Roger Wilbings occupied the other end with a bored technician who was preparing to record the proceedings. A fussy little man Wallace identified as the Superintendent of Education fluttered into the room, conferred briefly with Wilbings, and fluttered out.

"Most of 'em are fair," Wallace whispered. "They're honest, and they mean well. That's on our side. Trouble is, they don't know anything about education, and it's been a long time since they were kids."

From his position at the center of the table, the president called the meeting to order. He looked narrowly at Bernard Wallace. "This is not a trial," he announced. "This is merely a hearing to secure information essential for the board to reach a proper decision. We do not propose to argue points of law."

"Lawyer himself," Wallace whispered, "and a good one."

"You may begin, Wilbings," the president said.

Wilbings got to his feet. The flesh around one eye was splendidly discolored, and he smiled with difficulty. "The reason for this meeting concerns the fact that Mildred Boltz holds a contract type 79B, issued to her in the year 2022. You will recall that this school district originally became responsible for these contracts during a shortage of teachers on Mars, when—"

The president rapped on the table. "We understand that, Wilbings. You want Mildred Boltz dismissed because of incompetence. Present your evidence of incompetence, and we'll see what Miss Boltz has to say about it and wind this up. We don't want to spend the afternoon here."

Wilbings bowed politely. "I now supply to all those present four regular Trendex ratings of Mildred Boltz, as well as one special rating which was recently authorized by the board."

Papers were passed around. Miss Boltz looked only at the special Trendex, which she had not seen. Her rating was .2—two tenths of one per cent.

"Four of these ratings are zero or so low that for all practical purposes we can call them zero," Wilbings said. "The rating of twenty-seven constitutes a special case."

The president leaned forward. "Isn't it a little unusual for a rating to deviate so sharply from the norm?"

"I have reason to believe that this rating represents one of two things: fraud or error. I freely admit that this is a personal belief, and that I have no evidence that would be acceptable in court."

The board members whispered noisily among themselves. The president said slowly, "I have been assured at least a thousand times that the Trendex is infallible. Would you kindly give us the basis for this personal belief of yours?"

"I would prefer not to."

"Then we shall disregard this personal belief."

"The matter is really irrelevant. Even if the twenty-seven is included, Miss Boltz has a nine-week average of only five and a fraction."

Bernard Wallace was tilted back in his chair, one hand thrust into a pocket, the other twirling his keys. "We don't consider that twenty-seven irrelevant," he said.

The president frowned. "If you will kindly let Wilbings state his case—"

"Gladly. What's he waiting for?"

Wilbings flushed. "It is inconceivable that a teacher of any competence whatsoever could have ratings of zero, or of fractions of a per cent. As further evidence of Miss Boltz's incompetence, I wish to inform the board that without authorization she brought ten of her students to a studio in this building and attempted to teach them in class periods lasting an entire morning and an entire afternoon."

The shifting of feet, the fussing with cigarettes, the casual whispering stopped. Puzzled glances converged upon Miss Boltz. Wilbings made the most of the silence before he continued.

"I shall not review for you the probable deadly effect of this obsolete approach to education. All of you are familiar with it. In case the known facts require any substantiation, I am prepared to offer in evidence a statement of the physical damage resulting from just one of these class periods, as well as my own person, which was assaulted by one of the young hoodlums in her charge. Fortunately I discovered this sinister plot against the youth of our district before the effects of her unauthorized teaching became irreparable. Her immediate dismissal will of course put an end to it. That, gentlemen, constitutes our case."

The president said, "This is hard to believe, Miss Boltz. Would you mind telling the board why—"

Bernard Wallace interrupted. "Is it our turn?"

The president hesitated, looked along the table for suggestions, and got none. "Go ahead," he said.

"A question, gentlemen. How many of you secured your own elementary and/or secondary education under the deadly circumstances Wilbings has just described? Hands, please, and let's be honest. Eight, ten, eleven. Eleven out of fifteen. Thank you. Do you eleven gentlemen attribute your present state of degradation to that sinister style of education?" The board members smiled.

"You, Wilbings," Wallace went on. "You talk as if everyone is or should be familiar with the deadly effects of group teaching. Are you personally an authority on it?"

"I certainly am familiar with all of the standard studies and research," Wilbings said stiffly.

"Ever experience that kind of education yourself? Or teach under those conditions?"

"I certainly have not!"

"Then you are not personally an authority. All you really know about these so-called deadly effects is what some other windbags have written."

"Mr. Wallace!"

"Let it pass. Is my general statement correct? All you really know—"

"I am prepared to accept the conclusions of an acknowledged authority in the field."

"Any of these acknowledged authorities ever have any experience of group teaching?"

"If they are reputable authorities—"

Wallace banged on the table. "Not the question," he snapped. "Reputable among whom? Question is whether they really know anything about the subject. Well?"

"I'm sure I can't say just what bases they use for their studies."

"Probably not the only basis that counts: knowing their subject. If I could produce for you an authority with years of actual experience and study of the group-teaching system, would you take that authority's word as to its effects, harmful or otherwise?"

"I'm always happy to give proper consideration to the work of any reliable authority," Wilbings said.

"What about you gentlemen?"

"We aren't experts in education," the president said. "We have to rely on authorities."

"Splendid. I now give you Miss Mildred Boltz, whose twenty-five years of group teaching on Mars make her probably the most competent authority on this subject in the Western Hemisphere. Miss Boltz, is group teaching in any way harmful to the student?"

"Certainly not," Miss Boltz said. "In twenty-five years I can't recall a single case where group teaching was not beneficial to the student. On the other hand, TV teaching—"

She broke off as Wallace's elbow jabbed at her sharply.

"So much for the latter part of Wilbings's argument," Wallace said. "Miss Boltz is an expert in the field of group teaching. No one here is qualified to question her judgment in that field. If she brought together ten of her students, she knew what she was doing. Matter of fact, I personally would think it a pretty good thing for a school district to have one expert in group teaching on its staff. Wilbings doesn't seem to think so, but you gentlemen of the board might want to consider that. Now—about this Trendex nonsense."

Wilbings said coldly, "The Trendex ratings are not nonsense."

"Think maybe I could show you they are, but I don't want to take the time. You claim this rating of twenty-seven is due to fraud or error. How do you know those other ratings aren't due to fraud or error? Take this last one—this special rating. How do you know?"

"Since you make an issue of it," Wilbings said, "I will state that Miss Boltz is the personal friend of a person on the engineering staff who is in a position to influence any rating if he so desires. This friend knew that Miss Boltz was about to be dismissed. Suddenly, for one time only, her rating shot up to a satisfactory level. The circumstances speak for themselves."

"Why are you so certain that this last rating is not due to fraud or error?"

"Because I brought in an outside engineer who could be trusted. He took this last Trendex on Miss Boltz personally."

"There you have it," Wallace said scornfully. "Wilbings wants Miss Boltz dismissed. He's not very confident that the regular Trendex, taken by the district's own engineers, will do the job. So he calls in a personal friend from the outside, one he can trust to give him the kind of rating he wants. Now if *that* doesn't open the door to fraud or error—"

The uproar rattled the distant windows. Wilbings was on his feet screaming. The president was pounding for order. The board members were arguing heatedly among themselves.

"Gentlemen," Wallace said, when he could make himself heard, "I'm no Trendex authority, but I can tell you that these five ratings, and the circumstances surrounding them, add up to nothing but a mess. I'll take you to court cheerfully, and get you laughed out of court, if that's what you want, but there may be an easier way. At this moment I don't think any of us really know whether Mildred Boltz is competent or not. Let's find out. Let's have another Trendex, and let's have it without fussing around with samples. Let's have a Trendex on *all* of Miss Boltz's students. I won't make any promises, but if the results of such a rating were in line with this Trendex average, I would be disposed to recommend that Miss Boltz accept her dismissal without a court test."

"That sounds reasonable," the president said. "And sensible. Get Pargrin in here, Wilbings, and we'll see if it can be done."

Miss Boltz sank back in her chair and looked glumly at the polished tabletop. She felt betrayed. It was perfectly obvious that her only chance for a reprieve depended upon her refuting the validity of those Trendex ratings. The kind of test Bernard Wallace was suggesting would confirm them so decisively as to shatter any kind of a defense. Certainly Jim Pargrin would understand that.

When he came in, he studiously avoided looking at her. "It's possible," he said, when the president had described what was wanted. "It'll upset our schedule, and it might make us late with the next Trendex, but if it's important we can do it. Will tomorrow be all right?"

"Is tomorrow all right, Wilbings?" the president asked.

"Where Miss Boltz is concerned, I have no confidence in any kind of a rating taken by our staff."

Pargrin elevated his eyebrows. "I don't know what you're getting at, but if you've got doubts just send in that engineer of yours and let him help out. With this extra load the Trendex men probably would appreciate it."

"Is that satisfactory, Wilbings?" the president asked.

Wilbings nodded. "Perfectly satisfactory."

"Very well. Miss Boltz's class ends at eleven-fifteen. Can we have the results by eleven-thirty? Good. The board will meet tomorrow at eleven-thirty and make final disposition of this case."

The meeting broke up. Bernard Wallace patted Miss Boltz on the arm and whispered into her ear, "Now don't you worry about a thing. You just carry on as usual and give us the best TV class you can. It's going to be so tough it'll be easy."

She returned to her class, where Lyle Stewart was filling in for her. "How did you make out?" he asked.

"The issue is still in doubt," she said. "But not very much in doubt, I'm afraid. Tomorrow may be our last day, so let's see how much we can accomplish."

Her TV class that Wednesday morning was the best she'd ever had. The students performed brilliantly. As she watched them she thought with an aching heart of her lost thousands of students, who had abandoned her for jugglers and magicians and young female teachers in tights.

The red light faded. Lyle Stewart came in. "Very nice," he said.

"You were wonderful!" Miss Boltz told her class.

Sharon, the blind girl, said tearfully, "You'll tell us what happens, won't you? Right away?"

"I'll tell you as soon as I know," Miss Boltz said. She forced a smile, and then she turned away.

As she hurried along the corridor a lanky figure moved to intercept her—tall, pale of face, frighteningly irrational in appearance. "Randy!" she exclaimed. "What are you doing here?"

"I'm sorry, Miss Boltz," he blubbered. "I'm really sorry, and I won't do it again. Can I come back?"

"I'd love to have you back, Randy, but there may not be any class after today."

He seemed stunned. "No class?"

She shook her head. "I'm very much afraid that I'm going to be dismissed. Fired, you might say."

He clenched his fists. Tears streaked his face, and he sobbed brokenly. She tried to comfort him, and some minutes passed before she understood why he was weeping. "Randy!" she exclaimed. "It isn't your fault that I'm being dismissed. What you did had nothing to do with it."

"We won't let them fire you," he sobbed. "All of us—us kids—we won't let them."

"We have to abide by the laws, Randy."

"But they won't fire you." His face brightened, and he nodded his head excitedly. "You're the best teacher I ever saw. I know they won't fire you. Can I come back to class?"

"If there's a class tomorrow, Randy, you may come back. I have to hurry, now. I'm going to be late."

She was already late when she reached the ground floor. She moved breathlessly along the corridor to the board room and stopped in front of the closed door. Her watch said fifteen minutes to twelve.

She knocked timidly. There was no response.

She knocked louder, and finally she opened the door a crack.

The room was empty. There were no board members, no technician, no Wilbings, no attorney Wallace. It was over and done with, and they hadn't even bothered to tell her the result.

They knew that she would know. She brushed her eyes with her sleeve. "Courage," she whispered and turned away.

As she started back up the corridor, hurrying footsteps overtook her. It was Bernard Wallace, and he was grinning. "I wondered what kept you," he said. "I went to check. Have you heard the news?"

She shook her head. "I haven't heard anything."

"Your Trendex was ninety-nine and a fraction. Wilbings took one look and nearly went through the ceiling. He wanted to scream 'Fraud!' but he didn't dare, not with his own engineer on the job. The board took one look and dismissed the case. Think maybe they were in a mood to dismiss Wilbings, too, but they were in a hurry."

Miss Boltz caught her breath and found the friendly support of a wall. "It isn't possible!"

"It's a fact. We kind of planned this. Jim and I pulled the names of all of your students, and we sent letters to them. Special class next Wednesday. Big deal. Don't miss it. Darned few of them missed it. Wilbings played right into our hands, and we clobbered him."

"No," Miss Boltz said. She shook her head and sighed. "No. There's no use pretending. I'm grateful, of course, but it was a trick, and when the next Trendex comes out Mr. Wilbings will start over again."

"It was a trick," Wallace agreed, "but it's kind of a permanent trick. We figured it this way. The younger generation has never experienced anything like this real live class of yours. On the first day you told them all about school on Mars, and you fascinated them. You held their attention. Jim was telling me about that. Our hunch was that this TV class of yours would fascinate them, too. Wilbings took that special Trendex before you got your class going, but Jim has been sneaking one every day since then, and your rating has been moving up. It was above ten yesterday, and now that all of your kids know what you're doing, it'll jump way up and stay there. So—no more worries. Happy?"

"Very happy. And very grateful."

"One more thing. The president of the board wants to talk to you about this class of yours. I had dinner with him last night and filled him in, and today he came early and watched it. He's impressed. I've got a suspicion that he maybe has a personal doubt or two about this New Education. Of course, we won't tear down TV teaching overnight, but we're making a start. Now I have work to do. I'll be seeing you."

Twirling his keys, he shuffled away.

She turned again and saw Jim Pargrin coming toward her. She gripped his hand and said, "I owe it all to you."

"You owe it to nobody but yourself. I was up telling your class. They're having a wild celebration."

"Goodness—I hope they don't break anything!"

"I'm glad for you. I'm a little sorry, too." He was looking at her again in that way that made her feel younger—almost youthful. "I figured that if you lost your job maybe I could talk you into marrying me." He looked away shyly. "You'd have missed your teaching, of course, but maybe we could have had some children of our own—"

She blushed wildly. "Jim Pargrin! At our ages?"

"Adopt some, I mean."

"Really—I've never given a thought to what I might have missed by not having my own children. I've had a family all my life, ever since I started teaching, and even if the children were different every year I've loved them all. And now I have another family waiting for me, and I was so nervous this morning I left my history notes in my office. I'll have to run." She took a few steps and turned to look back at him. "What made you think I wouldn't marry you if I kept on teaching?"

His startled exclamation was indistinct, but long after she turned a corner she heard him whistling.

On the sixth floor she moved down the corridor toward her office, hurrying because her students were celebrating and she didn't want to miss that. Looking ahead, she saw the door of her office open slowly. A face glanced in her direction, and suddenly a lanky figure flung the door aside and bolted away. It was Randy Stump.

She came to an abrupt halt. "Randy!" she whispered.

But what could he want in her office? There was nothing there but her notebooks, and some writing materials, and—her purse! She'd left her purse on her desk.

"Randy!" she whispered again and walked forward slowly.

She opened the office door and looked in. Suddenly she was laughing—laughing and crying—and she leaned against the door frame to steady herself as she exclaimed, "Now where would he get an idea like that?"

Her purse lay on her desk, untouched. Beside it, glistening brilliantly in the soft overhead light, was a grotesquely large, polished apple.

THE DOUBLE-EDGED ROPE

It was already several minutes past the hour of noon, and from the little restaurant came an outpouring of tantalizing, palate-tingling odors that brought the hungry passerby to a hypnotic halt and caused those who had just eaten to slow their steps and sniff enviously.

In all other respects the restaurant was thoroughly unsavory—the square it faced upon, its appearance, its proprietor, its one tottering waiter, most of its customers, and the swarm of flies that passed freely through the open doorway. Its name, Le Favori des Rois, was more than merely disreputable. It was, in the enlightened atmosphere of a People's Democracy, a treasonous reminder of hated royalty combined with a degraded capitalistic penchant for exaggeration.

But the royal-blue letters had long since peeled and faded to illegibility. Few people noticed them and no one cared, least of all the proprietor, who was a capitalist himself and therefore politically suspect, the fact that his soup was the best to be had south of the Danube notwithstanding.

The foreigner was seated at his usual table when Serge Marzoff entered the restaurant. Of all the population of this teeming capital city, only the obscure Mr. Jones rated the privilege of a reserved table at Le Favori des Rois. He arrived in a taxi at the same hour each day, and he tipped well—a combination of circumstances that not only guaranteed him his favorite table, but even, on occasion, procured for him a wilted bunch of flowers for a centerpiece. Mr. Jones was indeed the favorite of The Favorite of Kings. For all Marzoff knew, he may have been the only patron of that filthy little restaurant who bothered to tip at all.

Marzoff's own entrance was carefully timed. Mr. Jones had arrived, he'd had time to order his meal and to light one of his expensive foreign cigars, and from this point all would proceed according to custom: Marzoff would look about the crowded restaurant in dismay. Mr. Jones would leap to his feet and offer to share his table. Marzoff would decline to inconvenience his distinguished friend. Mr. Jones would insist and would lead the protesting Marzoff to the side of the room and get him seated. Then they would eat together and talk.

It happened thus once each week—though not, to be sure, on the same day. Mr. Jones possessed an easygoing joviality and sometimes he seemed a bit simple-minded, but it would not do to stretch his credulity that much.

Unfortunately, the events of this day did not follow their usual smooth pattern. Mr. Jones was reading his mail, and he did not see Marzoff enter. Marzoff gave the room a casual survey and to his horror he found an empty table directly in front of him. He cursed his bad luck and pretended not to see it.

The vulture-eyed proprietor moved to meet him, executing a complicated series of starts, stops, and sidesteps to maneuver his protruding stomach through the narrow gaps between tables. He touched Marzoff's arm and indicated the vacant table. Marzoff ignored him. Mr. Jones continued to read his mail.

The proprietor jerked at Marzoff's arm. Marzoff nodded condescendingly. "I prefer a table at the rear," he said. The proprietor swept the room with a glance and threw up his hands. Into this impasse darted two new customers, a man and a woman, who saw the empty table and pounced upon it. The proprietor turned away, and at that moment Mr. Jones looked up, saw Marzoff, and leaped to his feet.

The relieved Marzoff permitted Mr. Jones to lead him away. He had narrowly averted disaster—double disaster. Had he allowed the proprietor to seat him at that unfortunately vacant table, he should have failed in his assignment and also committed himself to pay for his own meal.

"Nice to see you again," Mr. Jones murmured. He gathered up his letters and stuffed them into an inside pocket. He was a pleasant, gray-haired man with a ready smile, and Marzoff liked him more than his conscience would permit him to admit, even to himself.

"Nice to see you," Marzoff said. He could relax, now, and order from the top of the menu, with the assurance that the food would be paid for by the amazing device that Mr. Jones called an expense account. "And have you news from home?" he asked, ducking as the waiter unsteadily negotiated the passage by their table with a heavily laden tray.

"Nothing sensational," Mr. Jones said. "My daughter informs me that I am to be a grandfather—for the fifth time. There is a heat wave in my hometown and they would like some rain. Who wouldn't? A third cousin on my mother's side, whom I do not remember, has had a heart attack. My young nephew is interested in flying saucers and would like me to find a cheap telescope for him so he can watch for them. What's the matter?"

Marzoff had made a face. "Capitalistic nonsense," he said.

Jones puffed peacefully on his cigar. "I seem to recall hearing something about flying saucers over this country. Rumors, of course. You people at the Censorship Bureau wouldn't allow anything like that to get into print."

"The purpose of the Censorship Bureau," Marzoff said stiffly, "is to see that the people are not deluded by lies and idle rumors."

Jones made a conciliatory gesture with his cigar. "Of course. What other purpose would justify the existence of a Censorship Bureau? Nevertheless, a lie sometimes is a relative thing. There are degrees of falsehood, just as there are degrees of truth. Surely of all people a censor should be aware of that."

Jones's blue eyes fixed upon Marzoff with an expression that seemed guileless, but Marzoff twisted uneasily in his chair. He liked this foreigner, but he did not trust him. Jones always seemed to be joking when he was most serious, and serious when he was joking, and in either instance he could talk the bone out of a dog's mouth.

They were interrupted by the waiter, who stood over them silently until Marzoff gave him his order.

"Rumors," Jones said, when the waiter had tottered out of hearing, "are a natural creative expression of the people. It isn't wise to stifle such an important form of communication, for in most rumors there is at least an ingredient of truth. Is this not so?"

Marzoff shrugged his shoulders. He was not going to be trapped into admitting anything.

"Supposing," Jones went on, "that one of your peasants were to see a flying saucer land in some out-of-the-way place. What would he do?"

"Nothing," Marzoff said. "Because he wouldn't see it. Such things do not exist."

"How do you know?" Mr. Jones asked, pointing his cigar at Marzoff. "But you probably are correct that your peasant would do nothing. He has been told that such things do not exist. Therefore he would not believe his own eyes. If he were startled enough to run to the police, what would happen? Either he would be tossed into prison for discussing a forbidden subject, or he would be ridiculed. Naturally he would never mention flying saucers again.

"In my country it would be different. Word would spread quickly. Newspapermen would come with cameras. The authorities would investigate. Scientists would investigate. Even if they suspected that the man was lying, they would investigate. The truth would be confirmed or the hoax exposed, and quickly. I think this much the better way. Censorship is a two-edged sword. Or perhaps it is a two-edged rope. It can stifle that which it is supposed to protect."

"That is ridiculous," Marzoff protested. "Who needs protection against a thing that does not exist?"

To his intense relief he saw the waiter approaching. The old man placed a steaming plate of goulash in front of Jones, wiped his hands upon an apron that would never wear out from too-frequent washings, and silently limped away.

"Think it over," Jones said. "If this planet is ever invaded from outer space, it won't be my country that suffers the first blow. It'll be one of your People's Democracies—though not, I think, your friends the Soviets, because of their admirable technology. It'll be a country such as yours, backward, with an imperfect communications system, and with a people long trained to believe only what they are told to believe and do what they are told to do." He took a spoonful of goulash and sighed. "Amazing. In Paris or New York that cook could earn a fortune. Yet he labors in a place like this."

Marzoff sighed also, in his relief that Jones finally had changed the subject. His own food arrived. They ate; they discussed the weather, which had been warm; they considered the possibility of rain, which seemed remote; they talked at length about the restaurant's wine, which was very bad. They finished eating. Jones gave Marzoff a foreign cigar and insisted upon paying his bill. Marzoff protested, and Jones explained once again about the magic of his expense account. They parted at the door of the restaurant, Marzoff to walk back to his office and Jones to look for a taxi.

Marzoff felt disturbed. Uneasily he rolled a form into his typewriter, the same form that he filled out after each of his weekly meetings with Jones, and then he paused and gazed thoughtfully at his keyboard. Why this sudden interest in flying saucers, and where would Jones get the idea that a peasant would be afraid to mention a flying saucer even if he saw one?

Such a suggestion reflected on the morale of the populace and therefore was treasonable. If he reported the details of that conversation, Jones undoubtedly would be thrown out of the country. He would be sent home a failure, to whatever fate the capitalistic rulers dealt out to failures. Probably he would be shot, which would be a pity.

On an impulse Marzoff walked over to the board where new regulations were posted. He had been out of the office all morning, and it was possible—

Flying saucers.

Marzoff read and recoiled in horror. Flying saucers . . . written or verbal discussion . . . public or private . . . *the death penalty!* And he, Serge Marzoff, had just been discussing flying saucers in a public restaurant with a foreigner!

He staggered back to his desk and buried his face in his hands. Could they have been overheard? As usual they had kept their voices low, and in the noise and confusion of the restaurant—no, he thought not. But he was obligated to report their conversation, and if he did, was it not possible that he would be arrested along with Jones? Such things had happened. He would have to write an innocuous report and hope for the best. And the next time he saw Mr. Jones he would speak sharply to him for all but placing his silly double-edged rope around both their necks.

Marzoff typed. Mr. Jones had commented on the backwardness of the peasant comrades, and he had been interested in Marzoff's exposition of how the current Seven-Year Plan would correct that. Mr. Jones had many kind things to say about food in the restaurants of the capital city, but he did not like the native wines. Mr. Jones had complained of the arbitrariness of the Censorship Bureau, and Marzoff had taken some time to explain that drastic action was sometimes an unfortunate necessity. And so on.

He ripped the page from his typewriter, signed his name, and walked timidly into the presence of the bureau's director, Dimitri Storavieff. Storavieff said, "Ah, that newspaper correspondent," glanced at the report, and scribbled his initials. He dismissed Marzoff with a nod. The report, Marzoff knew, would be scrutinized intently by many interested persons and would eventually find its way into a bulging file, to join Marzoff's other reports and those from various sources, one of which was the sly young man who sometimes followed Jones to the restaurant.

Marzoff returned to his desk. A stack of copy had been plunked there during his absence, but he was much too perturbed to get down to work immediately. Could it be, he asked himself, that Jones was trying to tell him something? He dismissed the thought as ridiculous. If Jones had any information of importance, he would impart it to someone of consequence. Foreign newspapermen had contacts with all manner of high officials, and Marzoff was a nobody. It was true that his father had been Minister of Agriculture before he had been unfortunately assassinated by capitalistic hirelings, and his uncle was Deputy Director of the Police, but aside from obtaining him his lowly position in the Censorship Bureau this had not altered Marzoff's insignificant status. No, if Jones wanted to pass along information, he would not pick Marzoff as the recipient.

Then what was his purpose?

Marzoff shuffled through the papers on his desk and put them down again. He fussed with the keys of his typewriter. Suddenly the answer came to him, so startling, so overwhelmingly important, that he sprawled back in his chair and stared open-mouthed at the ceiling. "So!" he murmured.

So Mr. Jones had been fishing, dangling a tempting bait to see what would come to the surface. He had been trying to find out what Marzoff knew—what the Bureau of Censorship knew. Why had Jones picked that particular moment, just after the flying saucer order had been issued? The order itself was the reason. No doubt it was unexpected. It took the enemies of the state by surprise, and within two hours Jones was violating it in a public restaurant in an effort to find out what was behind it.

"So!" Marzoff murmured again. So there *were* flying saucers, or something like that. They *were* a capitalistic plot, and Jones was connected with it!

Five minutes later Marzoff stood again in the presence of the director. Storavieff glanced up impatiently. "What is it now?"

"Sir," Marzoff said, speaking with a much bolder tone of voice than was customary with him, "I think I have discovered a horrible conspiracy against our glorious People's Democracy and our Glorious Leader."

"One of the newspaper articles? Let's see it."

"It is not that. It is an outside matter that I myself have discovered."

"Then it concerns the police, not the Director of the Censorship Bureau."

"True. But it is best to be certain, and I am not yet—that is, I am certain, but there is lacking—I mean—" Marzoff flushed and broke off in confusion.

Storavieff looked at him sharply. "What is it you want?"

"A leave of absence," Marzoff blurted. "A few days, to investigate—"

Storavieff nodded. "Take a week. If that isn't enough, let me know."

Marzoff beamed. "Thank you, sir."

"But clean up the work on your desk before you go."

The next day Marzoff was sipping bad wine at a sidewalk table across the square when Mr. Jones arrived at Le Favori des Rois. He reflected sadly that he had only to present himself, and the fabulous expense account of Mr. Jones would automatically provide the best that the restaurant could offer. And would he not be better able to observe this suspected enemy agent at close range?

He thrust the temptation aside and turned his thoughts to what he knew about the art of trapping spies. Unfortunately, this was very little. Everyone knew that the People's Democracies were infested with such criminals, but to Marzoff's knowledge there was no manual of instruction detailing easy methods for catching them. He continued to sip wine and think, and when Mr. Jones at last strolled away in search of a taxi, Marzoff had accomplished nothing beyond a mild and extremely distasteful intoxication.

He finished his wine and walked slowly to the end of the square and back. He bought a small loaf of bread and munched on it as he made a complete circuit of the square. Finally he returned to his seat at the sidewalk table and—for the want of a better excuse—ordered more wine.

"Suppose—" he said to himself, "—just suppose that Mr. Jones's professed admiration for the food at Le Favori des Rois is feigned." Marzoff found the meals tasteful and ample, but surely an important man such as Mr. Jones, blessed with a magical expense account, would not eat in such degraded surroundings even if the food were as good as he said. Very well. Then why the daily visit to this sordid neighborhood?

Obviously he visited Le Favori des Rois to meet someone. The proprietor? A logical choice and therefore unlikely. The proprietor had little contact with his patrons except to wave them toward empty tables. On the other hand—

The waiter!

It would be a simple matter for the waiter to pass messages to Jones along with the food and for Jones to leave a message under his plate when he finished eating or conceal it with the money when he paid his bill. It had been going on for months, right under Marzoff's nose, and he hadn't suspected a thing!

He leaped to his feet and set out to explore the neighborhood. His wanderings terminated in the alley behind the restaurant, a narrow, littered passageway so foul smelling that it forced him into a hasty, nauseated withdrawal. He returned to the sidewalk table. Through the open restaurant door he could sometimes see the old waiter tottering about with his comical half limp. Marzoff performed a calculation on the probable hours worked by waiters and decided that spy catching could be a tedious occupation.

Darkness came at last. Marzoff, lurking in the shadows, watched the other business establishments close one by one, watched the square become deserted, watched lights wink out in the apartments above the shops. Midnight came and went. Finally even the stubborn proprietor of Le Favori des Rois accepted the inevitable and closed his door with an echoing slam. The rusty bolt shrieked a protest as it was driven home. Marzoff, his heart thumping violently, raced down the square to the jagged opening where the alley vented its vile odors. Such divine providence as deigned to watch over a People's Democracy was on his side, for the alley of Le Favori des Rois had only the one exit.

Minutes passed, and then the waiter shuffled into view. Marzoff clung to the shadowed wall of a building and allowed him to reach the end of the square before he started after him.

He was led on a stumbling, nightmarish ramble through narrow, unlighted streets. Once he tripped over a metallic object and fell with a crash that seemed to rattle the nearby windows. The old waiter evidently was deaf as well as lame, for he never looked back; but only his hesitant, uncertain pace enabled Marzoff to keep close to him in the darkness.

Finally the waiter turned into a narrow court, loomed for a moment against darker shadows, and disappeared. Marzoff sprinted after him. As he reached the end of the court, strong arms seized him, flung him to the ground, pummeled him. He came up fighting and was instantly slugged into unconsciousness. Minutes or hours later he opened his eyes in a crowded cell with a single, high, barred window and learned he was in the hands of the police.

"Your name," the officer said, shuffling Marzoff's papers, "is Serge Marzoff?"

"It is."

"My assistant informs me that you refuse to speak with such an underling as himself. Is my modest rank sufficient for your conversation, or must I call in my superior?"

There were snickers among the bystanders. Marzoff summoned his courage and spoke clearly. "I have information concerning an infamous conspiracy, and I demand an audience with our Glorious Leader."

The officer silenced the laughter with a gesture. "Marzoff," he mused. "You are not, by chance, related to General Marzoff?"

"He is my uncle."

In the silence that followed, feet shuffled uneasily. The officer eyed Marzoff warily. "And—our lately lamented Minister of Agriculture?"

"He was my father."

"I see." The officer twiddled his thumbs against a background of total silence. "If you would consent to speak with me in confidence, I would guarantee to use my small influence to place your information before the proper authority."

"Our Glorious Leader," Marzoff said firmly.

"Take him away," the officer said.

The scene was repeated four times during the day, before officials of dazzlingly ascending rank. Each scrutinized Marzoff's papers, contemplated the undeniable importance of his family connections and the probable unimportance of his information, and had him returned to a cell. After each interview the cell improved in quality. The last one, in which he spent the night, was almost comfortable.

On the second day he was left undisturbed, and his resolution slowly eroded into panic. He had absented himself from the service of the State in pursuit of a wild speculation, he had violated an unimaginable number of regulations, he had wasted the time of several high-ranking officials, and only his connection with a family that long since had written him off as worthless had prevented his summary execution.

He was jerked from his bed at midnight. He went trembling, expecting a firing squad, but instead he was hurried into a car and driven recklessly through dark streets. The car halted by an unfamiliar rear entrance, and he was led through endless corridors and at length into a dim room where a group of men waited to sit in judgment on him. Then he recognized one of them.

"Our Glorious Leader," he murmured and sank to his knees.

"On your feet, Comrade Marzoff," the familiar voice said. "We are all equal in our service to the people."

Marzoff stood and kept his eyes lowered.

"You have information for me, Comrade Marzoff?"

Marzoff took a deep breath. He had known this man for years, although the Glorious Leader certainly would not remember him. Marzoff had watched him in timid admiration back in the earliest days of his memory when the Glorious Leader, as well as his father and uncle, were fugitives from what a tyrannous government chose to call justice. The voice, and the face, were as familiar to him as those of a member of his family. His timidity fell away from him, and he stammered out the full account of his conversation with Mr. Jones and what it had led to.

The room was silent when he finished. The Glorious Leader cleared his throat ostentatiously and said, not unkindly, "Comrade Marzoff. Your motives are beyond reproach, your zeal is commendable, and your thinking is indescribably muddled. Flying saucers? Everyone knows they were invented by the capitalistic imperialists to cower their rebellious populations. Our citizens need no such fantasies to inspire their loyalty. As for your espionage work, I know I can rely on your discretion when I tell you that the man you were following is an agent of our police. You have made a nuisance of yourself, Comrade Marzoff, but you meant well, and you are the son of an old friend. You will return to the Censorship Bureau in the morning, and in the future you will be attentive to your duties there and leave the protection of the State to experts. I assure you that it is in good hands. Agreed?"

Marzoff nodded.

"Good."

The Glorious Leader got to his feet and walked away. Marzoff's admiring eyes followed him, drank in the familiar profile, gazed at his face as he turned to look back, contemplated his ears, odd-looking ears that seemed sculptured in low relief on the sides of his head—

"*You aren't the Glorious Leader!*" Marzoff blurted.

The man halted, all kindness drained from his face. He glared at Marzoff. Then he nodded, and that silent nod struck Marzoff as a thunderous clap of doom.

Which it was.

Dimitri Storavieff looked up impatiently and said, "Ah, Marzoff. You're back."

"Yes, sir."

"And what of this mysterious conspiracy?"

"There wasn't any, sir. I'm sorry to have wasted the time."

Storavieff nodded. Marzoff was a silly little fool, but on the other hand he had important relatives, and even fools had been known to stumble onto something important. But there was no harm done. Certainly the Censorship Bureau hadn't missed him.

"By the way," Storavieff said, "about that newspaper correspondent, Jones. He had an unfortunate accident last night. Most regrettable. There'll be all kinds of tiresome inquiries. It might be appropriate for you to write a note of regret to his family."

"Yes, sir."

"All right. You know what to do."

A moment later Storavieff was distracted by an altercation in the outer office. Marzoff had absently seated himself at the wrong desk. Storavieff watched him apologize and shuffle back to his proper corner.

"What peculiar ears that man has!" Storavieff thought suddenly. "Strange I never noticed it before."

Ears! He snapped his fingers. There was something about ears— yes, in a new regulation he had been reading when Marzoff interrupted him. He returned to his desk and picked up the list.

Ears. Certain capitalistic correspondents were ridiculing the shape of ears among citizens of the southern provinces. This treasonable activity was aimed at inciting racial strife in the People's Democracy similar to that which plagued the capitalistic nations. Any mention of ears henceforth would be a criminal offense.

"And properly so," Storavieff murmured and initialed the paper.

EYE FOR AN EYE

Walter Dudley and his wife paused at the top of the ramp for their
first glimpse of the independent world of Maylor. The bleak landscape stretched unbroken to the taut line of the horizon.

"It doesn't look very interesting," Dudley observed.

Eleanor Dudley was more emphatic. "It stinks."

"Maybe it'll be better in town," Dudley said, though he knew it
wouldn't. One could not expect to find much of the tinsel of civilization on a world that was, admittedly, the last refuge of the failure.

A noisy, vilely malodorous groundcar arrived in a choking swirl of
dust and fumes, and they climbed aboard with their hand luggage.
Minutes later, bounced and jolted to the verge of nausea, they were
deposited at the diminutive passenger terminal.

Hamal Bakr, the Galactic Insurance Company's temporary resident manager, was waiting for them. Dudley disliked him at sight.
Not only was he tall and handsome, but his casual afternoon robe
displayed his trim figure with the effectiveness of a military uniform.
Dudley had met his type before—met it frequently, and always to his
profound regret. Bakr would be the darling of his sector manager,
and even his infrequent failures would count more than other men's
successes.

He crushed Dudley's hand and bent low over Eleanor's, brushing
her fingers with his mustache and murmuring that this world of
Maylor's long-standing reputation as the abode of beautiful women
had been sheer fraud until the moment of her arrival. Eleanor tit-
tered.

"I've found an apartment for you," Bakr said. "You won't like it,
but it's the best I could do on short notice. There's a terrible housing
shortage here."

"Whatever it is, we've probably seen worse," Dudley said. But he
doubted that, too.

"I have my 'car waiting," Bakr said. "I'll drive you."

He herded them through customs, bullying officials, snarling at baggage attendants, and frightening porters. Then he loaded them and their luggage into his sleek groundcar and triumphantly roared away with them, trailing clouds of acrid white dust.

"In case you're in suspense," he said to Dudley, "I can summarize the present condition of our business in three words: There isn't any."

"I gathered that the situation wasn't healthy."

"The Maylor business is worse than just unhealthy. It's deceased. If you're thinking of doing anything except arrange a decent burial, forget it."

Dudley scratched his head perplexedly. "It shouldn't be that bad. What's the competition? I *know* no one has better air vehicular coverage than Galactic, and our fire coverages—"

"There aren't any air vehicles on Maylor. They're prohibited. Too dangerous. But this—" Bakr swerved, narrowly missing an oncoming 'car that crowded the center of the road. "This they consider safe."

"They must have an appalling accident rate. How many groundcar policies do we have in force?"

"One."

Dudley stared. "Just one policy? On the entire planet? You can't be serious!"

"But I am serious. The Galactic Insurance Company has one groundcar policy in force on this planet, and it's mine. I only bought it to be patriotic. Because of the peculiar customs and legalities of Maylor, its citizens consider insurance unnecessary or incomprehensible or both. They won't buy it at any premium or under any circumstances. Wasn't this explained to you? I thought you were being sent out to wind things up and close the office."

"Nothing was explained to me," Dudley said grimly. "I was sent out to make the business go here—or else."

"Old man, I had no idea, or I'd have broken the news gently."

Eleanor drawled, "Think nothing of it. This is Walter's ninth assignment in four years. You might say he's used to failing."

They drove on in silence.

The atmosphere of Maylor's capital city, when they finally reached it, was a nerve-shattering blend of dirt and noise and confusion. Factories vomited smoke, groundcar traffic was deafening, and the low buildings were hideous. Dudley appraised the shoddy frame dwellings with the eye of an insurance expert and shuddered.

"Fire insurance?"

"One policy in force," Bakr said. "Mine."

The architecture improved markedly as they approached the center of the city. Buildings were of brick, some of them two or three stories high. The traffic situation became increasingly disorganized. Pedestrians and vehicles shared the narrow street, the foot traffic usually, but not always, keeping to the sides. Buildings fronted directly on the street. It was possible to take one cautious step from one's doorway and be struck by a groundcar.

"Hazards like this and no insurance?" Dudley asked incredulously. Bakr did not answer.

Directly ahead of them, chaos swirled. Construction work was under way on one of the buildings. The workers and their equipment were scattered about in the street, and pedestrians and groundcars recklessly maneuvered among them.

"That's the place," Bakr said. "I might as well stop here." He edged to the side of the street, nudging pedestrians out of the way, and came to a stop almost grazing a building. "We'll get your stuff upstairs, and then I'll show you the office."

"What are they doing to the place?" Eleanor asked.

"They're adding another story."

"And we're supposed to live there with that racket on all sides?" she exclaimed.

"They only work during the day. It isn't a bad place, really. It's a luxury apartment, and it's within walking distance of the office—if you have the nerve to walk, that is. It could be a lot worse."

"I believe you," Dudley said gloomily.

Bakr and Dudley carried up the trunks and suitcases, and then, because Dudley wanted to look in at the office, they left Eleanor fuming in the three cramped rooms that constituted a luxury apartment on the world of Maylor. Back in the street, Dudley paused to watch the construction workers.

A man was hauling on a slender rope, which fed through a complex of pulleys and slowly raised an enormous load of brick. Pedestrians strolled indifferently beneath the swaying load. Dudley turned away, genuinely frightened. "Don't they take any safety precautions at all?"

"Sure. There's another workman standing by in case the one with the rope gets tired. If you'd ask them, they'd say they very rarely have an accident."

"Liability insurance?"

"They don't even understand what it is," Bakr said. "When you have a chance, take a close look at that rope. The hemp is of poor quality, and the rope only has two strands. If one parted, the other couldn't hold the load. Shall we go?"

Dudley nodded, and they climbed into Bakr's 'car.

"They're a fine-looking people, these Maylorites," Dudley observed. They were a sturdy, blond race, handsome and cheerful. Smiles greeted Dudley and Bakr from all sides.

"They are that," Bakr agreed. "Maylor *is* the abode of beautiful women. Good-looking men, too. But they're much too virtuous for my taste."

The Maylor office of Galactic Insurance was a small third-story room. It contained a desk, two chairs, and a row of empty filing cabinets. Unopened cartons of policy, endorsement, and record forms were stacked in a corner.

"No staff?" Dudley asked.

"No work," Bakr said. "I fired the one employee the day I took over."

"How long have you been here?"

"Three months. I was on my way back to the home office for reassignment when the Maylor resident manager was fired, and McGivern asked me to hold the fort until he assigned a new one. I've been recommending twice a week that the office be closed. I was afraid McGivern might promote me and give me the job. You have my sympathy, but there isn't much else I can do for you."

"You can fill me in on the situation. I understand that this office did very well when it first opened."

"Business was sensational. Galactic was the first insurance company on Maylor. Now it's the last. A couple of hundred others have come and gone."

"Stubbornness has made Galactic great," Dudley murmured.

"That's home office propaganda, and you know it. Stubbornness doesn't accomplish a thing on Maylor except to lose money. Business was sensational for the first six months. Then the claims started to come in, and in another six months the only policies in force were those of Galactic's employees."

"What happened? Were the claims rejected?"

Bakr shook his head. "A native holding a fire insurance policy had a fire. The company offered a generous settlement, but he wouldn't accept it. He demanded—and got—his premium refunded. Then he proceeded to scream long and loudly that Galactic's insurance was no good."

"If we offered to pay the claim, I don't understand why—"

"He'd insured himself against fire, and he had a fire anyway. Why carry fire insurance if it doesn't keep you from having fires?"

Dudley protested, "But surely if the principles of insurance were properly explained—"

"Not on Maylor. People here don't want money. They want to not have fires. Same thing happened with our life insurance. A native insured his life with Galactic, and he died anyway. Clearly the insurance policy wasn't worth the paper it was printed on, and the offer of money in the face of such an obvious failure constituted a form of bribery. I could go on and on. When a native of Maylor insures his life, he expects not to die. When he insures his groundcar against accidents, he expects not to have accidents. If the insurance won't keep him from dying or from having accidents or from anything else it claims to insure him against, why carry insurance? There are perfectly sound reasons for this attitude. You can study the legal and social and historical backgrounds if you like—you *will* study them—but all you'll get out of it will be a slightly better understanding of why you can't sell insurance."

"I see," Dudley said.

"I'm leaving on the next ship. I'd suggest that you come along."

"I can't do that. I've had some miserable luck, and I've been relieved of my last eight assignments, but I've never quit. And McGivern—"

Dudley turned away morosely. The mere recollection of that last interview with McGivern was enough to cost him a night's sleep.

"Damn McGivern," Bakr said. "Damn Galactic, if it holds you responsible for things beyond your control. There are other insurance companies."

"Which don't hire failures. Not in positions of responsibility."

"Did McGivern give you a time limit?"

"Three months, which means nothing at all. Once he gave me six months, and then he showed up on his private space yacht, the *Indemnity*, when I'd only been on the job for two weeks, hung around for a couple of days looking over my shoulder, and relieved me. It wouldn't surprise me if he turned up tomorrow wanting to know why the problem isn't solved yet."

Bakr got to his feet. "That's what can happen when the boss has a private yacht. Well, you know what you're up against. Any help I can give you in the next seven days you're welcome to."

"I'll need a groundcar, I suppose."

"You can rent one. I'll take care of it for you."

"And insurance on it."

Bakr grinned. "Certainly. Fire insurance on your personal property, too. Liability, accident, theft, health—write yourself a batch of policies. You can double Galactic's business your first day on the job.

When I leave I'll be canceling my policies, but for a week you'll have a sensational record."

From the room's one window Dudley watched him drive away. At the corner his car brushed the robe of a woman pedestrian, and she halted in the midst of traffic to smile after him sweetly. Shaking his head, Dudley retreated to the desk.

He had three months—maybe. He had no advertising budget and wouldn't have one until he produced a volume of business to support it. Within those limitations he had to contrive nothing less than a massive campaign to educate the people of Maylor to the value of insurance.

Personal salesmanship was the only answer, and he'd have to apply it quickly—pinpoint the area of most obvious need, devise a dramatic gimmick to catch people's attention, and hammer away with it. He could begin by tabulating recent losses. A rash of fires always put the public in a wonderfully receptive state of mind for fire insurance, and a series of break-ins never failed to soften a merchant's resistance to theft insurance.

He walked down the three flights of stairs to the general store that occupied the ground floor of the building and asked the clerk where he could buy a newspaper.

"I'm sorry, sir," the young man said. "We have none left."

"Is there someone else who'd have one?"

"I very much doubt it, sir. It's been out more than a week, you see."

"When will the next issue be available?"

The clerk looked surprised. "Why—not until next month!"

"Thank you."

Dudley introduced himself, and the clerk said blankly, "Galactic—Insurance? Oh, Galactic. You're upstairs."

Dudley agreed that when he was in his office he was upstairs. "Has this neighborhood been troubled by burglaries lately?" he asked.

"Burglaries? What is that?"

"Thefts, stealing—"

The clerk pondered this. "I'll ask," he said finally. He entered an office at the rear of the store. Through the open door Dudley watched him converse guardedly with an older man. A moment later the two of them bent over a book, the older man energetically flipping pages. Dudley moved closer and managed to identify the book. It was a dictionary.

The clerk returned and shook his head apologetically. "No, sir. We've never had anything like that."

On his way out, Dudley verified what he'd thought was a faulty observation when he entered. The store's street door had no lock. Neither were there locks on the entrances to the adjoining stores. Neither, now that he thought about it, was there a lock on the door of his office.

No insurance company managed by sane men would underwrite theft insurance on a business establishment that had no lock on its door, but the clerk claimed there were no losses by theft. He did not even know what the word meant!

Dudley dropped the subject of theft insurance and went back to his office to stand at the window and meditate on the perilous groundcar traffic.

Bakr returned, settled himself comfortably in the desk chair, and announced that Dudley's groundcar would be ready for him in a couple of days. "That's fast service for Maylor," he said.

"I'll need lessons," Dudley said. "I've never driven one before."

"That needn't worry you. The natives don't know how to drive, either."

"Even so—"

"Right. I'll supervise your instruction myself. It'll give me something to do. And tonight I want you and Eleanor to be my guests for dinner. Afterward I'll take you on a comprehensive tour of Maylor City's nightlife. About twenty minutes will do the job. Is there anything else I can do for you?"

"I'd like to see a newspaper."

Bakr scowled. "That *is* a problem. The thing only publishes once a month. I'll try to dig one up."

"I've never heard of a city of this size without a daily paper. Is there a shortage of newsprint?"

"There's a shortage of news. Nothing happens on Maylor."

"What about advertising?"

"It's limited to disgustingly polite announcements," Bakr said. " 'Thomas Peawinkle and Son are pleased to announce that they will have no imported shoes for sale until the next consignment arrives.' That sort of thing."

"I'm beginning to understand why you call the situation impossible."

"My friend, even now you have absolutely no idea how impossible it is!"

"I'll have to do some thinking."

"If you're a religious man, you might pray for divine guidance. That's the only thing that's likely to help. I'll call for you and Eleanor at seven."

He left Dudley to his despondent window gazing.

The restaurant was so spotlessly clean and so starkly unadorned that Dudley was reminded of a hospital ward. The young waitresses had a rosy, freshly scrubbed appearance.

"Bland is the word for it," Bakr said. "Everything and everybody on Maylor is bland. That includes the food."

"It smells delicious," Eleanor remarked, as a waitress moved gracefully past their table with a steaming tray.

"Wait'll you taste it. I come forearmed, though, and you're welcome to share." Bakr placed a small flask on the table in front of him.

"What is it?" Eleanor asked.

"Sauce. It's a special blend mixed to my specifications. It's hot. Most people think it blisters their mouths, but that's the way I like it."

He unscrewed the cap and passed the flask to Eleanor, who sniffed cautiously. "It smells—interesting."

She handed it to Dudley, and one quick whiff brought tears to his eyes. "Whew! Do you *eat* this stuff?"

Bakr laughed. "If *you* think it's strong, you should see how the natives react to it. For all their sturdy appearances, every one of them has a weak stomach. I suppose that accounts for the bland food."

Their order arrived, a large tureen of a thick, creamy stew. It had dumplings floating in it, and it looked and smelled delicious. Bakr deftly served the three of them, and then he applied his custom-made sauce to his portion with gusto. Dudley tasted the food, grimaced, and agreed that it lacked something.

"The commissary out at the port has some imported spices and sauces," Bakr said. "I should have told you to stock up. You can't buy such things anywhere else. Try a little of this."

Eleanor added a light dash of Bakr's sauce and praised the result enthusiastically. Dudley took the flask, miscalculated as he tilted it, and spilled a gush of sauce into his bowl. He regarded it with dismay as it stained the food an unappetizing brown.

"Clumsy!" Eleanor snapped.

Dudley shrugged, stirred the stew, tasted it. Instantly he doubled up, eyes watering, choking, gasping for breath, while Bakr pounded him on the back.

"You put twice as much on!" he said accusingly to Bakr.

"But I'm used to the stuff," Bakr said. "And I like it. You'd better have a fresh bowl and try again."

Dudley permitted Bakr to serve him a second time, but he flatly refused a second offer of the sauce. He ate glumly and finished his meal in silence. Eleanor mockingly added more sauce to her food and devoted her full attention to Bakr.

"Now, then," Bakr said, when they had finished eating. "A nightspot or two. Some dancing such as you've never seen before, where the partners exchange affectionate glances from across the room. Singing to a weird musical scale that approximates a banshee's howling. Comedians who have contests to see who can tell the most pointless story, and the more pointless it is, the louder the natives laugh. Nonalcoholic liquor that tastes like water laced with extract of prunes. Maylorian nightlife is about as wide open as a prison camp, but you might as well sample it now and see what you're in for."

"No, thank you," Dudley said. "I want to work on this insurance problem."

"I vote for the nightlife," Eleanor said.

Dudley glared at her.

"We'll drop Walter at the apartment," Eleanor told Bakr. "He works better when I'm not around."

"I can understand that," Bakr said.

Bakr stopped his 'car at the apartment entrance, and Dudley walked away without a backward glance. His anger at Eleanor's transgressions long since had dulled to indifference. He was thinking, rather, about McGivern. How would McGivern go about selling insurance to the citizens of Maylor? Better—how would McGivern expect Dudley to proceed?

He made himself comfortable on the narrow sofa, his inhalator at his elbow, and confronted the problem through fragrant puffs of smoke. His objective, as he saw it, was to condition the natives to think of personal injury or property loss in monetary terms. Once they grasped the concept of financial compensation, their awareness of the need for insurance would follow inevitably. One claim, properly settled, would establish a precedent; two would set a pattern.

But how could he properly settle a claim if there was no insurance in force?

He dug Galactic's *Underwriting Handbook* from a suitcase and began listing endorsements to standard policy forms that might make them more appealing to the Maylorites. He found so few that seemed appropriate that he began to create his own endorsements. When Bakr and Eleanor finally returned, potently trailing alcoholic fumes, the floor of the small living room was littered with paper, and Dudley was nursing a headache.

"I thought there was no alcohol on Maylor," he said sourly.

"Officially there isn't," Bakr said. "It does such appalling things to

those delicate Maylorian stomachs that it's banned as a poison. Fortunately the Maylorites are such innocent, trusting souls that smug-
gling is child's play. I brought my private stock with me. How are
you making out?"

"I'm not," Dudley admitted.

"You'll have to face the facts, old man. Insurance, and the
Maylorites, are absolutely incompatible. They're a disgustingly ethi-
cal race. They not only don't want something for nothing, but they
positively refuse to accept it. They're also disgustingly well balanced.
There isn't a mental hospital or a psychiatrist on Maylor. They
aren't afraid of the future, or of fate, or of the so-called 'acts of God.'
They aren't even superstitious. Take away greed and fear, and what
motives do you have left for buying insurance?"

"That takes us back to lesson number one in the sales manual,"
Dudley mused. "Motivation. If the old standbys won't work, we'll
have to think up some new motives."

"*You'll* have to think them up, old man. I resigned from thinking
about the Maylor situation a long time ago. Naturally I wish you
luck, and if I can help in any way except by thinking, let me know."

For the next two days Dudley spent most of his waking moments
in futile thinking. He thought lying on the sofa, hands clapped to his
ears to filter out some of the racket caused by the construction work
going on just above his head. He thought leaning from the window,
watching the tangle of traffic in the street below and waiting with
bated breath for a load of brick to snap the slender rope and crush
an innocent passerby. The load passed his window, and on one as-
cent he noticed that it bumped the side of the building frequently
and that the bumping had frayed the rope sling on all four sides. If
one strand parted—he turned away, shaking his head. No consci-
entious insurance underwriter would accept coverage on such a risk,
and yet he would have to do so if he wanted to sell insurance on
Maylor. There were no better risks.

When he tired of the apartment, he went to the Galactic office
and spent tedious hours contemplating the lockless door. Bakr
helped tremendously by entertaining Eleanor, but by the end of that
second day she was complaining that she had seen all of Maylor City
that she wanted or intended to see.

On the third day Dudley's rented groundcar was delivered, and
Dudley and Bakr took it out for a driving lesson. Dudley drove
slowly, horrified at the risks taken by the nonchalant pedestrians,
and Bakr chuckled repeatedly at his discomfiture.

"How are you doing with the insurance situation?" Bakr asked.

"I haven't been able to come up with anything," Dudley confessed. "If I could manage a proper settlement of just one claim, I'd have a strong selling point to work with. But how can I settle a claim if there's no insurance in force?"

"One claim," Bakr said thoughtfully. "Yes, a claim would be a help—if you could talk the claimant into *being* a claimant."

They had turned into a quiet residential section, and the 'car was bouncing wildly on the irregular cobblestones. "One claim," Bakr said again. "You have insurance on yourself, don't you? Didn't you write a liability policy on this groundcar?"

"Of course. But a claim involving myself—"

"A claim is a claim, no matter who it involves. And—" Bakr grabbed at the steering wheel, "—here it is!"

The 'car veered crazily. A woman screamed, and Dudley frantically dug at the brake pedal. He brought the 'car to a halt inches short of a flimsy wood dwelling and leaped out to bend over the young woman who lay pinned under it.

"Why didn't you use your brake?" Bakr hissed. "You've killed her!"

Dudley turned his back on the crushed body, valiantly trying not to be sick. "Is she dead?"

"They don't come any deader," Bakr said grimly. "Look—I'll have to get to Eleanor right away. Hide her somewhere."

"Eleanor?"

"Leave it to me. I'll take care of it."

He pushed through the gathering crowd of spectators and broke into a run. Dudley leaned against the car and miserably contemplated the still form that lay beneath its ponderous wheels.

A young doctor arrived from somewhere. With the help of the spectators he pulled the body from under the 'car, clucked his tongue sadly, and sacrificed his white robe to cover the dead woman. Three police officers trotted up looking ridiculously gay in their checkered robes. One took charge of the situation and sent the other two hurrying off on urgent errands. He accepted Dudley's identification and recorded the information on a report form. The crowd of spectators continued to grow. Dudley searched the circle of faces for indications of the indignation he expected, and to his intense surprise he found them regarding him with polite sympathy.

The police officer patted him on the shoulder. "The judge should be here soon."

"Judge?" Dudley exclaimed.

"Why don't you wait in the 'car?"

Dudley swallowed his protest and staggered to the 'car. His knees had been on the verge of collapse since he first saw the woman's body. He eased himself into the rear seat and waited, and soon the woman's husband appeared, escorted by a police officer, and the judge arrived from the opposite direction in a flurry of scarlet robes. The husband, a sturdy, honest-looking young man in a tradesman's robe, bent resignedly over his dead wife and then quietly stepped aside. The judge, a robust old man with formidably sagging jowls, studied Dudley's papers with a scowl.

"An Alien! Now we shall have all manner of tiresome complications. Have you a wife, Alien Dudley?"

"Certainly," Dudley said.

"You have a wife but no manners at all!" the judge snapped.

"You must stand before the judge," the police officer whispered.

Dudley scrambled from the car and faced the judge.

"And you must say, 'Your Wisdom,' when you answer," the police officer whispered.

"Now, then," the judge said. "It would be entirely too much to expect that your wife would be here on Maylor. Where is she?"

"Here on Maylor," Dudley said, belatedly remembering to add, "Your Wisdom."

"Excellent!" The judge's glum expression vanished. He flashed a plump smile at Dudley and examined the papers again. "Then we can settle this matter before lunch. Is your wife at this address?"

"She was there when I left this morning, Your Wisdom."

"Excellent!"

"Do you wish her to be brought here, Your Wisdom?" the police officer asked.

"We shall go there. At once."

"In the violator's 'car, Your Wisdom?"

"Of course. Otherwise, I shall be late for lunch."

Dudley rode in the rear seat with the bereaved husband; the judge rode in front beside the police officer, who drove. Dudley uneasily watched the husband, who had not spoken. If the young man was not dazed by shock, his composure was truly heroic.

Dudley turned away and sought to convince himself that he had nothing to worry about. He had insurance—very good insurance. He said, "Your—Wisdom?"

The judge turned.

"I have insurance, Your Wisdom."

The judge considered this. "What is insurance?" he asked.

"It's—well—it's insurance, you see, and when there's an accident—"

He broke off lamely. The judge had returned his attention to the clutter of traffic that surrounded them. They continued the trip in silence.

The police officer parked the 'car a short distance from the apartment entrance, and they moved toward it in single file, Dudley making a cautious circuit of the area beneath an ascending load of brick. The judge stoically marched straight ahead.

They climbed the stairs. Dudley opened the door of the apartment —which, like his office, had no lock—and called, "Eleanor!"

There was no answer. The apartment was empty. Dudley examined the luggage and noted that a suitcase was missing.

"She isn't here, Your Wisdom," he told the judge.

"Indeed. She is visiting a neighbor, perhaps? Or gone purchasing?"

"I guess she's just—gone. She took a suitcase."

"Indeed." The judge seated himself on the sofa and looked at Dudley severely. "It seems that I shall after all be late for lunch." He nodded at the police officer. "You will make inquiries. At once."

"Yes, Your Wisdom."

"And you." The judge pointed at Dudley. "I warn you. If this case is not settled promptly, I intend to charge my maximum fee."

"I don't mind paying your maximum fee, Your Wisdom," Dudley said. "I don't really see what Eleanor has to do with this. After all, I *do* have insurance."

"Eleanor is your wife's name? She has everything to do with it. On this world we follow the Rule of Justice."

"But my insurance—"

"You have deprived this man of his wife. You must give him your wife. If he is willing to accept her, that is. It is only simple justice."

"Eleanor might not consent to that," Dudley protested.

"She has no choice in the matter."

"But my insurance—"

"What *is* this insurance?"

"It will pay him a cash settlement for his loss, Your Wisdom."

"Cash!" the judge screamed. "You would substitute money for justice? What barbarous customs you Aliens have!"

The return of the police officer saved the judge from the attack of apoplexy that seemed imminent. The two conferred in whispers, and the judge's expression gradually changed from one of anger to amazement. "A conspiracy?" he demanded.

"It would appear so, Your Wisdom."

"But the Alien Dudley could not have warned his wife. He did not even know our Rule of Justice."

"The fact remains, Your Wisdom—"

"True. The fact remains. And if the Alien Dudley is involved in the conspiracy, I shall be harsh with him. What are we to do with him in the meantime, if I am not to miss my lunch altogether?"

"I don't know, Your Wisdom."

"You should know. Justice is your profession, too. We must incarcerate him. That is the Rule—incarceration after the event and before the judgment. The question is where? In all of my judicial experience such a thing has never happened. Do you have any knowledge of a judge incarcerating a violator?"

"No, Your Wisdom."

"We once had special places of incarceration, but because of our present commendable efficiency in applying the Rule of Justice, they are no longer needed. Several legal histories mention them. They don't assist us in the present dilemma, however. I leave the entire problem in your hands, officer. Incarcerate the violator!"

"Yes, Your Wisdom."

"And continue your search for the wife, of course. For the next three hours I shall be at lunch."

After a lengthy conference with his colleagues, the police officer decided to incarcerate Dudley in his own apartment. The only other place available, it seemed, was his own home, and he saw no reason to take a violator into his home when the violator had a home of his own to be incarcerated in.

"You must not leave until the judge orders your release," the police officer said. He left, taking the bereaved husband with him, and Dudley found himself officially incarcerated by an unlocked door. The remainder of the day he paced the small apartment, counted the bricks that were hoisted past his window, cursed Hamal Bakr's thoughtless blundering, and, when he could force himself to concentrate, gave fleeting thought to the insurance problem.

What Maylor needed, he decided, was an entirely different concept of the insurance claim settlement: a type of barter arrangement where the insurance company restored a loss without reference to money. It would create endless complications, and it would require the training of an entirely new breed of claims adjustor, but he thought he could, given sufficient time, develop claim procedures that would meet the requirements of Maylor's strange Rule of Justice.

Thaddeus McGivern was not in the habit of allowing anyone sufficient time for anything. The plaque on his office wall read, "RESULTS—NOW!"

The police officer called again the next day—not to see if Dudley had escaped his incarceration, which possibility evidently had not even occurred to him, but to see if Eleanor had returned.

"The judge is becoming impatient," he announced. "I apologize for the reflection on your honesty, but he has asked me to determine if you are hiding your wife."

"Certainly not," Dudley said. "Eleanor isn't the kind of wife one would hide when there's a good chance of getting rid of her. I haven't the vaguest notion of where she is. Unless—you might ask an Alien named Hamal Bakr. He probably knows."

"We have asked Alien Bakr. He says he does not know."

"Did you search his apartment?"

"What would be the point of that when he has said she is not there?"

"I have a feeling," Dudley said, "that this is going to be a long incarceration."

The following morning Dudley was awakened by a violent pounding on his door. Sleepily he stumbled to open it, and the enraged apparition that greeted him shocked him into instant, terrified wakefulness. "McGivern!" he gasped.

The apparition remained—as large as life and several degrees angrier. McGivern's purple suit was immaculate, but he'd crushed his hat in his hand. He pointed with it. "Dudley!" he bellowed. "Why aren't you at the office?"

"Where did you—I mean, how—"

"I just arrived. On the *Indemnity*, of course, and my first stop was the Galactic office to see how my special troubleshooter was proceeding with the revitalization of our business on this planet. I'd like to hear about this new technique that enables you to sell insurance while in bed."

"There's been some trouble," Dudley said lamely.

"Nonsense! Get dressed, man, and come along. There's *work* to do!"

"I can't come," Dudley said. "I've been—well—arrested."

"Arrested? Have you let this bunch of hicks—" McGivern waddled across the room and sank his weight into the protesting sofa. "I've been patient with you, Dudley, far too patient, but I've reached the end. You won't learn. You have enough ability to fill even my shoes, someday, but you lack gumption, and without gumption your ability isn't worth a damn. What sort of trouble?"

"It's rather complicated."

"I'll bet it is. You're under house arrest, I take it." He scratched fretfully at the polished dome of his bald head. "I'd hate to let you go, Dudley, but you just won't learn. Take that situation on Himil. All you had to do was bribe a few legislators, and you funked it."

"I thought I could find an honest way—"

"Dudley, we are not moralists or philosophers. We're practical businessmen." He pointed his hat again. "Be *ruthless*, Dudley. Chart your objective and smash anyone that gets in the way. You aren't playing school games, Dudley. You don't give back the marbles you win at the end of the day. Here's an entire planet without insurance. It's an opportunity to make any ambitious resident manager drool. What have you done about it?"

"I've worked out a plan for an entirely new—"

"Bah! What have you *done*? Galactic can't pay stockholders' dividends with plans." He struggled out of the cavity in the sofa and thrust a fistful of money at Dudley. "Here—fix this arrest thing. I'm going to nose around and get the feel of the situation."

"I don't think—"

"Good. You waste entirely too much time thinking. Stop it and start *doing* a few things. The hotels in this town stink, so I'll be staying on the *Indemnity*. As soon as you've fixed the police, report there. I can't give you more than a couple of days, Dudley. If you aren't straightened out by then, you're through."

He left Dudley nervously fingering the bribery money.

Dudley spent the remainder of the day alternately pondering the insurance problem and wondering what the police officer would do if he left the apartment. He had no intention of offering a bribe, either to the police or to the judge. The only thing that would secure his prompt release was finding Eleanor. She'd never consent to being ordered into a marriage, but if she were found, the police would have no further claim on Dudley. Their problem would be with Eleanor, and they were welcome to it.

He wondered, though, if he would be ruthless enough to turn her over to the police even if he did locate her. She was not to blame for Bakr's muddled attempt to create an insurance claim.

He went to bed early that night, and he slept very badly.

The next morning the police officer came with the startling news that Eleanor had surrendered voluntarily. Her marriage to the dead woman's husband had been recorded, and Dudley's incarceration was terminated. The judge would, when he got around to it, bill Dudley for his fee.

"Am I divorced—legally separated—from Eleanor?" Dudley demanded.

"Certainly not! What if her new husband should divorce her? Just because you have deprived that man of his wife is no reason for your wife to be deprived of a husband. In order to be separated from her, you would have to divorce her yourself."

"Thank you for explaining it so clearly," Dudley said.

He drove his groundcar to the spaceport. McGivern's yacht, the *Indemnity*, was parked in a choice location near the terminal building where a sign said, "No Landing Permitted in This Area." McGivern was having breakfast. His temper had not improved since the previous day. The steward set a place for Dudley, and McGivern said, snarling around a mouthful of toast, "I've been up all night. Did you know that this crummy planet doesn't even have an underworld?"

"No," Dudley said, "but it doesn't surprise me."

"All I need is an arsonist and a few thieves. With organization, they could create an overwhelming need for insurance within a week." He raised a steaming cup of beverage to his lips, drained it, and slammed it down again. "Nothing. I can import them, of course, but I'd much prefer to patronize the local underworld. What do you have?"

"What is needed," Dudley said, "is an entirely different concept of claim settlement. A type of barter arrangement that would replace a lost object without reference to money. For example, where the liability insuring clause reads, 'The Company will pay in behalf of the insured,' we could change it to read, 'The Company will *furnish* in behalf of the insured.'"

"I don't like it," McGivern said. "These people are basically no different from people anywhere. Get them accustomed to the idea, and they'll gladly take money. You won't be able to stop them. But I agree that there are two aspects to this problem. The fire rate is unbelievably low. There aren't any thefts at all. There are hardly any groundcar accidents, and that isn't just unbelievable, it's impossible. We'll have to bring about enough losses to make insurance necessary, and we'll have to establish a precedent or two for settling losses with money. You take the second one. I'll look in on you tomorrow and see what you've done with it."

"I still think we should hire a local attorney to draw up new insurance policies to conform with local practices."

"There aren't any attorneys on Maylor," McGivern snapped. "I looked into that the first thing—which is what you should have done. Get a move on and find me that claim precedent."

Late the next morning Dudley sat at his desk in the Galactic office, nervously contemplating a blank sheet of paper. He'd been up all night, and the blank sheet of paper was the same one he'd started with the previous day. He leaped to his feet in panic when the door opened, but it wasn't McGivern—it was Hamal Bakr.

"Come home, old man," Bakr said with a grin. "All is forgiven. Eleanor has lunch waiting."

"What are you talking about?" Dudley demanded. "Eleanor just married—"

"Her new husband divorced her this morning."

"It didn't take him long to get acquainted with her."

"Oh, he didn't *want* to divorce her," Bakr said. "He couldn't help himself."

"Eleanor frequently affects people that way."

"Nonsense. Have you looked into the divorce laws on Maylor? You should. If a husband refuses to eat the food his wife prepares, that's grounds for divorce. Eleanor fixed the guy's breakfast yesterday morning, right after the marriage ceremony. She laced the food with that special sauce of mine. The guy got sick and had to be pumped out. For lunch she gave him more of the same, and his sensitive Maylorian stomach put him in the hospital overnight. This morning he refused to eat breakfast, and she called in a judge and got her divorce."

"Obviously some woman thought up that law."

"You may be right. A man can divorce his wife any time he likes, just by refusing to eat, but there's no divorce unless she makes the complaint herself and proves there's nothing wrong with the food by eating it herself. Fortunately Eleanor has developed a taste for my sauce. It solved the problem neatly."

"Very neatly," Dudley agreed. "Have you seen McGivern?"

"Saw him yesterday. He gave me my new assignment—resident manager on Nunquad. It's a pushover, and I leave tonight as planned. Now come to lunch."

They walked back to the apartment, Dudley maintaining a glum, meditative silence, and Bakr cheerfully commenting on Maylorian social customs and several times plucking Dudley bodily from the menacing traffic. Eleanor met them at the apartment door, kissed Dudley gushily, and escorted him to the luncheon table.

"Maylorian stew," she said brightly. "The recipe was the property of the deceased wife of my ex-husband."

"Too bad she didn't take it with her," Dudley muttered. He poked doubtfully with his spoon, took a small amount to sample—and doubled up in agony.

"You put that sauce in it!" he exclaimed, when he had rinsed out his mouth and wiped his eyes.

"Delicious, isn't it?" Eleanor asked. "Have some more."

"I can't eat the stuff, and you know it."

"This is a terrible blow to a woman's pride," Eleanor said. She went to the apartment door and opened it. The old judge stood there scowling.

"At lunchtime, too," he grumbled. "You Aliens have no innate sense of decency. Why can't you divorce your wives at breakfast?"

"Your Wisdom," Eleanor said, "my husband refuses to eat the food I have prepared."

"Is this true?" the judge demanded. "I ask you now, in the presence of a witness, to eat."

Dudley glared at Eleanor. He clenched his teeth and firmly shook his head.

"You will now eat of the food to demonstrate that it is properly prepared," the judge said to Eleanor.

"Certainly," Eleanor said. She took Dudley's bowl and ate noisily. "Delicious stuff," she said.

"The witness will note that the husband has refused to eat and that the wife has eaten. Present yourself at my office with your witness, and I shall draw up your bill of divorcement."

"Certainly, Your Wisdom," Eleanor said. "Shall we come now?"

"After lunch," the judge said. "That'll be in about three hours." He went out, banging the door behind him.

"I still have some packing to do," Eleanor said. She flitted into the bedroom.

"I suppose Eleanor is leaving Maylor with you," Dudley said to Bakr.

Bakr nodded. "The ship leaves at midnight. We'll have the captain marry us as soon as we go on board."

"You're entirely welcome," Dudley said.

"Glad you feel that way, old man—though I can't understand why you're so eager to give up a wife like Eleanor. She was afraid you'd fight it."

"She flatters herself."

"At least we can part friends. And we wish you luck with the insurance problem and especially with McGivern. I've never seen the old boy in such a violent mood. It's too bad we didn't think of that divorce gimmick earlier. We could have saved a lot of trouble."

"Bakr!" Dudley exclaimed. "You killed that woman deliberately!"

Bakr grinned. "So what? Have you worked for McGivern all these years without his sermon getting through to you? Hasn't he ever pointed his finger and said, 'Be ruthless!'?"

"He has. Quite recently, in fact."

"You should have listened. Men at the home office have been

wondering for years when their bright boy Dudley will grow up and start doing a man's work. The groundcar accident was Eleanor's idea. She wanted to get you incarcerated so you couldn't keep her from leaving Maylor. Apart from divorce, the law on this planet is entirely on the husband's side. But neither of us bore you any ill will, and when we thought of that divorce gimmick we used it to get the judge and the police off your back. We didn't have to, you know. I could have smuggled Eleanor away from Maylor and left you incarcerated indefinitely. Ready, Eleanor?"

"Ready," Eleanor said, bringing two suitcases from the bedroom. "You can junk the rest of the stuff, Walter, unless you want to keep it as a memento. Bye, bye. Keep a grip on yourself and don't be *too* ruthless."

Dudley went to the window and looked out. He saw Bakr and Eleanor leave the building together and walk slowly through the construction area. There was a momentary lull in the street traffic; the two of them were alone except for the workers, who were raising another load of brick.

The impulse struck Dudley so suddenly, the timing was so perfect, that he acted before he quite knew what he was doing. He whipped his penknife from his pocket, leaned out, sliced the nearest strand of rope. The sling collapsed instantly and the entire load of brick poured down upon Bakr and Eleanor.

The horrified workers ran forward. Dudley turned away, seated himself on the sofa, and waited. His only thought was that the pathetic body under his groundcar had somehow been revenged, and he almost looked forward to suffering whatever penalty this queer Maylorian legal system imposed for killing one's soon to be ex-wife.

Then McGivern burst into the room. "You idiot!" he panted. "Have you lost your mind?"

Dudley smiled calmly. "I've never felt saner."

"I was across the street—saw the whole thing." McGivern flopped down beside him. "I don't blame you for getting rid of that alley cat, but—in broad daylight, with fifty witnesses about? There's bound to be a scandal, your connection with Galactic will be publicized, and it'll be bad for business. Had you thought about that?"

"I hadn't thought of it in precisely that way."

"You wouldn't. Consider yourself fired as of yesterday. If you can manage this so Galactic isn't mentioned, I'll furnish any money you need for your defense and buy you a one-way ticket to the world of your choice when—or if—they let you go."

"That's magnanimous of you."

"I think so. Why'd you have to kill Bakr, too? I'll admit he wasn't much more than an ornament, but he had his uses. Of all the stupid, asinine, irrational things to do—"

There was a knock at the door. Dudley calmly admitted a police officer.

"There's been a most unfortunate accident," the officer said.

"*Accident!*" McGivern exclaimed.

The police officer looked at him doubtfully. "Which of you is the Alien Dudley?" Dudley nodded gravely. "A clumsy oaf of a workman has managed to kill your wife," the officer said. "Would you oblige us by identifying the body?"

"Is that necessary?" Dudley asked.

"No. Two of your neighbors already have done so. I have sent for a judge and the workman's wife."

"The *workman's* wife?" McGivern sputtered. "What the devil for?"

"The workman has killed Alien Dudley's wife. He must, therefore, give his wife to Alien Dudley. Are you not familiar with our Rule of Justice?"

For one of the few times in his life, McGivern was speechless.

"I shall return when all is ready for the marriage ceremony," the police officer said.

"Thank you," Dudley told him.

He returned to the window. A crowd of spectators had blocked off the street. Workmen were reloading the bricks, and a doctor's robe was spread over the two bodies.

"*Marriage ceremony!*" McGivern said hoarsely. "What are you up to?"

"Does it matter? You just fired me."

McGivern was silent for a long time. Finally he said, "Does this fiasco have anything to do with solving the insurance problem?"

"Certainly," Dudley told him. "What did you think I was working on?"

He intended the words as sarcasm, but even as he spoke he realized that a possible solution was in his grasp. In all of their previous cases they had been in the awkward position of offering a financial settlement to a claimant who didn't want it. Supposing the claimant demanded such a settlement?

Lost in thought, he paced the floor energetically while a strangely subdued McGivern looked on. "Can I help?" McGivern asked finally.

Dudley shook his head. "It's a long shot."

"I like men who play long shots. I like them even better when they win."

Another knock sounded, and Dudley admitted the police officer, a young judge, and an attractive young Maylorian woman.

"Alien Dudley?" the judge asked. "Are you ready for the ceremony?"

"I'm not completely familiar with your customs, Your Wisdom," Dudley said. "This procedure seems very strange to me. Where I come from, the custom is for the violator to pay financial compensation."

"Such a thing is unheard of on Maylor," the judge said. "How could money compensate for the loss of a wife?"

"Nevertheless, Your Wisdom, I would like to know if I cannot request compensation according to my own custom."

The judge frowned. "I don't know. I can't recall such a thing ever happening."

"Is there any law that would forbid such a thing, Your Wisdom?"

The police officer was regarding Dudley with open-mouthed amazement. The young woman modestly kept her eyes on the floor, as though the conversation could not possibly concern her. The judge had his eyes closed in thought.

"The Rule requires only that justice be done," the judge announced finally. "I should have to consider whether or not it would be unjust to deny you justice according to your own custom. To my knowledge no such request has ever been made of a violator, but if such a request were made, I should—yes, I should feel obliged to honor it. Do you now make this request?"

"I do, Your Wisdom."

"And what amount of compensation do you request?"

"Your Wisdom should establish the amount."

"That would require much thought on my part. There is no precedent, none at all. I shall have to postpone settlement of this case until I am able to reach a decision as to the amount."

"That will be satisfactory, Your Wisdom."

Judge, police officer, and workman's wife filed out solemnly. Dudley closed the door and turned to find himself the recipient of one of McGivern's rare smiles. "Dudley, I badly underestimated you. This is the most brilliant stroke I've ever seen." McGivern scrambled to his feet and waddled about the room excitedly. "And I was telling *you* to be ruthless! You've wrapped the whole thing up nicely. This gives us our legal precedent. One more case—"

"We have it," Dudley said. "My groundcar killed a woman a few days ago. That's why I was under house arrest. The husband—it's a rather complicated story—the husband ended up with nothing because of Eleanor's maneuvering. Now I'll offer him a cash settlement for the death of his wife, the amount to be determined by the judge. He'll refuse, but I'll tell him my own customs demand that I give it to him. He'll end up accepting it if only to oblige me. The Maylorites are a very obliging people."

"Well done, my boy. *Well done!*"

"And what progress have you made with *your* problem?"

McGivern started. "That's what I came to see you about. These people are so naïve that hiring professional underworld men would be a waste of money. Last night I took a few crewmen from the *Indemnity*, and we set a dozen fires and looted twenty shops. Did you know that they don't even lock their doors?"

Dudley nodded.

"I've arranged to stay on for a few days. I'm going to take a ground-floor office in a conspicuous location and get out some advertising circulars. We'll hit different neighborhoods tonight and tomorrow night, and after that you won't have to sell insurance. They'll come demanding it."

"You may be underestimating them."

"Nonsense. You take care of those claims, and then I want you to start canvassing the northwest section and explain fire insurance to the neighbors of the people who had fires last night. I'll be looking for that new office. I'll meet you back here this evening."

"Right," Dudley said.

McGivern was waiting when Dudley returned to the apartment. He said quickly, "How'd you make out?"

Dudley seated himself wearily. "I *think* I've established an entirely new legal principle. And I'm worn out."

"You *think?* Is that the best you could do?"

"The judges are coming tonight to give me their verdicts. I've been to the northwest section. Whatever you used to start those fires was darned effective."

"The *Indemnity's* engineering officer made some incendiary bombs. He could only get a dozen ready on short notice, but tonight there'll be twice as many."

"If you'd planted them differently, you could have had much better results," Dudley said.

"I suppose. We don't want to burn down the city, though. A small fire is better for our purposes than a large one." He chuckled. "It wouldn't do to burn so much that they have nothing left to insure."

"What'd you do with the stuff that was stolen?"

"It's stashed away on the *Indemnity*. We'll dump it as soon as we get into space."

"Then tonight you'll start twenty-four fires?"

"Right," McGivern said. "And we'll loot about fifty shops. Southwest section this time."

"And the new office?"

"Couldn't find anything I liked. I'll look again tomorrow. What is this legal principle you're working on?"

"I finally found out what was behind the Maylorian Rule of Justice. On this world the husband has to put up a sum of money when he's married—a kind of bride fee. The whole point in giving the violator's wife to the husband of the victim is that it supplies him with another wife without cost. Actually it's much more complicated than that, and the practice is encrusted with all manner of historical twists and precedences. What I'm trying to establish is that this is not a Rule of Justice—it's manifestly unjust because it breaks up a marriage and forces unknown and probably unwanted new spouses on the violator's wife and the victim's husband, who are innocent parties. The problem could be solved easily and justly by requiring the violator—or his insurance company—to supply the marriage money so the husband of the victim can choose his own wife."

McGivern nodded thoughtfully. "If they accept that, we'll certainly have a basis for selling insurance."

Dudley said tiredly, "They've already accepted it on an optional basis. They're not ready to dump a time-tested social custom on the world of an Alien, but they're willing to let the victim's husband demand the price of a new wife in compensation if he prefers it that way. What I'm trying to get from them is a legal requirement that all groundcar drivers carry insurance—in the interest of justice."

McGivern's eyes bulged with excitement. "Gad! And Galactic is the only insurance company on Maylor!"

A knock sounded. "Want to hear the verdict?" Dudley asked.

"I can't wait!"

Dudley opened the door and brought in the two judges and an escort of three police officers. The old judge muttered, "Tomorrow would have done just as well. I'll be late for dinner."

"Have you reached a decision, Your Wisdom?" Dudley asked.

"We have. Your petition is granted. Settlement in the two cases in which you are involved shall be as you requested, and we take note of your generous offer to accept a token settlement from the workman whose clumsiness killed your wife. Your petition is also granted as to the insurance requirement, which will be presented to the Council tomorrow, along with the charter application of the Maylorian Insurance Company."

"*Maylorian* Insurance Company?" McGivern exclaimed.

"Thank you, Your Wisdom," Dudley said. "Did you record in full the conversation that took place while you were waiting?"

The judge sighed. "We did. We found it difficult to believe, but the facts you have revealed to us support it completely. We accept your recommendations. The charter of the Galactic Insurance Company will be revoked tomorrow. Clearance will be denied Alien McGivern's yacht until the stolen articles are returned and compensation paid for the fire damage. We will arrange with the Interplanetary Authority to securely incarcerate him at the port until justice has been fulfilled. Is this satisfactory?"

"Perfectly satisfactory," Dudley said. "I'd like a few words in private with Alien McGivern, and then you can have him."

"Certainly."

Dudley closed the door after them. It was the first time he'd ever been able to face McGivern without being afraid of him, and he'd looked forward to this moment with intense pleasure. The expected blast of anger did not materialize, however. McGivern said quietly, "You're out of your mind."

"On the contrary, the longer I stay on Maylor the saner I seem to get."

"I suppose you realize that you're fired."

"I've already sent my resignation to the *Indemnity*."

"I won't accept it. You're fired. I feel a little sorry for you, Dudley. You've ruined what might have been a brilliant career. You'll never hold another job with an insurance company—I can promise you that."

"I already have one," Dudley said. "You're speaking with the new president of the about-to-be-chartered Maylorian Insurance Company. Since I'll have an absolute monopoly of this world's insurance business, I expect to do rather well. I also expect to create an insurance industry aimed at serving the people instead of itself."

"If there was a psychiatrist available I'd have you examined," McGivern said bitterly. "But I don't suppose this damned planet has one. You're sick. Something's happened to you."

Dudley nodded. "You're right. Something did happen to me. Today, for the first time in my entire career, you gave me your wholehearted approval for something I'd done. And all I had to do to get that approval was to ruthlessly exploit a double murder. The more I thought about it, the more I wondered what sort of business this is that downgrades my real accomplishments and rewards me for the worst thing I've ever done. Up to that moment I certainly needed a psychiatrist, but since then I've made a remarkable improvement. Perhaps it's the result of associating with people who aren't greedy or afraid and who have healthy minds." Dudley smiled complacently. "They're so grateful for this exposure of the infamous Galactic Insurance plot that they've given me a public appointment. I'm a member of a committee charged with the guardianship of public morals and customs, and I've already squelched the recommendation by an Alien engineer that Maylor City install one-way streets and traffic lanes."

McGivern glared at him tight-lipped.

"I'm not—really—being *too* ruthless," Dudley murmured as he turned him over to the police.

They took McGivern away, and Dudley left immediately afterward and walked through the crush of rush-hour traffic toward the restaurant where Bakr had taken them that first night. The atmosphere would be sterile, and the food would be disgustingly bland, and this time Dudley expected to enjoy it.

FIRST LOVE

Walt Rogers laid aside his brush, pushed back the easel, and switched off the dim light. The storm had faltered momentarily, and now it surged back with a pounding torrent of rain. Walt stepped to the open window and stood there, oblivious of the water that flooded against his eager young face.

Flashes of lightning ripped aside the darkness and laid bare a familiar landscape twisted strangely. Towering trees bowed submissively before the angrily moaning wind. Water veiled the accumulated filth of the barnyard, and cattle huddled pathetically under a shelter. The rain blurred the outlines of the barn and gave it a somber loveliness.

Lightning flashed again, and thunder snapped and rumbled after it, and Walt leaned forward with his elbows on the windowsill and whispered, "Beautiful! Beautiful!"

But how to paint it?

Of course he could paint how it looked. Any darned fool could paint *that*. But how to paint the sound of it, and the feel of it, and the wonderful, glorious, fresh-breathing smell of it?

He turned away and kicked disgustedly at the easel, and at that moment the thunder struck. It came with a thickening roar that impaled him in clinging fright against the windowsill. As he stood crouched in numbed astonishment, it swelled to a bloated, consuming agony of sound until he winced in pain and clapped his hands to his ears, and still it grew and crescendoed until, at the instant it seemed no longer bearable, it exploded.

He was lying on the floor under the window, in the full blast of the driving rain. Glass tinkled as he moved, and cascaded from his back as he got to his feet. His first thought was to close the window, and he cut his hand on a sliver of glass that remained attached to the empty frame. His ears rang painfully, and the wild roar of the storm now seemed only a subdued mutter. As he stared into the night, fire glowed in the distance, sent an exploring tongue of flame up into the rain, and suddenly leaped skyward.

He ran from his room and down the hallway. As he reached his parents' room his father opened the door, flashlight in hand.

"The lights are out," his father said. "Did your window break? Ours did." He flashed the light into a spare bedroom. "That one's broken, too."

"Dad," Walt said breathlessly, "something happened over by the quarry. There's a big fire. The flames are shooting way up."

"Damn the flames. What happens at the quarry is Zengler's business, not ours." He was looking into the bathroom. "Every window in the house is broken. In this storm, too. We'll be flooded out. Mother, get some plastic, or oilcloth, or anything you can dig up. Get a hammer and some tacks, Walt. We'll have to work fast."

"Shouldn't we telephone?" Walt asked. "About the fire, I mean."

"I've tried the telephone," Walt's mother called from the bedroom. "It's out of order."

Walt turned obediently to go for a hammer and tacks. His father's sharp exclamation halted him. "Walt, your back is cut. It's covered with cuts. What were you doing? Standing by the window?"

"I—yes—"

"What on Earth for?"

"I was watching the storm."

"Good God! At three in the morning—fix him up, Mother. I better get started on those windows."

There was no more sleep for the three of them that night. They covered windows, and swept up broken glass, and mopped. Walt slipped away once to open a door a crack and peer out into the continuing storm. "The quarry—" he began.

"Damn the quarry!" his father said.

"It's still burning."

By the time they finished their cleaning, the storm had passed and a pink dawn was staining the horizon. Walt went out with his father, and they walked across the yard with the water-soaked grass squishing underfoot. Before they entered the barn to check for damage there, they stood looking toward the quarry.

"Whatever it was," Jim Rogers said, "it's burned out now. I'll go take a look. Maybe Zengler had some gasoline stored over there—though I wouldn't know why. But if he's responsible for this, he's going to pay for these windows or he'll never get another lease."

But it seemed that Zengler was not responsible. The fire had burned out a corner of the north pasture, where Zengler certainly had nothing stored. The quarry, and Zengler's property, were undamaged. Neighboring farmers had heard the explosion as a distant roar, and it had done no damage except to their sleep. No one but the Rogers family had seen the fire.

The net result was a brief item in that week's edition of the Harwell *Gazette*, under "Local Briefs." "A mysterious explosion, which might have been a clap of thunder, broke windows at the James Rogers farm during the storm last Monday night."

On the Saturday following the storm, Walt helped his father with the morning chores, as he usually did, and then he took the cows to the pasture. As they lurched away, he cut diagonally across the pasture toward the quarry. The morning was warm, even for early June. White wisps of cloud drifted serenely across the purest of blue skies.

"Beautiful," Walt whispered and wished he had brought his paints.

The mysterious fire had scarred a circle almost a hundred yards in diameter. At the point nearest the quarry it had ruined the fence, and Walt had come out with his father on Tuesday after school to string new strands of barbed wire. The haste had been unnecessary. The cows, for strange cow reasons comprehensible only to themselves, refused to approach the burned area.

Walt climbed through the fence and walked over to the quarry. Water filled a vast hollow that had been excavated long before Walt's birth. The little lake was said to be fifty feet deep at its deepest point. Beyond it, the hill had been sliced away neatly where Zengler's men were blasting out the rock.

Walt sat down by the water and amused himself with the reflections, imagining how he would put them on canvas. The clouds overhead, the one towering oak tree, the mass of the hill beyond—all were mirrored splendidly in the dark, still water. His own image had an amusing, elongated perspective.

He seized at an inspiration. "I'll come this afternoon," he thought, "and do a self-portrait, using the water instead of a mirror. I wonder if it's ever been done."

He felt gloriously happy. School had ended the day before, and he had the entire summer before him. There would be the farm work, of course, but he'd be able to find plenty of time to paint, and paint, and—

He looked longingly at the water. The morning was warm, but it was too early in the year for swimming. The water would be icy. His mother was waiting breakfast for him.

He was out of his clothes in an instant, carelessly dropping them on the rocky bank, and he turned and stepped off into ten feet of water. The chilling shock spurred him to a frantic churning of arms and legs. He broke water, wiped his eyes, and turned to strike out for the opposite side.

Suddenly he whirled and threshed wildly for the bank. He pulled himself out and turned to stare at the water. He could see nothing but his own reflection, peering back at him quizzically.

But he had seen something, something long and dark, drifting up out of the deepest water and nosing purposely toward him. A fish? But there never had been any fish in that water, and a fish of that size would be a monster.

Then he saw it again, a long, sinister-looking shadow that drifted slowly toward the bank and then hung motionless, too deep for him to see it clearly. He waited breathlessly. It tilted and slowly coasted toward the surface, and he found himself gazing into the face of a girl.

He sucked his breath in sharply, and it was seconds before he realized that she was staring at him, too, and that he was nude. Moving slowly, he got to his knees and stretched out on a flat rock, moving his face close to the water.

She remained well below the surface, but by watching her intently he began to make out her features. Her dark mass of hair swayed gently in the water, stretching back the length of her body. A smooth material, greenish even in the dark water, covered her body, molding the contours of her small breasts so distinctly that he felt himself blushing. The water gave her face a curiously flattened appearance, but he measured its perfect oval with an artist's eye and wondered what mysterious color her eyes might have.

Then he noticed the gills.

One of her hands, with delicately webbed fingers, made a circle and pointed to her open mouth. It circled and pointed again. The third time he understood. She was hungry.

Even as he watched, his alert sixteen-year-old mind was probing the imponderable with relentless logic. She was hungry. Of course she was hungry. The storm had been Monday night, so whatever it was that had brought her had crashed and burned Monday night, and this was Saturday. She must be starved. There was nothing in that water for her to eat.

He had read of flying saucers and possible life on other worlds, and he did not pause to speculate. He *knew*. She could not be of this world, so she must have come from another world. How had she come? The charred edge of the pasture was a mere two hundred yards from the water. Could her people, water people, have mastered the intricacies of space flight? She was here. That was answer enough. She was here, and her ship had consumed itself in that mysterious fire that had tossed flames high but seemed to have produced relatively little heat.

He extended one hand slowly, toward her face. She darted backward in alarm, approached again as he withdrew his hand, and repeated her signal. Her webbed hand moved toward her mouth. She was hungry.

Walt leaped to his feet and pulled on his clothing. With one last glance at the face in the water, he started back across the pasture, running.

Edna Rogers took in her son's disheveled appearance and wet mop of curly hair and exclaimed, "What *have* you been doing?"

"Dad," Walt said breathlessly, "I'd like to go fishing. Could I take the car?"

"By yourself?"

"Why—yes."

"Well," Jim Rogers said easily, "I guess summer's officially here. Things are pretty well in hand, and a mess of fish would taste good. Where are you going?"

"I know some good places," Walt said evasively.

Fishing had never interested him. Nothing had interested him except painting and drawing, but he remembered a submerged tree stump in the river south of town. Once when he was out sketching he had seen a boy catch several sunfish there. It was as good a place to start as any.

The girl was hungry. But what could she eat? Raw meat or fresh? What about fruit and vegetables? She lived in the water, so he would get her some fish, if he could. And then he could try some other things.

He left the car parked by the road and cut across the Malloy farm to the river. No one was about, which pleased him. Tense with excitement, he baited his hook and dropped it into the water.

Nothing happened. The bobber drifted idly with the current and eventually snagged Walt's hook on the stump. He freed it and tried again, impatiently counting the minutes. The girl was starving. He told himself that he should have taken her something else. His mother wouldn't miss one steak from the deep freezer. He had to do something quickly, and if the fish weren't going to co-operate—

He whipped his line from the water and ran back to the car. Two miles down the road he pulled in at Marshall's Service Station. Old

Ed Marshall sat by the door of the weathered frame building, tilted back in a chair, reading and enjoying the sunshine.

"Minnows?" he said. "I can let you have some. But if you'd rather get your own, you know where the net is. Take it any time you want it. And say—Sadie'd like another of those pictures of yours. She wants to put it in the guest room."

"She'll get one," Walt said fervently.

He found the neatly folded net in the shed behind the station. He was on his way back to his car when Old Ed called after him, "Sure you can manage by yourself?"

"I can manage," Walt said.

The net was twenty-five feet long and a rather large-meshed affair for capturing minnows. There were those who thought maybe Old Ed used it on larger prey, and Walt, who had seen him in action one morning, was certain of it. And everyone knew about the way the Marshall family lived on fish during the summer.

Old Ed got to his feet and walked over to the car. "I'll tell you, Walt," he said with a confidential grin. "It's a little late in the morning to start out with that thing. And you have to know where to go. If you want fish, why don't you come with me tomorrow?"

"I'd like to give it a try," Walt said.

"I could let you have a few for today."

"And—tomorrow?"

"I go every morning. You're welcome to come along any time you like."

"Thanks," Walt said.

Minutes later he was driving wildly toward the quarry with three healthy-sized bass splashing in a bucket.

Fortunately Zengler's men did not work on Saturday. The quarry was deserted, the water dark and lifeless. Walt leaned over and splashed frantically with his hand. Then he saw her, gliding swiftly toward him. She halted well below the surface.

He caught one of the fish and held it low over the water. She did not move until he lowered it into the water, and then she backed slowly away. Suddenly the fish jerked and slipped from his clutching fingers. He gasped in dismay as it darted away.

But in a flash the girl was after it. She overtook it with dazzling speed, captured it deftly, and with a graceful twist headed downward and disappeared. It all happened in an instant—a blur of movement in the water directly below him, and then he saw only her long, shapely legs receding as she sped away from him.

He waited for a time, and then, when she did not reappear, he released the other fish. It would be humiliating for her, he thought, to be summoned for her food like a trained animal. And if the fish were there, he now had no doubt that she could catch them.

Then, off to one side, he saw the dark form lying motionless in the water. She was watching him. He stretched out on the bank, his face close to the water, and looked at her.

"Beautiful," he murmured.

There was a strange, unearthly loveliness about that water-shrouded face, and in the blurred gracefulness of her slender figure, and in the long, flowing hair. The hair fascinated him. Most of the girls of his acquaintance were wearing their hair in disturbingly short, boyish styles. He considered girls formidable enough when they looked like girls.

He wondered how he appeared to her through the shimmering veil of water. Did he possess an alien ugliness that fascinated her? Suddenly the question became very important. He told himself bitterly that he was only her provider, her meal ticket, and she could not possibly have any interest in him beyond that; but he lingered long that morning, and he was back again after the evening chores, lying on the bank as the sun vanished and the shadow of the scraggly old oak tree that lay quietly on the water sank into invisibility. He stayed on until the dusk deepened and her face was no longer visible.

He remembered a poem he had once seen in an old schoolbook of his mother's when he went through it looking for subjects to draw. It suggested rich colors and strange scenes to him, but he had not understood it. Now he found it again.

> Come live with me, and be my love,
> And we will some new pleasures prove,
> Of golden sands, and crystal brooks,
> With silken lines, and silver hooks.
>
> There will the river whispering run
> Warm'd by thy eyes, more than the Sun.
> And there th'enamour'd fish will stay,
> Begging themselves they may betray.
>
> When thou wilt swim in that live bath,
> Each fish, which every channel hath,
> Will amourously to thee swim,
> Gladder to catch thee, than thou him. . . .

He dreamed that night of a sheltered mountain stream, pure, crystal clear, deep, where young lovers could splash and play and love in the tumbling torrent. He awoke in a chill of fright. What would be-

come of her? He could care for her during the summer. With Old
Ed's help, he could get plenty of fish. But winter would come, and
thick ice would cover the water. Even if she could survive the cold, it
would be difficult to get food to her. It might be impossible.

And she might die a lonely death in the cold, stagnating water of
the quarry.

The river? He rejected the thought instantly. He knew instinc-
tively that she needed deep water, that she would be helpless and at
the mercy of any passerby in the shoals of that small stream. It was
thirty miles to the nearest lake, which was small. But in the opposite
direction, fifty miles would take him to Lake Michigan. That was
where she should be, with the vast, connecting waters of the Great
Lakes to conceal and protect her solitary life on this strange planet.
But how could he get her there?

He would have to think of something.

He was out before dawn with Old Ed and his net, and they
brought in fish by the milk can full. Walt swore him to eternal secrecy and confided that he wanted to try to stock the quarry. Old Ed
allowed that he didn't think it would work, that the fish would lack
their natural food and the water might be queer for them. But if
Walt wanted to try, why, he enjoyed catching fish, and he'd never
rightly caught all he wanted to catch because he hated to waste
them. Walt saved out enough fish for the Rogers' table and triumphantly dumped the rest into the quarry with the shadowy face
watching him silently from the depths.

Walt took advantage of a lull in the dinner-table conversation to
say cautiously, "Mother, I'd like one of those aqualung outfits."

Edna Rogers set down the steaming dish of mashed potatoes and
stared at him. "Did you ever! What would you do with it?"

"Go in the water," Walt said.

Jim Rogers seemed interested. "Now where around here is there
water for a thing like that?"

"There's the river," Walt said evasively, "and the quarry—"

"You couldn't swim long under water in the river without your
tail fins sticking out. And the quarry's deep enough, but there's nothing there to see. If there was, you probably couldn't see it in that
water. Those lung things are for places where there's lots of water
and lots of fish and things to see."

"Mr. Moore has some of that equipment in," Edna Rogers said,
giving Walt a worried look. "It wasn't very expensive."

"He just has goggles and the things you wear on your feet," Jim
Rogers said. "I told him he'd never sell them. Walt's talking about

these outfits where you have a tank of air on your back and you can
stay under for hours. No sense in it around here. But if you want the
goggles, Walt, go ahead and buy them. You've got your own money,
and if you want to waste it—"

"Thanks, Dad."

"Take some more potatoes, Walter," Edna Rogers said. "You're
burning up a lot of energy these days. All this fishing and swimming—"

"Does him good," Jim Rogers said.

Walt's mother shook her head. "What about your painting,
Walter? You haven't touched it for a week."

Walt said impatiently, "There'll be plenty of time for painting
when I can't go fishing or swimming."

"He spends too much time by himself," Edna Rogers said. "Walt,
Virginia Harlon asks about you every time I see her, and she felt aw-
fully bad because you wouldn't go to her party when she asked you.
She'd teach you to dance, if you'd let her. Then you could go to the
Saturday dances."

Jim Rogers chuckled dryly. "He's young. He'll have plenty of time
to chase after girls."

"I still think he spends too much time by himself." Edna Rogers
shrugged resignedly and changed the subject. "What did Mr.
Zengler want?"

Jim Rogers laughed and laid down his fork. "His boy thinks he
saw some fish over at the quarry. He tried to catch them and didn't
get a nibble, so he wants to dynamite and see what will come up.
Zengler wanted to know if I had any objections."

"Dynamite?" Walt blurted. "Dynamite—the quarry?"

"Yeah. I told Zengler there'd never been any fish there and
couldn't be any, and if he wanted to waste the dynamite that was all
right with me."

"Did you ever!" Edna Rogers said. "Is he going to do it?"

"I don't think so. Zengler's not one to waste anything. What's the
matter, Walt?"

"I've finished," Walt said, getting to his feet. "I'm not very
hungry."

"You might excuse yourself."

"Excuse me, please," Walt said humbly and fled before they could
answer.

The quarry was a blending of dim shadows. In the gathering darkness, the motionless water looked like a smooth extension of the pasture. Walt circled around it and went directly to the shack that
served Zengler as office and storehouse. Zengler's four trucks were

parked haphazardly nearby, three of them battered hulks and the fourth new, its sleek lines evident even in the dusk.

Walt sat down next to the shack and waited.

He knew Roy Zengler. The kid was a young punk who did what he pleased, and if his father told him not to use dynamite, he'd be sneaking around the first chance he got to do it. And old man Zengler would think it was a joke, afterward, and laugh it off.

Crickets chirped busily, and a rabbit loped slowly past, hesitated, and scampered away. The ground became insufferably hard, and Walt finally got to his feet and leaned against the shack. He did not know what to do. If Roy didn't come, Walt could see him in the morning and warn him off, but that would make him much more certain to try it.

A light bounced toward him on the quarry road. A bicycle lurched and skidded in the sand, and its rider leaped off and wheeled it forward. He leaned it against the shed and moved toward the door, keys jingling. Walt stepped out and faced him.

"Roy?"

"Oh, it's you, Walt. Jeez, you scared me. Gonna have a little fun —want to join me?"

"Those fish are mine," Walt said. "I put them there. You let them alone."

"Like hell they're yours. Dad leases this place, doesn't he? You got no business—"

Walt swung. His fist spattered against Roy's face and sent him sprawling. Walt was on him in a flash, his hands found the throat and circled it, and he applied pressure. "Try dynamiting those fish," Walt said grimly, "and I'll kill you."

"All right," Roy said weakly.

Walt released him, and Roy got up slowly. "All right," he said again. "I didn't know. Your old man said—you could have been nice about it. Why didn't you tell me?"

"You let them alone."

"All right."

Roy went to his bicycle, wheeled it out to the road, and mounted. "You can't watch this place all the time," he shouted. "I'll be back. You'll see."

Walt fumbled frantically on the ground, found a stone, and threw it.

"Missed!" Roy shouted. "I'll be back! Just you wait!"

He vanished into the darkness, and Walt stood looking after him, white-faced and trembling with rage and fright, knowing he would be back.

"Your mother and I would like to go over to Coleville tomorrow," Jim Rogers said. "She wants to see her sister, and maybe we'll take in a movie. Think you could manage the evening chores all right?"

Walt, lost in thought, said nothing.

"Walt? Did you hear what I said?"

"What? Oh, sure. I can manage. I always have, haven't I?"

Jim Rogers chuckled. "Sure you have. I was just wondering if you were still with us."

"Will you stay overnight?"

"Nope. We won't be back very early, though. Don't wait up for us."

Walt nodded absently, looked up, found his father regarding him with a troubled frown.

"Something bothering you, Walt?"

"No. Why?"

"You've been acting odd. Your mother's worried about you. So—when you went out last night, I followed you. Don't look so guilty," he went on, as Walt started and flushed crimson. "She was afraid you were getting into trouble, the way you've been staying out nights. I reckon maybe she was more afraid you were getting some girl into trouble. Anyway, I don't see much point in sitting over there by the quarry until after midnight, but if you want to do it, I can't see that any harm can come of it. I know you've always enjoyed going off by yourself. It isn't our way, your mother and I, but we try to understand. So I want you to know we're on your side, and if you have something on your mind we'll try to help."

Walt moistened his lips and swallowed. "Thanks, Dad."

"You're sure there isn't something bothering you?"

"No. Nothing."

"Well—you weren't over there to meet someone, were you? A girl, maybe?"

"No!" Walt said defiantly.

"If you have a girl, or when you have one, you don't have to sneak off and meet her. Bring her here, and we'll make her welcome. Otherwise, well, you're young. There are lots of problems in this life, and you'll run smack into them soon enough. There's no point in rushing around trying to tangle with them now. Might as well enjoy yourself. And—are you sure it's all right about the chores?"

"It's all right," Walt said.

Later, when his parents were safely out of hearing, Walt risked a telephone call. Carl Reynolds, a friend Walt's age, accepted his request as a matter of course. "Sure," he said. "Sure—I'll do chores for you Saturday night. I owe you one, you know. I'll have to clear it with the old man, though."

"Carl," Walt said tremulously, "tell him you're going to help me. Don't tell him I won't be here."

There was a moment of silence, and then Carl laughed. "Sure. I'll tell him that. And I wish you luck, old fellow. Do I know her?"

"No," Walt said. "You don't know her."

Late Saturday afternoon, Walt walked slowly over to the deserted quarry. Somewhere in the depths *she* was—doing what? He knew that he had only to splash, and she would come. But instead he sat down under the oak tree and thoughtfully studied the quiet, dark water. He had come to realize that his was a hopeless love, that there was no middle ground where a creature of the air and one of the water could meet. He had gone swimming in the quarry twice since he had found her. The first time she had fled in seeming panic, and when she did return she kept her distance cautiously.

He wanted only to touch her, to caress the beautiful, flowing hair. She eluded him easily, and then, when she found how awkward his movements were, she circled around him with dazzling speed. He dove to the depths with her, but in the dim, uncertain light it was only a nimble shadow that cavorted about him. His second effort had been as frustrating as the first, and he had not tried again.

True love, he told himself, must be selfless. The happiness of the loved one was the important thing. He had spent hours trying to think of some place, some way for her to live in comfort and safety, where he could still visit her from time to time, even if only to see her through the blurring water. There was no such place. He would have to get her to Lake Michigan, and once those vast waters closed over her he must accept the fact that he could never see her again.

He glanced at his watch and walked toward Zengler's shack. "Has to be timed just right," he reminded himself. A single blow with a rock snapped open the flimsy padlock. There weren't—never had been—any thieves around Harwell, and that lock had served Zengler for years.

Walt lifted the rings of keys from a nail inside the door and ran an appreciative eye over Zengler's new truck. Gas? He could siphon some out of the other trucks if there wasn't enough. Anything else? A bucket. He found two in the corner and set them aside.

Looking up at the truck's high tailgate, he started apprehensively. How would she get in?

In the shack were tools and nails. Scattered about were lengths and scraps of lumber. Walt nailed frantically, fearful that now he might be too late. He should have thought of it sooner. He could have made something easier for her than this rough ramp with strips nailed across it. But this would have to do. He carried the ramp, and the buckets, down to the water, to the spot he had picked out, and then he ran back to the truck.

He drove slowly at first, getting the feel of the truck, timidly testing its deep-throated power. Dusk was settling on the town when he reached Harwell. Nearly everyone would be uptown, but he took no chances. He followed a circuitous route toward the business section, using alleys as much as he could, driving without lights, crossing side streets cautiously.

He kept glancing at his watch. Mr. Warren always closed up promptly at nine, Saturday night or no Saturday night. He couldn't be late, but he didn't dare be too early.

He turned into the alley paralleling Main Street and carefully backed into position. "A. J. Warren and Sons, Farm Implements," the weathered sign over the rear door said. Walt glanced at his watch again, went to the door, and looked in. There were several farmers up front, casually inspecting a new tractor. One of the Warren boys was sweeping up. Walt dropped back into the shadows and waited nervously.

The farmers left one by one. Not until Mr. Warren followed the last one to the door, and locked it, did Walt step forward. Mr. Warren turned and saw him.

"Evening, Walt," he said. "Just closing. Can I do something for you?"

Walt fought to make his voice sound normal. "Dad's decided to take that big stock tank you were talking to him about."

Mr. Warren beamed. "Glad to hear it. What changed his mind?"

"Ours sprung another leak."

"I told him it wouldn't last much longer. I'll send the new one out Monday morning. That be all right?"

"I'll take it now, if you don't mind," Walt said. "I borrowed a truck. It's out back."

"Why, sure. Tank's out in the shed."

"I know," Walt said. "And—Mr. Warren—"

"Yes?"

"Dad will be in Monday to see you about—about—"

"Sure thing, Walt. Your pa's credit is good as gold. Come on, and we'll get it in the truck."

It was easy—so easy that Walt giggled hilariously when he got the truck out of Harwell and pointed toward the quarry. Then he soberly reminded himself that this was only the beginning, and he stopped laughing.

At the quarry he drove down to the water, set his brakes, and got Zengler's pump going. The ancient gasoline engine made a racket that should have been heard for miles, and Walt felt panicky as he directed the stream of water into the tank. Across the fields he could see the lights in the barn, where Carl Reynolds would be finishing the milking. It was taking him longer than Walt had expected. Supposing he heard the pump when he took the cows to the pasture, and came to investigate?

It couldn't be helped. It would take forever to fill the tank by hand.

When the water reached the brim, he cut off the motor and slowly backed the truck into position where he had left the ramp and the buckets. It took him some jockeying to place the truck so that the ramp just reached the edge of the water, and he had to be careful about it. A false move, and Zengler might never find out what had happened to his truck.

He set the brakes. He dropped the tailgate and wedged the ramp into position. Then he leaned over and splashed the water.

She did not come.

"The pump must have frightened her," he muttered.

He splashed again and again.

Suddenly he saw her, a dark shadow in the darker water. He waited for her to edge closer, and then he mounted the ramp. Looking down at the water, alarm gripped him. How could he make her understand what he wanted? He could scarcely see her, and he could only hope that she could see him better. But even if she could, if she understood what he wanted, would she trust him?

He gestured. He moved up and down the ramp. He splashed the water in the tank. And all the while her shadowy form hung motionless in the water below him.

"Oh, God," he pleaded, "make her understand!"

It was getting late. He had to drive fifty miles, and drive fifty miles back, and leave Zengler's truck and get home before his parents got there. And somehow he'd have to explain about the tank.

The darkness deepened, and the moon had not yet appeared. Lights went off in the barn as Carl finished up and headed for home. He could hear the cattle on the other side of the pasture. He stumbled frantically up and down the ramp. There must be some way—

He leaped down and ran for Zengler's shed. Maybe a rope—

He stopped before he got there and turned back. How could a rope help? He couldn't drag her out of the water. Was she afraid of the air? But she'd gotten from the place the ship came down over to the water. He turned back toward the truck, turned again. A light— perhaps if he could light the tank she could see what he wanted her to do. Even a match might help. He fumbled wildly about the shed, knocking things down and finding nothing.

A new fear splashed over him coldly. Perhaps there were others there. Perhaps she wouldn't want to leave by herself. Suppose there were dozens of them?

He started to run back to the truck, and the sound of—something —brought him to a halt. Something, followed by a splash. He ran again.

A wet trail led up the ramp and into the truck. The truck was flooded with the tank's overflow. "She did it!" he gasped. He leaped up the ramp and looked into the tank. She was there, the closest he had ever seen her, a dark form somehow shimmering and dimly luminescent. He threw the ramp and the buckets into the truck and put up the tailgate. With a wild song of joy throbbing in his throat, he started the motor and got the truck into gear.

He took a route that would carry him around Harwell on back roads. He had studied maps—how he had studied them!—and he wanted to keep to lightly traveled roads most of the way. But he would have to hurry. He had no idea how long the girl could live in that tank without having the water changed.

He had been under way only a few minutes when, topping a hill, his lights picked out a car parked by the roadside. He recognized the long lines of Zengler's new cadillac, the only one in the township. He caught a glimpse of a pair of heads close together in the front seat and guessed that it would be Roy Zengler, out with some girl too young to know better.

His foot dug hard at the accelerator. As the truck picked up speed he glanced at the side-view mirror. He saw the light flash on in the Cadillac as Roy flung open the door and leaped out. As long as Walt could see him he was standing in the road, staring after the disappearing truck.

Walt thought with reckless abandon, "He'll tell. They'll go to the quarry, just to make sure, and they'll find the truck gone. They'll think some kids took it for a joy ride, and they'll be looking for them around Harwell, so they'll probably catch me on the way back." He felt a twinge of uneasiness, but he told himself boldly that what happened didn't matter—on the way back. The truck roared on smoothly, powerfully.

He was only ten miles from the lake when he had to risk a stretch of main highway. He was worrying about the girl and trying to decide whether to look for fresh water for her or try to get to the lake as quickly as possible. He kept going because that was easiest, but he continued to worry.

Traffic on the highway was light, and Walt was so engrossed in his concern for the girl that he did not notice the car approaching him from the rear. He did not notice it until it pulled alongside and the red light flashed, and he realized that a state trooper was ordering him to stop. His numbed hands and feet obediently made the proper motions. The truck eased off the road and halted. The police car stopped behind him. Then, as the trooper got out and walked forward, he stepped on the accelerator.

For precious seconds the trooper seemed bewildered. He stood outlined in the lights of his car, waving his hands. Then, as Walt glanced again at the mirror, one hand spouted fire. Walt thought wildly, "The tires—if he hits a tire—"

Glass tinkled behind him as the rear window shattered, and the bullet thudded into the roof of the cab. The fire flashed again, and then the truck nosed over a rise and was safe. Walt drove with the accelerator crushed to the floor, peering anxiously beyond the racing beams of his headlights. A dirt road veered off at a sharp angle to the right, and he made the turn with screaming brakes. He found himself on a winding country road. Around a curve and out of sight of the highway, he switched off his lights. A farmhouse beckoned, and he slowed and skidded into the driveway, rolled as far as the barn, and turned sharply to come to a stop between the barn and a corn crib. Seconds later the police car roared past and disappeared.

A yard light came on. A man opened the farmhouse door and stood looking out at him. Walt backed up, turned, and drove back to the highway. He followed the highway for a short distance, took the first turn to the left, and breathed freely once more as the truck bounced along a rough dirt road. At the next crossroad he turned right and headed for the lake.

In the moon's half light the gently tossing water was beautiful. Walt drove past an unoccupied summer cottage, turned at the edge of the beach, and backed toward the water. A few yards short of his goal, his wheels spun in the loose sand and dug themselves in.

Walt leaped out and dropped the tailgate. Water soaked his knees as he hauled himself up. He placed the ramp in position, and then, as he turned, a stream of water brushed his foot. He knelt, fumbled in the darkness, and found the holes. The trooper's last shots had struck the tank.

And the tank was two-thirds empty.

With a moan he seized the buckets and ran for the lake. For the moment he had no thought that the shots might have struck the girl. He thought only of life-giving water. He splashed into the lake, dipped the buckets, and raced back to the truck. Again and again he made the trip, until his breath came in tormented jerks and his aching legs could carry him no faster than a plodding walk. Still he worked on, dumping water into the tank and seeing it gush forth through the holes.

He lost all sense of time. The water level in the tank was rising slowly—too slowly, he feared—and when finally it occurred to him that she might be wounded or dead, he could not bring himself to look and see. Like an automaton, he continued to carry water.

Then, turning once more with full buckets, he saw her. She stumbled down the ramp and staggered toward him—toward the lake. She moved awkwardly, her feet churning in the sand, and as he hurried to meet her she fell at his feet with weird, whistling gasps.

He bent over to help her and fell back with a cry of horror.

Her face was a gruesome, rubbery mask, her eyes large and sunken. She had no nose. Needlelike fangs protruded from her gaping, gasping mouth. Her hair, her lovely, flowing hair, was short tufts of fur that covered her back from the crown of her head to the base of her spine. The glimmering dark green fabric that she wore was her flesh, spongy and slimy to the touch.

As he stared helplessly, she lurched to her feet, staggered forward, and sprawled at the water's edge with her head submerged. A moment later her webbed feet kicked and tore at the sand, and she slid into the water and disappeared.

Stunned to paralysis, Walt looked after her, unable to move, or think, or do anything but stare bewilderedly at the ruffled sand and the lapping waves. He did not hear the car drive up and stop. He did not notice the lights that pinioned him against the watery horizon. He heard nothing at all until the trooper approached with a sharp command. Then he turned slowly and raised his hands.

The trooper moved forward cautiously, shined a light into his face, and exclaimed, "Why, you're only a kid!"

Walt said nothing.

The trooper searched him deftly, stepped back, and signaled him to drop his hands. "That wasn't very smart. What were you trying to do?"

Walt shook his head. The enormity of what he had done horrified him. The truck, stolen and damaged. The tank, which his father would have to pay for. Running away from the police. And now he'd have to face his parents. What could he tell them? What could he tell anyone?

A few yards out from shore, something broke water with an echoing splash—something big. The trooper whirled. "Good God! What was that?"

Walt shrugged wearily. "Only a fish," he said.

WHO'S ON FIRST?

Priority Rating: Routine
From: Jard Killil, Minister of Juvenile Affairs
To: All Planetary Police Organizations
*   All Interplanetary Patrol Units*
Subject: Juvenile detention escapee Muko Zilo
Enclosures: Character analysis, filmstrips, retinal patterns
*   All law-enforcement agencies are hereby informed of the*
escape of Muko Zilo from the Juvenile Rehabilitation Center on
Philoy, Raff III, Sector 1311. Escapee is presumed to have fled
the planet in a stolen space yacht, Stellar Class II, range
unlimited. His probable destination is unknown.
*   Escapee is not considered dangerous. He possesses low-*
grade intelligence and has no psi ability higher than Class F.
*   Kindly notify Philoy JRC immediately upon detention.*

The major-league baseball season of 1998 was only two weeks old,
and Manager Pops Poppinger wished it was over and done with.
Since opening day his Pirates had managed to lose fourteen games
while winning none, and Pops had only the Baseball Managers'
Tenure Act of 1993 to thank for the fact that he was still gainfully
employed. He'd had that same act to thank for his regular paychecks
during the 1996 and 1997 seasons.

"But it can't last," he muttered. "Congress will repeal the thing
and cite me as the reason."

He strode through the locker room without a glance at his loung-
ing ballplayers, entered his private office, and slammed the door. He
did not want to talk to anyone, especially if that anyone happened to
be wearing a Pirates' uniform. He dropped an armful of newspapers
onto his desk, tilted back in his chair until he could plant his size
thirteen feet in a comfortable position, and opened the top paper to

the sports pages. The headline made him wince. "WHEN IS A PIRATE?" it demanded. Pops stuck a cigar in his mouth as he read and forgot to light it.

"In the venerable days of yore," the article said, "when professional athletic organizations found it necessary to attach themselves to some unfortunate city in the mistaken belief that civic loyalty would induce the population to attend games in person and pay for the privilege, the fair city of Pittsburgh spawned two notable gangs of thieves, the baseball Pirates and the football Steelers. Both organizations had their days of glory. Within the memories of men now living, if you care to believe it, the Pirates won five consecutive world championships and the Steelers four.

"Those days of myth and fable are far behind us. If the Steelers stole anything worth mentioning during the football season just concluded, it escaped this writer's attention. The 1998 Pirates are so far removed from thievery that they will not take a game as a gift. They emphatically demonstrated their moral uprightness yesterday, when their opposition was stricken with that most tragic of baseball diseases, paralytic generosity. The Dodgers committed six errors and presented the Pirates with nine unearned runs. The Dodgers won the game, 27 to 9."

Pops crumpled the paper and tossed it over his shoulder. "Bah! Let 'em rave. It's for sure I ain't got any ballplayers, but I got lots of tenure."

The telephone rang, and he picked it up and growled a response.

"Who's pitching today, Pops?" a cheerful voice asked.

"I dunno," Pops said. "If you reporters find some guy in the press box that ain't got a sore arm, send him down."

He slammed down the phone and reached for another paper. "PIRATES STILL IN REVERSE," the headline said. Pops tossed that one aside without reading it.

A knock rattled the door. Pops ignored it. The knock sounded again, and the door opened wide enough to admit the large, grinning face of Dipsey Marlow, the Pirates' third-base coach.

"Scram!" Pops snapped.

"Some kid here to see you, Pops."

"Tell him I got a batboy. I got a whole team of batboys."

"He's older than that—I think. He says he's got a letter for you."

Pops straightened up and grinned. "From Congress?"

"He says it's from Pete Holloway."

"Send him in."

The kid shuffled in awkwardly. His dimensions looked to be about five feet, five inches—in both directions. Oddly enough, he was not fat. There was an unhealthy thinness about his freckled face, and his overly large ears gave his features a whimsical grotesqueness, but he was shaped like a box and moved like one. He dragged to a stop in front of Pops's desk, fumbled through four pockets, and came up with a letter.

"Mr. Poppinger?"

The high, squeaky voice made Pops's ears ring. "I'm ashamed to admit it," Pops said, "but that's my name."

"Mr. Holloway told me to give this to you."

"The last I heard of Pete Holloway, he was lost in the woods up in Maine."

"He still is, sir. I mean, he's still in Maine."

"You came clear out here to California just to give me this?"

"Yes, sir."

Pops took the envelope and ripped it open.

"Dear Pops," he read. "This here kid Zilo is the most gawdawful ballplayer I ever see on two legs. He also is the luckiest man south of the North Pole. Put him in center with a rocking chair and a bottle of beer and every ball hit to the outfield will drop in his lap. He'll even catch some of them. Sign him, and you'll win the pennant. Yours, Pete. P.S. He also is lucky with the bat."

Pops scratched his head and squinted disbelievingly at Zilo. "What d'ya play?"

"Outfield," Zilo said. He quickly corrected himself. "Outfield, sir."

"Where in the outfield?"

"Anywhere, sir. Just so it's the outfield, sir."

Pops wasn't certain whether he should throw him out or go along with the gag. "I got three outfielders that get by. How about second or short? Between first and third I got nothing but grass."

"Oh, no, sir. Mr. Holloway had me play short, and I made nine errors in one inning. Then he moved me to the outfield."

"I'm surprised he didn't kill you," Pops said. He continued to eye Zilo disbelievingly. "You actually played baseball for Pete?"

"Yes, sir. Last summer, sir. I went to see him a week ago to find out when I could start playing again, and he said he thought you could use me because your season starts before his does."

"What'd you bat?"

"Six-forty, sir."

Pops winced. "What'd you field?"

"A thousand, sir. In the outfield. In the infield it was zero."

Pops got up slowly. "Son, Pete Holloway is an old friend of mine, and he never gave me a bad tip yet. I'll give you a tryout."

"That's very kind of you, sir."

"The name is Pops. And it ain't kind of me after what happened yesterday."

Pops was standing in the corner of the dugout with Ed Schwartz, the club secretary, when the new Pirate walked out onto the field. Pops took one look, clapped his hand to his forehead, and gasped, "My God!"

"I told you I'd find him a uniform," Ed said. "I didn't guarantee to find him one that fit. He just isn't made the way our uniforms are made, and if I were you I'd make sure I wanted to keep him before I called the tailor. Otherwise, if you release him we'll have a set of uniforms on our hands that won't fit anyone or anything except maybe that oversized water cooler in the league offices."

Pops walked over to the third-base coaching box, where Dipsey Marlow was standing to watch batting practice. The Dodger dugout had just got its first incredulous look at Zilo, and Pops waited until the uproar subsided somewhat before he spoke.

"Think Pete is pulling my leg?" he asked.

"It wouldn't be like Pete, but it's possible."

"The way things is going, he ought to know better. I'll look him up when the season is over and shoot him."

Dipsey grinned happily. He was rather pleased with himself in spite of yesterday's loss. As third-base coach he'd been the loneliest man in the Western Hemisphere for seven straight days while the Pirates were being shut out without a man reaching third. Even if his team was losing, he liked to have some traffic to direct.

"You got nothing to lose but ball games," he said.

Zilo had taken his place in the batter's box. He cut on the first pitch, and the ball dribbled weakly out toward the pitcher's mound.

"He's a fly swatter," Dipsey said disgustedly.

Zilo poked two more lazy ground balls and lifted a pop fly to the third baseman. Apparently satisfied, he borrowed a glove and wandered out to left field. He dropped a couple of balls that were hit right at him and stumbled over his own feet when he tried to go a few steps to his left.

"It's a joke," Pops said. "Pete must have seen him catch one. That's what he meant by him being lucky."

Dipsey walked out to left field to talk with Zilo. He came back looking foolish. "The kid says it's all right—he's just testing the atmosphere. It'll be different when the game starts."

"He says he hit six-forty," Pops said dreamily.

"You going to use him?"

"Sure I'll use him. If I'm gonna shoot Pete, I gotta have a reason that'll stand up in court. As soon as we get ten runs behind, in he goes."

Pops headed back toward the dugout, and some tourists in box seats raised a lusty chorus of boos as he passed. Pops scowled and quickened his pace. The dratted tourists were ruining the game. There had been a time when a manager could concentrate on what he was doing, but now he had to operate with a mob of howling spectators literally hanging over his shoulder and shouting advice and criticism into his ears. It got on the players' nerves, too. There was the Giants' Red Cowan, who'd been a good pitcher until they opened the games to tourists. The noise so rattled him that he had to retire.

"Why can't they stay home and see it on TV, like everybody else?" Pops growled.

"Because they pay money, that's why," Ed Schwartz said. "There's a novelty or something in seeing a ball game in the flesh, and it's getting so some of these tourists are planning their vacations so they can take in a few games. Bill Willard—the L.A. *Times* man—was saying that the National League now is California's number one tourist attraction. The American League is doing the same thing for Arizona."

The boos sounded again, and Pops ducked into the dugout out of sight. "I don't mind their watching," he said, "if only they'd keep their mouths shut. When I started managing there wasn't anyone around during a game except the TV men, and they were too busy to be giving me advice. Even the sportswriters watched on TV. Now they camp here the whole season, and you can't go out after the morning paper without finding one waiting for an interview."

"The tourists are here to stay, so you might as well get used to them," Ed said. "There's even some talk about putting up hotels for them, so they won't have to commute from Fresno to see the games."

Pops sat down and borrowed Ed's pen to make out his lineup. Ed looked over his shoulder and asked, "How come you're not using that new guy?"

"I'm saving him until we get far enough behind."

"You mean until the second inning?" Ed said and ducked as Pops fired a catcher's mask.

"That's the trouble with those tenure laws," Pops said. "They had to go and include the club secretaries."

The game started off in a way sadly familiar to Pops. The Dodgers scored three runs in the first inning and threatened to blast the Pirates right out of the league. Then, with the bases loaded and one out, the Pirates' third baseman managed to hang onto a sizzling line drive and turn it into a double play. Pops's breathing spell lasted only until the next inning. Lefty Effinger, the Pirates' pitcher, spent a long afternoon falling out of one hole and into another. In nine innings he gave up a total of seventeen hits, but a miraculous succession of picked-off runners, overrun bases, and double plays kept the Dodgers shut out after those first three runs.

In the meantime, Dodger pitcher Rip Ruster was having one of his great days. He gave up a scratch single in the second and a walk in the fourth, and by the ninth inning he had fanned twelve, to the gratification of the hooting, jeering tourists.

The last of the ninth opened with Ruster striking out the first two Pirates on six pitches, and the Pirates in the dugout started sneaking off to the dressing room. Then first baseman Sam Lyle ducked away from an inside pitch that hit his bat and blooped over the infield for a single. Pops called for the hit and run, and the next batter bounced the ball at the Dodger shortstop. The shortstop threw it into right field, and the runners reached second and third. Ruster, pacing angrily about the mound, walked the next batter on four pitches.

Pops jumped from the dugout and called time. "Hit six-forty, did he?" Pops muttered and yelled, "Zilo!"

The beaming Zilo jumped up from the far end of the bench. "Yes, sir?"

"Get out there and hit!"

"Yes, sir!"

He shuffled toward the plate, and the uproar sent up by the tourists rocked the grandstand. Dipsey Marlow called time again and hurried over to the dugout.

"You off your rocker? We got a chance to win this one. Get that thing out of there and use a left-hander."

"Look," Pops said. "You know derned well the way Ruster is pitching we're lucky to get a loud fowl off of him. That hit was luck, and the error was luck, and the base on balls happened only because Ruster got mad. Now he'll cool off, and the only thing that keeps this going is more luck. Pete says the kid's lucky, and I want some of it."

Marlow turned on his heel and stalked back to the coaching box.

Ruster coiled up and shot a bullet at home plate. Zilo swatted at it awkwardly—and popped it up.

The second baseman backed up three steps, waved the rest of the infield away, and got ready to end the game. The base runners, running furiously with two out, came down the stretch from third in a mournful procession. Zilo loped along the base path watching the Dodger second baseman and the ball.

The ball reached the top of its arc and suddenly seemed to carry. The second baseman backed confidently into position, changed his mind, and backed up again. The ball continued to float toward the outfield. The second baseman turned and raced toward center field with his eyes on the misbehaving ball. The center fielder had been jogging toward the infield. Now he broke into a run. The second baseman leaped for the ball. The center fielder dove for it. Neither man touched it, and they went down in a heap as the ball bounced and frolicked away.

The lumbering Zilo crossed home plate before the startled right fielder could retrieve the ball. The Pirates had won, 4 to 3, and they hoisted Zilo to their shoulders and bore him off to the dressing room. The Dodgers quitted the field to an enthusiastic chorus of boos.

Pops went out to the third-base coaching box, where Dipsey Marlow still stood gazing vacantly toward the outfield.

"Luck," Pops said and gently led him away.

Rodney Wilks, the Pirates' brisk little president, flew over from L.A. that evening and threw a victory celebration in the ultramodern building that housed the National League offices. All of the players were there, and those who had families brought them. Women and children congregated in one room and the men in another. Champagne and milk shakes flowed freely in both rooms.

National League President Edgar Rysdale looked in on the party briefly but approvingly. A team in a slump was bad for all the teams —bad for the league. When the race was a good one, fans frequently paid a double TV fee, watching two games at once or, if they had only one set, switching back and forth. If one team was floundering, National League fans would watch only one game. They might even patronize the American League. So the victory pleased the league president and also the other owners, who stopped by to sample the champagne and talk shop with Wilks.

Fred Carter, the Dodger manager, also looked in on the party. Zilo's freak pop fly had ruined a nine-game winning streak for him, but he seemed more puzzled than mournful. He backed Pops into a corner and said with a grin, "I been watching pop flies for thirty-five years, and I never saw one act like that. Did the kid magnetize his bat, or something?"

Pops shrugged. "I been watching baseball forty-five years, and I see something new seven times a week."

"Just the same, the next time that kid bats against me I'm passing out butterfly nets. He don't look like much of a hitter. Where'd you get him?"

"Pete Holloway sent him out."

Carter arched his eyebrows. "He must have something, then."

"Pete says he ain't got a thing except luck."

"Isn't that enough? I'm going over to watch the Reds and Giants. Want to come?"

"Nope. Now that I finally won one, I'm gonna get some sleep tonight."

Pops saw Ed Schwartz talking with Zilo, and he went over to see what line the club secretary might be handing out. Ed was talking about the old days, and Zilo was listening intently, his dark eyes sparkling.

"Each team had its own city," Ed said, "and its own ball park. Think of the waste involved! Eventually there were twenty-four teams in each league, which meant forty-eight ball parks, and even during the playing season they were in use only half the time, when the teams were playing at home. And the season only lasted six months. And there was all that traveling. We froze one day in Montreal and baked the next in New Orleans. Our hotel bill for the season used to look like the national debt, not to mention the plane fares. It was rough on the players in other ways. They only saw their families when they were playing at home, and just as they got settled somewhere they'd be traded and maybe have to move clear across the country—only to be traded again the next season or even the next week. Putting the entire league in one place solved everything. The climate is wonderful, and we almost never have a game postponed because of bad weather. We're down to eight teams in a league, which anyway is as many as the fans can keep track of. We have two fields, and they're used twice a day, for two afternoon and two night games. Each team has its own little community. Baseball, Cal is growing, boy, and lots of players are settling here permanently and buying their own homes. You'll want to, too. It's a wonderful place."

"It's a soft place for club secretaries," Pops growled. "Ed used to have to worry about baggage, plane schedules, hotel reservations, and a million and one other things. Now all he has to do is get the equipment moved a couple of hundred yards from one park to the other, now and then, and he gripes about it. Has he stopped talking long enough to get you settled?"

"Oh, yes, sir," Zilo said. "I'm rooming with Jerry Fargo."

"All right. Come out early tomorrow. You gotta learn to catch a fly ball without getting hit on the head."

Dipsey Marlow nudged Pops's arm and pulled him aside. "Going to play him tomorrow?"

"Might. We could use a little luck every day."

"I been listening to the big boys. Know what they're going to do? Put up a flock of temporary stands at World Series time. They think they might get fifteen thousand people out here for every game."

"That's their business," Pops said.

"Just tell me why anyone wants to take a trip and pay a stiff price to see a ball game when he can sit at home and see it for fifty cents."

"People are funny," Pops said. "Sometimes they're almost as funny as ballplayers."

President Wilks came over and placed a full glass in Pops's hand. Pops sipped the champagne and grimaced. "It's all right, I guess, but it'll never take the place of beer."

"Finish in first division," Wilks said, "and I'll buy you enough beer to take you through the off season."

Pops grinned. "How about putting that in my contract?"

"I will," Wilks promised. "Do you want it in bottles or kegs?"

"Both."

"I'll take care of it first thing in the morning." He grinned and prodded Pops in the ribs, but behind the grin his expression was anxious. "Do you think we have a chance?"

"Too early to say. Sure, we only won one out of fifteen, but we're only ten games out of first. We been looking like a bunch of schoolkids, and if we keep that up we finish last. If we snap out of it —well, the season's got a long way to go."

"I hope you snap out of it," Wilks said. "Managers have tenure, but club presidents haven't."

Pops found a bottle of beer to kill the taste of the champagne, and he made a quiet exit after instructing Marlow to get the players home to bed at a reasonable hour. The National League's two playing fields were a blaze of light, and the shouts of the two crowds intermingled. There seemed to be a lot of tourists in attendance—and tourists at night games made even less sense than tourists at afternoon games. It'd be midnight before some of them got back to their hotels. Pops walked slowly back to Pirateville, grumbling to himself. The large mansion intended for the manager Pops had turned over to Dipsey Marlow, who needed the room for his eight kids. Pops lived in a small house a short distance down the street. His middle-aged daughter Marge kept house for him, and she was already in bed. She didn't like baseball.

Priority Rating: Routine
From: Jard Killil, Minister of Juvenile Affairs

To: All Planetary Police Organizations, Sectors 1247; 2162; 889; 1719
    All Interplanetary Patrol Units, Sectors 1247; 2162; 889; 1719
Subject: Juvenile Detention Escapee Muko Zilo
Reference: Previous memorandum of 13B927D8 and enclosures
    Information from several sources indicates that an unidentified ship, possibly that of escapee Zilo, traveled on a course roughly parallel to Trade Route 79B, which would take it into or through your sectors. Because of the time elapsed since his escape, it is assumed that Zilo has found an effective planetary hiding place. Immediate investigation is requested. Escapee is not—repeat not—dangerous.
    Kindly notify Philoy JRC immediately upon detention.

Pops opened a three-game series against the Cubs with Zilo in left field. He figured the youngster would do the least damage there, since he was pitching Simp Simpson, his best right-hander, and the Cubs had seven left-handed batters in their lineup. At least that much of his strategy worked. In the first six innings only two balls were hit to left. One was a line-drive single that Zilo bobbled for an error as the runner reached second. The other was a foul fly on which Zilo seemed about to make a miraculous catch until his feet got tangled and spilled him. At the plate he waved his bat futilely and struck out twice while the Cubs were taking a five-run lead.

In the last of the sixth, the Pirates got men on first and second. It was Zilo's turn to bat. Dipsey Marlow called time, and as the tourists hooted impatiently, he strode to the dugout. "Take him out," he said.

"Why?" Pops asked. "He's still batting .333. That's better than the rest of these dopes."

"You gotta understand this luck thing. Yesterday it was luck to put him in. Today it's luck to take him out. I found a spider in my locker, today, and that means—"

"Hit and run on the first pitch," Pops said.

Zilo fanned the air lustily and dribbled a grounder toward the first baseman. Suddenly it took an unaccountable eight-foot bounce over his head and rolled into the outfield, picking up speed. Zilo pulled up at first, breathing heavily, and the two runners scored.

Sam Lyle followed with a lazy fly ball to right. Zilo moved off first base and halted to watch the progress of the ball. The right fielder seemed to be having difficulties. He wandered about shading his eyes, backed up, and finally lost the ball in the sun. The center fielder had come over fast, and he shouted the right fielder away, backed up slowly, and finally turned in disgust to watch the ball drop over the fence. Lyle trailed the floundering Zilo around the bases, and the Pirates trailed by a run, 5 to 4.

Three fast outs later, Dipsey Marlow returned to the dugout and squeezed in beside Pops. "I take it all back," he said. "I won't argue with you again the rest of the season. But this spider of mine—"

Pops cupped his hands and shouted, "Let's HOLD 'em now! Let's WIN this one!"

"—this spider of mine was in my sweat shirt, and my old mother always used to say spider in your clothes means money. Will the players get a cut of what those fifteen thousand tourists pay to watch a Series game?"

"The World Series is still a couple of hundred games away," Pops said. "Let's worry about it later. Get to work and pick us off a sign or two."

In the eighth inning, Zilo got a rally started with a pop fly that three infielders chased futilely. He moved to second on a ground ball that took a bad hop, and he scored on a soft line drive that curved sharply and landed between the outfielders. The Pirates pushed over two more runs on hits that were equally implausible and took a two-run lead into the ninth.

The Cubs came back with a vengeance. The first two batters lashed out sizzling singles. Pops prodded his bullpen into action and went out to talk with Simpson. They stood looking down at the next Cub batter, the burly catcher Bugs Rice.

"Don't let him pull one," Pops said.

"He won't pull one," Simp said determinedly through clenched teeth.

Rice did not pull one. He didn't have to. He unloaded on the first pitch and drove it far, far away into left field, the opposite field. Pops sat down with the crack of the bat and covered his face with his hands.

"Now we gotta come from behind again," he moaned. "And we won't. I know we ain't *that* lucky."

Suddenly the men on the bench broke into excited cheers, and a scattering of applause came from the tourists. Pops looked up, saw runners on second and third, saw the scoreboard registering one out.

"What happened?" he yelped.

"Zilo caught it," Dipsey Marlow said. "Didn't think he had it in him, but he backed up to the fence and made a clean catch. Took so much time getting the ball back to the infield that the runners had time to touch up and advance, but he caught it."

"He didn't. I heard it hit the bat, and I saw it go. It should have cleared the fence by twenty feet."

"Your eyes and ears aren't as young as they used to be. Zilo caught it against the fence."

Pops shook his head. He huddled down in a corner of the dugout while Simpson fanned one batter and got another on a tap to the infield, and the Pirates had won two in a row.

That was the beginning. The Pirates pushed their winning streak to twelve, lost one, won eight more. They were twenty and fifteen and in fourth place. Zilo became a national sensation. Lucky Zilo Fan Clubs sprang up across the country, and he kept his batting average around the .450 mark and even got another home run when a solid fly ball to the outfield took crazy bounces in nineteen directions while Zilo lumbered around the bases. The rest of the team took courage and started playing baseball.

But not even a lucky Zilo could lift the Pirates above fourth place. Pops's pitching staff was a haphazard assortment of aching, overage veterans and unpredictable, inexperienced youths. One day they would be unhittable; the next day they'd be massacred, and Pops found to his sorrow that luck was no answer to a nineteen-run deficit. Still, the season drifted along with the Pirates holding desperately to fourth, and Pops began to think they might even stay there.

Then Zilo sprained his ankle. The trainer outfitted him with crutches and applied every known remedy and a few unknown ones that Zilo suggested, but the ankle failed to respond.

"It beats me," the trainer said to Pops. "Things that should make it better seem to make it worse."

"How long will he be out?" Pops asked gloomily.

"I won't even guess. The way it's reacting, it could last him a lifetime."

Pops breathed a profane farewell to first division.

Zilo hobbled to every game on his crutches and watched with silent concentration from a box behind the dugout. Oddly enough, for a time the team's luck continued. Ground balls took freakish bounces, fly balls responded to unlikely air currents, and on some days opposition pitchers suffered such a loss of control that they would occasionally wander in and stare at home plate, as though to assure themselves that it was still there. Ollie Richards, the Reds' ace and one of the best control pitchers in either league, walked seventeen batters in three innings and left the game on the short end of a 6 to 3 score without having given up a hit.

Zilo's good-natured, freckled face took on an unhealthy pallor.

Wrinkles furrowed his brow, and his eyes held a tense, haunted look. As the team's luck began to fade, he grew increasingly irritable and despondent. On the day they slipped to fifth place, he met Pops after the game and asked, "Could I speak with you, sir?"

"Sure," Pops said. "Come along."

Pops held the door as Zilo swung through on his crutches. He got the youngster seated, and then he settled back with his own feet propped up on his desk. "Ankle any better?"

"I'm afraid not, sir."

"Takes time, sometimes."

"Sir," Zilo said, "I know I'm not a good ballplayer. Like they say, I'm just lucky. Maybe this will be the last season I'll play."

"I wouldn't say that," Pops said. "You're young, and luck has took a lot of men a long way in baseball."

"Anyway, sir, I like to play, even if I'm not good. And I'd like to have us win the pennant and play in the World Series."

"Wouldn't mind having another winner myself, before I retire."

"What I'd like to do, sir, is go home for a while. I think I could get my ankle fixed up there, and I'd like to bring back some friends who could help us."

Pops was amused. "Ballplayers?"

"I think they'd be better than I am, sir. Or maybe luckier. Do you —would you give them a trial?"

"I'd give anybody a tryout," Pops said seriously. "Especially short-stops and second basemen and pitchers, but I'd have a look at anybody."

Zilo pushed himself erect on his crutches. "I'll get back as soon as I can."

"All right. But leave a little of that luck here, will you?"

Zilo turned and looked at Pops strangely. "I wish I could, sir. I really wish I could."

Ed Schwartz took Zilo to L.A. and put him on a plane for the East. For Maine. And at Baseball, Cal, the Pirates won two more games and went into a cataclysmic slump. They lost ten straight and slipped to sixth place. Pops put through a phone call to the Maine address Zilo had given him and was informed that there was no such place. Then he called Pete Holloway.

"I wondered what was happening to you," Pete said. "No, I haven't seen the kid. He dropped out of nowhere last summer and played a little sandlot ball for me. He never told me where he came from, but I don't think it was Maine. If he shows up again, I'll get in touch with you."

"Thanks," Pops said. He hung up slowly.

Ed Schwartz said thoughtfully, "I suppose I better get a detective on it."

"Detectives," Pops said and wearily headed for the field and another shellacking.

Two more weeks went by. The detectives traced Zilo to Maine, where he seemed to have vanished from the ken of mortal man. The Pirates were tottering on the brink of last place.

Then Pops received an airmail letter from Zilo—from Brazil.

"I got lost," he wrote plaintively. "We crashed in the jungle and they won't let us leave the country."

Pops called President Wilks into conference, and Wilks got on the phone to Washington. He knew enough of the right people to make the necessary arrangements and keep the matter out of the papers. Zilo was flown back on a chartered plane, and he brought four friends with him.

Ed Schwartz met them in L.A. and rushed them out to Baseball, Cal, in President Wilks's own plane. They arrived during the fourth inning of another Pirate beating.

"How's the ankle?" Pops demanded.

Zilo beamed. "Just fine, sir."

"Get in there, then."

Zilo got his friends seated in the president's box, and then he went out to loft a long fly ball over the fence for a home run. The Pirates came to life. Everyone hit, and a 10 to 0 drubbing was transformed like magic into a 25 to 12 victory.

After the game Zilo introduced his friends. They were John Smith, Sam Jones, Robert White, and William Anderson. Smith and Jones, Zilo said, were infielders. White and Anderson were pitchers.

Ed Schwartz took in their proportions with a groan and went to work on the uniform problem. They were built like Zilo but on a much more lavish scale. They towered over Pops, answered his questions politely, and showed a childlike interest in all that went on about them.

Pops called one of his catchers over and introduced him to White and Anderson. "See what they got," he said. The catcher led them away, and Pops took Smith and Jones out for infield practice. He watched goggle-eyed as they covered ground like jet-propelled gazelles and made breathtaking leaps to pull down line drives.

The catcher returned, drew Pops aside, and said awesomely, "They got curves that break three feet. They got sliders that do a little loop-the-loop and cross the plate twice. They got fast balls I'm scared to catch. They got pitches that change speed four times between the mound and the plate. If you're figuring on pitching those guys, you can get yourself another catcher."

Pops turned the ceremony of signing them over to Ed Schwartz, handed releases to four players who weren't worth the space they were taking up on the bench, and went home to his first good night's sleep in more than a month.

Priority Rating: Urgent
From: Jard Killil, Minister of Juvenile Affairs
To: All Planetary Police Organizations
    All Interplanetary Patrol Units
Subject: Juvenile detention escapees
Enclosures: Character analyses, filmstrips, retinal patterns
    All law-enforcement agencies are hereby informed of the escape of four inmates of the Juvenile Rehabilitation Center on Philoy, Raff III, Sector 1311. Escapees have high psi ratings and may use them dangerously. Kindly give this matter top-priority attention and notify Philoy JRC immediately upon detention.

The next day Pops started Anderson against the Braves. The Pirates bounced forty hits over and through and around the infield and scored thirty-five runs. Anderson pitched a no-hit game and struck out twenty-seven. White duplicated the performance the following day. Thereafter Pops pitched them in his regular rotation. He wasn't sure whether they hypnotized everyone in the park or just the ball, but as Dipsey Marlow put it, they made the ball do everything but stop and back up.

Pops's other pitchers suddenly looked like champions with Smith and Jones playing behind them. In spite of their boxlike builds, they ranged about the infield with the agility of jackrabbits. No one ever measured exactly how high they went up after line drives, but one sportswriter claimed they were a hazard to air traffic and should be licensed as aircraft. They sped far into the outfield after fly balls. Jones made more catches in right field than the right fielder, and it was not an unusual sight to see Jones and Smith far out in center contesting the right to a descending ball while the center fielder beat a hasty retreat. And both men swung murderous bats.

The Pirates had won fifty-seven games in a row and rewritten the record book when Zilo timidly knocked on the door of Pops's office. He was carrying a newspaper, and he looked disturbed.

"Sir," he said anxiously, "it says here that we're ruining baseball."

Pops chuckled. "They always say that when one team starts to pull away."

"But—is it true?"

"Well, now. If we keep on winning the way we are now, that won't do the game any good. People like to see a close race, and if one team wins too much, or loses too much, a lot of people stop watching the games. But don't let it worry you. We'll do our best to go on winning, but we'll drop a few, one of these days, and things will be back to normal. Your friends been playing over their heads and we've been luckier than usual."

"I see," Zilo said thoughtfully.

That evening Pops ruefully wished he'd kept his big mouth shut. Talk about jinxing a winning streak!

Anderson got knocked out in the first inning and lost his first game. White failed the next day, and the Pirates dropped five straight. Then they got off on another winning streak, but the talk about their ruining the game had quieted down. Pops never bothered to remind Zilo about how right he'd been. He wasn't going to jinx the team again.

"Those baseball players of yours," his daughter said to him one evening. "You know—the funny-looking ones."

"Sure, I know," Pops dead-panned. "What about 'em?"

"They're supposed to be pretty good, aren't they?"

Pops grinned wickedly. "Pretty fair." It would have been a waste of time referring Marge to what was left of the record book.

"I was over at the bowling alley with Ruth Wavel, and they were there bowling. They had everybody excited."

"How'd they do?"

"I guess they must be pretty good at that, too. They knocked all the pins over."

Pops grinned again. Marge's idea of a sport was crossword puzzles, and she could go through an entire season without seeing a single game. "Nothing unusual about that," he said. "Happens all the time."

She seemed surprised. "Does it? The people there thought it was something special."

"Someone was pulling your leg. How many strikes did they get?"

"How many what?"

"How many times did they knock all the pins down?"

"They knocked all of them down every time. All evening. It was the first time they'd ever bowled, too."

"Natural athletic ability," Pops muttered. They'd never played baseball before, either, except that Zilo had coached them a little. The more he thought about it, the odder it seemed, but he wasn't one to argue with no-hit games and home runs and sensational fielding plays.

"What'd you say?" Marge asked.

"Never look a gift ballplayer in the mouth," Pops said and went to bed.

TO ALL SHIPS OF THE SPACE NAVY SECTORS 2161, 2162, 2163 [] GENERAL ALERT [] FIVE ESCAPEES JUVENILE REHABILITATION CENTER PHILOY RAFF III PILOTING STOLEN SPACE YACHT STELLAR CLASS II RANGE UNLIMITED HAVE BEEN TRACED THROUGH SECTOR 2162 [] DESTINATION UNSURVEYED QUADRANT C97 [] CONTACT BASE HEADQUARTERS SECTOR 2162 FOR PATROL ASSIGNMENTS [] ACKNOWLEDGE [] ZAN FIRST ADMIRAL.

The pennant race leveled into a five-team contest for first place. The Pirates stayed in first or second, playing sometimes with unbelievable brilliance and sometimes with incredible ineptitude. Pops took the race stoically and tried to ignore the tourist hysteria that enveloped Baseball, Cal. He was doing so much better than anyone expected—so much better than he had thought possible even in his wildest moments of preseason optimism—that it really didn't matter where he finished. He was a cinch to be Manager of the Year. He might add a pennant and a World Series, or he might not. It didn't matter.

Another season might see him in last place again, and a smart manager went out as a winner—especially a smart manager who was well along in his sixties. Pops called a news conference and announced his retirement at the end of the season.

"Before or after the World Series?" a reporter asked.

"No comment," Pops said.

The club owners erected their World Series stands early, and the tourists jammed them—fifteen thousand for every game. Pops wondered where they came from. National League President Rysdale wandered about smiling fondly over the daily television receipts, and President Wilks sent Pops a load of beer that filled his basement.

Over in Baseball, Arizona, the American League officials were glum. The Yankees, who were mainly distinguished for having finished last more frequently than any other team in major-league history, had suddenly and inexplicably opened up a twenty-game lead, and nobody cared any longer what happened in the American League.

"Three weeks to go," Pops told his team. "What d'ya say we wrap this thing up?"

"Right!" Zilo said happily.

"Right!" Smith, Jones, Anderson, and White chorused.

The Pirates started another winning streak.

TO ALL SHIPS OF THE SPACE NAVY PATROL-ING UNSURVEYED QUADRANT C97 [] PREPARE LANDING PARTIES FOR PLANETARY SEARCH [] THIS MESSAGE YOUR AUTHORIZATION TO INVES-TIGATE ANY PLANET WITH CIVILIZATION AT LEVEL 10 OR BELOW [] CONTACT WITH CIVILI-ZATIONS HIGHER THAN LEVEL 10 FORBIDDEN [] SPACE INTELLIGENCE AGENTS WILL BE FURNISHED EACH SHIP TO HANDLE HIGH-CIVILIZA-TION PLANETS [] ACKNOWLEDGE [] ZAN FIRST AD-MIRAL.

The last week of the season opened with the Pirates in first place, two games ahead of the Dodgers. A provident schedule put the Dodgers and Pirates in a three-game series. The league hastily erected more stands, and with twenty-two thousand howling tourists in attendance and half of Earth's population watching on TV, White and Anderson put together no-hit games and the Pirate bat-ters demolished the Dodger pitching staff. The Pirates took all three games.

Pops felt enormously tired and relieved that it was finished. He had won his pennant and he didn't see how he could lose the World Series. But he never had felt so old.

President Wilks threw another champagne party, and the sportswriters backed Pops into a corner and fired questions.

"How about that retirement, Pops? Still going through with it?"

"I've gone through with it."

"Is it true that Dipsey Marlow will take your place?"

"That's up to the front office. They ain't asked my opinion."

"What if they did ask your opinion?"

"I'd faint."

"Who'll start the Series? Anderson or White?"

"I'll flip a coin," Pops said. "It don't matter. Either of them could pitch all thirteen games and not feel it."

"Does that mean you'll go all the way with just Anderson and White?"

"I'll use four starters, like I have most of the season."

"Going to give the Yankees a sporting chance, eh?"

"No comment," Pops said.

President Wilks and League President Rysdale rescued him from the reporters and took him to Rysdale's private office.

"We have a proposal from the American League," Rysdale said. "We'd like to know what you think of it and what you think the players would think of it. They want to split up the Series and play part of the games here and part of them in Arizona. They think it would stir up more local interest."

"I wouldn't like it," Pops said. "What's wrong with the way it is now? Here one year, there the next year, it's fair to both sides. What do they want to do—travel back and forth between games?"

"We'd start out with four games here, and then we'd play five in Arizona and the last four back here. Next year we'd start out with four in Arizona. It used to be done that way years ago."

"One ball park is just like another," Pops said. "Why travel back and forth?"

"They think we would draw more tourists that way. As far as we're concerned, we're drawing capacity crowds now. It might make a difference in Arizona, because there are fewer population centers there."

"They suggested it because it's in California this year," Pops said. "Next year they'd want to change back."

"That's a thought," Rysdale said. "I'll tell them it's too late to make the change this year, but we might consider it for next year. That'll give us time to figure all the angles."

"For all I care, you can play in Brazil next year," Pops told him.

In the hallway, Pops encountered half a dozen of his players crowding around infielder Jones. "What's up?" he asked Dipsey Marlow.

"Just some horsing around. They were practicing high jumps, and Jones cleared three meters."

"So?"

"That's a world record by almost half a meter. I looked it up."

TO JARD KILLIL [] MINISTER JUVENILE AFFAIRS [] SPACE SHIP PRESUMED THAT OF JRC ESCAPEES FOUND IN JUNGLE UNSURVEYED QUADRANT C97 PLANET [] HAS TYPE 17D CIVILIZATION [] INTELLIGENCE AGENTS CALL SITUATION CRITICAL [] AM TAKING NO ACTION PENDING RECEIPT FURTHER INSTRUCTIONS [] REQUEST MINISTRY TAKE

CHARGE AND ASSUME RESPONSIBILITY [] ZAN
FIRST ADMIRAL.

Pops retired early the night before the Series opened. He'd ordered
his players to do the same. Marge was out somewhere. Pops hadn't
gone to sleep, but he was relaxing comfortably when she came in an
hour later.

She marched straight through the house and into his bedroom.
"Those ballplayers of yours—the funny-looking ones—they were at
the bowling alley."

Pops took a deep breath. "They were?"

"They'd been drinking!"

Pops sat up and reached for his shoes. "You don't say."

"And they were bowling, only—they weren't bowling. They'd pretend to throw the ball but they wouldn't throw it, and the pins
would fall down anyway. The manager was mad."

"No doubt," Pops said, pulling on his trousers.

"They wouldn't tell anyone how they did it, but every time they
waved the ball all the pins would fall down. They'd been drinking."

"Maybe that's how they did it," Pops said, slipping into his shirt.
"How?"

"By drinking."

He headed for the bowling alley at a dead run. The place was
crowded with players from other teams, American and National
League, and quite a few sportswriters were around. The writers
headed for Pops, and he shoved them aside and found the manager.
"Who was it?" he demanded.

"Those four squares of yours. Jones, Smith, Anderson, White."

"Zilo?"

"No. Zilo wasn't here."

"Did they make trouble?"

"Not the way you mean. They didn't get rough, though I had a
time getting them away from the alleys. They left maybe ten minutes ago."

"Thanks," Pops said.

"When you find them, ask them how they pulled that gag with
the pins. They were too drunk to tell me."

"I got some other things to ask them," Pops said.

He pushed his way through the crowd to a phone booth and called
Ed Schwartz.

"I'll take care of it," Ed said. "Don't you worry about a thing."

"Sure. I won't worry about a thing."

"They may be back at their rooms by now, but we won't take any chances. I'll handle it."

"I'll meet you there," Pops said.

He slipped out a side door and headed for Bachelor's Paradise, the house where the unmarried Pirates lived with a couple of solicitous houseboys to look after them. All the players were in bed—except Smith, Jones, Anderson, White, and Zilo. The others knew nothing about them except that Zilo had been concerned about his friends and gone looking for them.

"You go home," Ed said. "I'll find them."

Pops paced grimly back and forth, taking an occasional kick at the furniture. "You find them," he said, "and I'll fine them."

He went home to bed, but he did not sleep. Twice during the night he called Ed Schwartz, and Ed was out. Pops finally reached him at breakfast-time, and Ed said, trying to be cheerful, "No news is supposed to be good news, and that's what I have. No news. I couldn't find a trace of them."

The reporters had picked up the story, and their headlines mocked Pops over his coffee. PIRATE STARS MISSING!

Ed Schwartz had notified both President Wilks and President Rysdale, and the league president had called in the FBI. By ten o'clock, police in every city in the country and a number of cities in other countries were looking for the missing Pirates, but they remained missing.

When Pops reached the field for a late-morning workout, there still was no word. He banned newsmen from the field and dressing room, told Lefty Effinger he might have to start, and went around trying to cheer up his players. The players remembered only too vividly their fourteen-game losing streak at the beginning of the season and the collapse that followed Zilo's departure. Gloom hung so thickly in the dugout that Pops wished he could think of a market for it. He could have bottled and sold it.

An hour before game time, Pops was called to the telephone. It was Ed Schwartz, calling from L.A. "I found them," he said. "They're on their way back. They'll be there in plenty of time."

"Good," Pops said.

"Bad. They're still pretty high—all except Zilo. I don't know if you can use them, but that's your problem."

Pops slammed down the phone.

"Did they find 'em?" Dipsey Marlow asked.

"Found 'em dead drunk."

Marlow rubbed his hands together. "Just let me at 'em. Ten minutes, that's all I ask. I'll have 'em dead sober."

"I dunno," Pops said. "These guys may not react the way you'd expect."

The delinquent players were delivered with time to spare, and Marlow went to work enthusiastically. He started by shoving them into a cold shower, fully dressed. Zilo stood looking on anxiously.

"I'm sorry," he said to Pops. "I'd have stopped them, but they went off without me. And they never had any of that alcohol before and they didn't know what it would do to them."

"That's all right," Pops said. "It wasn't your fault."

Zilo had tears in his eyes. "Do you think they can play?"

"Leave 'em to me," Marlow said. "I'm just getting started." But when he emerged later, he looked both confused and frustrated. "I just don't know," he said. "They tell me they're all right, and they look all right, but I think they're still drunk."

"Can they play?" Pops demanded.

"They can walk a straight line. I won't say how long a straight line. I suppose you got nothing to lose by playing them."

"There ain't much else I can do," Pops said. "I could start Effinger, but what would I use for infielders?"

Even Pops, who had seen every World Series for forty-five years as player, manager, or spectator, had to admit that the winter classic had its own unique flavor of excitement. He felt a thrill and a clutching emptiness in his stomach as he moved to the top step of the dugout and looked out across the sunlit field. Along both foul lines, the temporary stands were jammed with tourists. Beyond them, areas were roped off for standees, and the last tickets for standing room had been sold hours before. There was no space left of any kind.

Ed Schwartz stood at Pops's elbow looking at the crowd. "What is it that's different about a submarine sandwich when you buy it at the ball park?" he asked.

"Ptomaine," Pops growled.

Clutching his lineup card, he strode toward home plate to meet the umpires and Yankee manager Bert Basom.

Basom grinned maliciously. "Your men well rested? I hear they keep late hours."

"They're rested well enough," Pops said.

A few minutes later, with the National Anthem played and the flag raised, Pops watched critically as Anderson took his last warmup pitches. He threw lazily, as he always did, and if he was feeling any aftereffects it wasn't evident to Pops.

But Anderson got off to a shaky start. The Yankees' leadoff man clouted a tremendous drive to left, but Zilo made one of his sensational, lumbering catches. The second batter drove one through the box. Jones started after it, got his feet tangled, and fell headlong. Smith flashed over with unbelievable speed, gloved the ball, and threw to first—too late. Anderson settled down, then, and struck out the next two batters.

Zilo opened the Pirates' half of the first with one of his lucky hits, and Smith followed him with a lazy fly ball that cleared the fence. The Pirates led, 2 to 0.

The first pitch to Jones was a called strike. Jones whirled on the umpire, his large face livid with rage. His voice carried over the noise of the crowd. "You wouldn't know a strike zone if I measured it out for you!"

Pops started for home plate, and Jones saw him coming and meekly took his place in the box. Pops called time and went over to talk to Dipsey Marlow.

"Darned if I don't think he's still tight. Maybe I should lift him."

"Let him bat," Dipsey said. "Maybe he'll connect."

The pitcher wasted one and followed it with a curve that cut the outside corner. "Strike two!" the umpire called.

Jones's outraged bellow rattled the center-field fence. "What?" he shrieked. He stepped around the catcher and stood towering over the umpire. "Where's the strike zone? Where was the pitch?"

The umpire gestured impatiently to show where the ball had crossed the plate. Pops started out of the dugout again. The umpire said brusquely, "Play ball!"

Still fuming, Jones moved back to the batter's box. His high-pitched voice carried clearly. "You don't even know where the strike zone is!"

The pitcher wound up again, and as the ball sped plateward Jones suddenly leaped into the air—and stayed there. He hovered six feet above the ground. The ball crossed the plate far below his dangling legs, was missed completely by the startled catcher, and bounced to the screen.

The umpire did not call the pitch. He took two steps forward and stood looking up at Jones. The crowd came to its feet, and players from both teams edged from their dugouts. A sudden, paralyzed hush gripped the field.

"Come down here!" the umpire called angrily.

"What'd you call that pitch? Strike, I suppose. Over the plate between my knees and armpits, I suppose."

"Come down here!"

"You can't make me."

"Come down here!"

"You show me where it says in the rules that I have to bat with both feet on the ground!"

The umpire moved down the third-base line and summoned his colleagues for a conference. Pops walked out to home plate, and Zilo followed him.

"Jones," Zilo said pleadingly.

"Go to hell," Jones snarled. "I know I'm right. I'm still in the batter's box."

"Please," Zilo pleaded. "You'll spoil everything. You've already spoiled everything."

"So what? It's time we showed them how this game should be played."

"I'm taking you out, Jones," Pops said. "I'm putting in a pinch-hitter. Get back to the dugout."

Jones shot up another four feet. "You can't make me."

The umpire returned. "I'm putting you out of the game," he said. "Leave the field immediately."

"I've already left the field."

Pops, Zilo, and the umpire stood glaring up at Jones, who glared down at them. Into that impasse came Smith, who walked slowly to home plate, soared over the heads of those on the ground, and clouted Jones on the jaw. Jones descended heavily. Smith landed nearby, calmly drying his hands on his trousers.

Effective as his performance was, nobody noticed it. All eyes were on the sky, where a glistening tower of metal was dropping slowly toward the outfield. It came ponderously to rest on the outfield grass while the outfielders fled in panic. The crowd remained silent.

A port opened in the tower's side, and a landing ramp came down. The solitary figure that emerged did not use it. He stepped out into midair and drifted slowly toward the congregation at home plate. There he landed, a tremendous figure, square like Zilo and his friends but a startling nine feet tall and trimly uniformed in a lustrous brown with ribbons and braid in abundance.

Zilo, Jones, and Smith stood with downcast eyes while the others stared. Anderson and White moved from the dugout and walked forward haltingly. The stranger spoke one crisp sentence that no one understood—except Zilo, Jones, Smith, Anderson, and White.

Smith and Jones lifted slowly and floated out to the ship, where they disappeared through the port. Anderson and White turned obediently and trudged to the outfield to mount the ramp. Only Zilo lingered.

A few policemen moved nervously from the stands and surrounded the ship. The hush continued as the tourists stared and half of Earth's population watched on TV.

Zilo turned to face Pops. Tears streaked his face. "I'm sorry, Pops," he said. "I hoped we could finish it off for you. I really wanted to win this World Series. But I'm afraid we've got to go."

"Go where?" Pops asked.

"Where we came from. It's another world."

"I see. Then—then that's how come you guys played so well."

Zilo blubbered miserably, trying to wipe his eyes. His good-natured, freckled face looked tormented. "The others did," he sobbed. "I'm only a Class F telekinetic myself, and that isn't much where I come from. I did the best I could, but it was a terrible strain keeping the balls I hit away from the fielders and stopping balls from going over the fence and holding balls up until I could catch them. When I hurt my ankle I tried to help out from the bench, and it worked for a while. Sometimes I could even control the ball enough to spoil a pitcher's control, but usually when the ball was thrown fast or hit hard I couldn't do anything with it unless I was in the outfield and it had a long way to go. So I went home where I could get my ankle fixed, and when I came back I brought the others. They're really good—all of them Class A. Anderson and White—those are just names I had them use—they could control the ball so well they made it look like they were pitching. And no matter how hard the ball was hit, they could control it, even when they were sitting on the bench."

Pops scratched his head and said dazedly, "Made it *look* like they were pitching?"

"They just pretended to throw, and then they controlled the ball —well, with their minds. Any good telekinetic could do it. They could have pitched just as well sitting on the bench as they did on the pitcher's mound, and they could help out when one of our other pitchers was pitching. And Smith and Jones are levitators. They could cover the ground real fast and go up as high as they wanted to. I had a terrible time keeping them from going too high and spoiling everything. I was going to bring a telepath, too, to steal signs and things, but those four were the only ones who'd come. But we did pretty good anyway. When we hit the ball, Anderson and White could make it go anywhere they wanted, and they could control the balls the other team hit, and nothing could get past Smith and Jones unless we wanted it to. We could have won every game, but the papers said we were spoiling baseball, so we talked it over and decided to lose part of the time. We did the best we could. We won the pennant, and I hoped we could win this World Series, but they

had to go and drink some of that alcohol, and I guess Jones would
have spoiled everything even if we hadn't been caught."

The stranger spoke another crisp sentence, and Zilo wiped the
tears from his face and shook Pops's hand. "Good-bye, Pops," he
said. "Thanks for everything. It was lots of fun. I really like this
baseball."

He walked slowly out to the ship, passing the police without a
glance, and climbed the ramp.

Reporters were edging out onto the field, and the stranger waved
them back and spoke English in a booming voice. "You shall have a
complete explanation at the proper time. It is now my most unpleas-
ant duty to call upon your nation's President to deliver the apologies
of my government. Muko Zilo says he did the best he could. He did
entirely too much."

He floated back to the ship. The ramp lifted, and the police scattered as the ship swished upward. The umpire-in-chief shrugged his
shoulders and gestured with his mask. "Play ball!"

Pops beckoned to a pinch-hitter, got a pitcher warming up to replace Anderson, and strode back to the dugout. "They been calling
me a genius," he muttered to himself. "Manager of the year, they
been calling me. And how could I lose?"

A sportswriter leaned down from the stands. "How about a statement, Pops?"

Pops spoke firmly. "You can say that the best decision I made this
year was to resign."

An official statement was handed out in Washington before the
game was over. That the Yankees won the game, 23 to 2, was irrelevant. By that time, even the players had lost interest.

Priority Rating: Routine
From: Jard Killil, Minister of Juvenile Affairs
To: Milz Woon, Minister of Justice
Subject: Escapees from the Juvenile Rehabilitation Center,
    Philoy, Raff III, Sector 1311.

*A full report on the activity of these escapees no doubt has
reached your desk. The consequences of their offense are so serious they have not yet been fully evaluated. Not only have
these escapees forced us into premature contact with a Type
17D civilization for which neither we nor they were prepared,
but our best estimate is that the escapees have destroyed a notable cultural institution of that civilization. I believe that their
ages should not be used to mitigate their punishment. They are
juveniles, but they nevertheless are old enough to know right*

*from wrong, and their only motive seems to be that they were
enjoying themselves. I favor a maximum penalty.*

Baseball, as students of the game never tired of pointing out, was
essentially a game of records and statistics. The records were there
for all to see—incredible records, with Jones and Smith tied with 272
home runs and batting above .500, with Anderson and White each
hurling two dozen no-hit games, and with the strikeouts, and the ex-
tra-base hits, and the double plays, and the games won, and the total
bases, and the runs batted in, and the multitudinous individual and
team records that the Pirates had marked up during the season. The
record book was permanently maimed.

Who had done this? Four kids, four rather naughty kids, who—according to the strange man from outer space—were not especially
bright. And these four kids had entered into a game requiring the ultimate in skill and intelligence and training and practice, entered
into it without ever playing it before, and made the best adult ballplayers the planet Earth could produce look like a bunch of inept
Little Leaguers.

The records could be thrown out, but they could not be forgotten.
And it could not be forgotten that the four kids had made those records when they weren't half trying—because they didn't want to
make Earth's ballplayers look too bad. No one cared to consider
what would have happened had the people from outer space sent a
team made up of intelligent adults.

The Yankees took the World Series in seven straight games, and
few people cared. The stands were empty, and so sparse was the TV
audience that the Series ended as a financial catastrophe. A committee met to decide what to do about the aliens' records and reached
no decision. Again, no one cared.

The baseball establishment, fussing futilely with long-range plans
to correct the damage, suddenly realized that the awards for the
Most Valuable Players and Managers of the Year and the various individual championships had not been made. The oversight was not
protested. People had other things on their minds.

And when a dozen TV comedy teams simultaneously resurrected
an ancient, half-legendary, half-forgotten comedy sketch, they got no
laughs whatsoever. The sketch was called, "Who's on First?"

ROUND TRIP TO ESIDARAP

Jeff Allen pressed his nose against the door and steamed the glass with an angry snort. "A bomb would do it," he said. "Something big enough to make a nice bang and clean out the office but not big enough to knock over the building. Ann, where can we get a bomb?"

His wife looked up from her typewriter and smiled. "Don't be ridiculous. You're getting all riled up over nothing."

Allen turned gloomily. "You know very well that Centralia is too small to support *two* travel agencies."

"Business hasn't fallen off since he opened up. In fact, it's improved."

"That's a temporary fluke. It's bound to fall off. If he does any business at all, it has to cut into our business. Where else would it come from? So where can I get a bomb?"

She laughed, and he leaned over to kiss her before he went despondently back to his desk. Things probably had been going too smoothly, he told himself. He was just fifteen hundred dollars short of a down payment on that rambling, California redwood, ten-room ranch house with a rustic lake view, and he and Ann had been working and planning ever since their marriage three years before—working hard—to build the business to a point where she could retire from her role as clerk and personal secretary and concentrate on being a housewife with perhaps a robust crop of little Allens.

And now everything they'd worked for was threatened by a villainous-looking man with a brownish-red beard and a spectacularly bald head, who had appeared suddenly in Centralia and opened a new travel agency directly across the street from Allen's Globe Travel Agency. And he'd had the infernal nerve to name his business the Gloob Travel Agency.

"What did the Chamber of Commerce say?" Ann asked.

"They're puzzled. Gloob seems to be an obvious infringement on

Globe. On the other hand, he says his name is Gloob, so how can we keep him from using his own name? They're going to investigate. On my way back I stopped by for a brief conversation with Mr. Gloob. Charming gentleman. He seemed deliriously happy to meet me. He feels confident that we'll get along fine, and he even promises to send me any business he can't handle himself—which I take as evidence of a fiendish sense of humor." He shook his head. "I suppose we'll have to let Doris go. We might as well tell her now. She's entitled to a month's notice."

"But the business hasn't fallen off!" Ann protested. "Let's wait and see what happens. There'll be plenty of time—"

She broke off as a tiny, gray-haired old lady pushed open the door and stepped briskly to the counter. "I wish immediate accommodations for Sirap," the caller said.

Ann winced. "For—what was the place?"

"Sirap."

"What country is that in?"

The old lady cocked her head to one side and cast puzzled glances about the office. "Oh, I'm so sorry!" she said suddenly. "I must have the wrong—"

She walked away briskly, and the door whipped shut behind her, cutting off the blast of warm air from the street.

Ann's golden head bent studiously over an atlas. "There's a Siret in Rumania," she announced, "but it's a river."

"I thought there was something decidedly fishy about her," Allen said. He moved to the window and watched her cross the street and march confidently into the Gloob Travel Agency. She did not emerge, but as he continued to watch, a portly-looking gentleman came out, crossed the street, and followed an unerring path to the Globe Travel Agency. He paused inside the door, sniffed deeply at the air conditioning, and uttered a sigh of appreciation.

"Feels good in here," he announced. He walked to the counter and smiled down at Ann. "I'd like to arrange an extended tour of the United States. Could you handle it for me?"

Ann caught her breath. "Yes, sir."

"This is what I'd like to do. Start out with a week in Detroit, and then move on to Chicago—"

His voice rumbled on, and Ann took notes feverishly. "It will take a little time to arrange this," she said. "Where can we reach you?"

"At the Centralia Hotel."

"All right, Mr.—"

"Smith. John Smith."

"Mr. Smith. We'll get to work on it immediately."

"Excuse me," Allen said. "Didn't I see you coming out of the Gloob Travel Agency?"

The gentleman turned and beamed at him. "Indeed you did. The young man there recommended you."

Allen returned to his desk, leaned back in his chair, and gnawed fretfully on a pencil.

There was a brawny, bald-headed man who drawled with a foreign-sounding accent and seemed nervously anxious to get to Nilreb with all possible haste. There was a sedate, middle-aged woman who hovered in the background while two teen-aged girls inquired with assorted giggles as to whether Dnalsi Yenoc was actually anywhere near Kroywen, and whether they could go direct or by way of Nylkoorb. And there were others.

Eventually Ann stopped fumbling with the atlas, and in time she even grew weary of explanations. She contented herself with pointing, and when people with odd destinations sighted along her unwavering finger and glimpsed Mr. Gloob's Gloob sign, they invariably bounded away with unconcealed enthusiasm.

In between these visitations, the Globe Travel Agency's business boomed in a way that defied rational explanation. Allen made the down payment on the ranch house, and when Ann insisted that they were too busy for her to consider taking up housekeeping, he hired two new office girls. And the boom continued.

"Have you noticed," he said to Ann two weeks later, "that more than eighty per cent of our customers are not residents of Centralia?"

She nodded. "I've been wondering about that."

"And have you noticed that we're getting fewer inquiries from people with out-of-this-world destinations?"

"There was only one yesterday," Ann said.

She paused as a white-haired, scholarly-looking man stopped on the sidewalk outside, scrutinized them doubtfully through the window, and finally entered to ask for reservations to Kroywen. Ann pointed at the Gloob sign, and he left muttering apologies.

"Kroywen," Allen mused. "I've heard that one before."

"It seems to be one of the more popular destinations."

"Ann," Allen said, "I've got to get to the bottom of this. Mr. Gloob knows me, but I've noticed that he goes out to lunch at twelve-thirty. About a quarter to one I'm going over to the Gloob Travel Agency and see if I can arrange a fast trip to Kroywen."

"Not without me, you aren't," Ann said.

They left the mystified Doris with instructions to carry on if they should be delayed, bank the money, and forge Allen's signature on any necessary checks. At one forty-two they marched across Main Street, invaded the Gloob Travel Agency, and were met by Mr. Gloob's smiling young assistant.

"Kroywen," Allen said. "Make it snappy."

"Two for Kroywen," the young man said complacently. "That will be sixty-two dollars and fifty cents."

Allen counted it out. By coincidence, he had the exact change in his pocket.

The young man smiled appreciatively. "Had it all ready, I see. Do you have any money to exchange?"

"Why, ah—no," Allen said.

"No luggage?"

"No. You see—"

"I quite understand. It's best that way. Now if you will receipt these papers—"

With one deft motion he took Allen's right hand, inked his thumb, rolled a thumbprint onto the paper, and wiped the thumb clean. "And yours, please," he said to Ann. "Thank you. Did you have a nice tour?"

"Very nice."

"But you found the people a bit backward, I suppose."

He chuckled, and Allen said cheerfully, "Just a bit."

"Most people do. Right this way, please."

They followed him through a rear door, rode an escalator down to the basement, and paused in front of a metallic bulge in the wall. He opened it.

"Be seated, please," he said. "Remain seated until the door opens."

They sat down, and he smiled and told them to come again. The door closed. They were in a tubelike chamber that had six rows of seats dipping across the curved floor.

"Mr. Gloob is running a carnival," Ann said. "Thirty-one and a quarter for a tour of the chamber of horrors. Or could this be a subway car?"

"All things considered, it certainly could. But what's it doing in Centralia, Ohio? I wonder if the Interstate Commerce Commission knows about Mr. Gloob."

There was a jerk, so insignificant that they would not have noticed it had they not been tensed in anticipation. A light flashed red and faded slowly. They looked blankly at each other as the door opened. Another smiling young man was peering in at them.

"Some ride," Allen said.

"Destination," the young man told them. "Kroywen Terminal. All out, please."

They stepped out and followed him.

They paused at a desk marked "Customs," and a young lady noted their lack of baggage, glanced in a cursory manner at the contents of Ann's purse, and waved them past. They walked out into what obviously was the concourse of a large transportation terminal. There were ticket windows, travelers wandering about with bags, and an enormous board that listed arrivals and departures from and to tongue-twisting locations. Allen looked back at the door they had just emerged from and saw a large sign.

BOOLG, INCORPORATED
Specialists in Travel Curiosities

"Understatement of the year," he said.

They settled themselves on uncomfortable seats at the far end of the concourse and looked about them. Allen glanced at a large clock, glanced again, and then stared. "Screwy time they have here," he said. "That clock says five after eleven. My watch says five to one. How about yours?"

"Five to one," Ann said.

"I guess we've proved there is such a place as Kroywen. What do we do now? Turn around and go back?"

"It might look funny if we went back right away."

"True," Allen agreed. "And even if we've proved there is a Kroywen, we still don't know where it is or what it is. I'd like to walk around a bit. What's the matter?"

Ann's elbow had dug sharply at his ribs. "The second hand on that clock is running backward," she said.

Allen studied it. "So is the minute hand," he announced. A short time later, he added, "So is the hour hand."

Ann looked at her watch. "Then they have eleven o'clock when we have one o'clock. And when we have two, they have ten. It's just like our time, only backward." She turned to the distant Boolg, Incorporated, sign. "Boolg," she said. "Now, if you spell that backward—"

Allen did so, mouthing the letters slowly. "Gloob!" he exclaimed. "The Gloob Travel Agency!"

"And this town. Kroywen. Could that be—"

"New York!"

"It must be."

"This whole setup is someone's idea of a joke."

"We're here, aren't we?" Ann asked.

"But where are we? Something like twenty seconds from Centralia, and New York is nearly six hundred miles. And which way did we go? East, or west, or straight down?"

Ann giggled. Allen looked at her perplexedly, and she said, "I was just thinking of something Gloob's assistant said. Remember? He asked us if we found the people a bit backward. Referring to us, of course. So it shouldn't be surprising that we find things a bit backward here."

"Shall we take a quick look at the town?"

"We might as well. I've never been to New York."

"You still haven't been to New York."

They rode an escalator up three stories and found an exit. A man in uniform called out, "Taxi?" as they went out the door.

"They speak English," Allen said.

"How clever of you to notice," Ann told him.

The street was a brightly illuminated tunnel, with a high, arched ceiling. There were throngs of people on the walks, and throngs of vehicles in the street.

"The underside," Ann said. "Maybe like reflections in the water. Maybe somewhere straight up is the real New York." Allen had stopped to watch passengers boarding a bus. "We can't take it," Ann said. "You didn't get any money changed. Remember?"

"How was I to know what we'd find here? Anyway, I was just looking. The traffic moves on the left side. And the bus drivers sit in the rear. How do you suppose they see where they're going?"

"Maybe they have front-view mirrors."

They turned away as the bus rumbled off. They walked for what seemed to be miles along the tunneled streets, wandering about aimlessly, spelling the names of buildings and places and streets backward and finding some that they recognized. They found Broadway, and Fifth Avenue, and the Etats Eripme Building, one hundred two stories deep and the second lowest building in the world. They resisted the temptation to visit the meditation gallery on the hundred and second level, remembering at the last moment that they had no money.

"It's just another big city," Ann said. "Too many people and too much noise."

"And no blue sky," Allen said. "They must have some sky somewhere. Where do you suppose they keep it?"

When they next thought about the time it was after five—or before seven, Kroywen time. They were tired and hungry and definitely ready to leave. They found their way back to the terminal and rode the escalator down to the concourse. Ann turned suddenly and clutched Allen's arm. "How are you going to buy tickets?"

"I've got plenty of money."

"Dollars. But you didn't get any money changed. What if they won't take dollars?"

"Anyone will take dollars," Allen said. "They took dollars at the other end, didn't they? And if they won't, there should be somewhere we can get them changed."

"I hope you're right," Ann said. "Thinking backward is all right for one afternoon, but I'm too old to try it permanently."

Allen grinned down at the young face she called old, and they walked hand in hand across the concourse to Boolg, Incorporated. At the door they halted in consternation. Boolg, Incorporated, was closed. "Hours three to seven," read the crisp sign on the door.

Allen counted on his fingers. "Which means nine to five. My watch says five-twenty."

"So what do we do now? Sit in the station all night?"

"Certainly not. We'll go to a hotel."

"How are you going to pay the hotel bill?"

"I can get some money changed in the morning."

"All right," she said.

They advanced self-consciously on the registration desk of the Notlih Reltats Hotel and faced the suspicious scrutiny of the room clerk. He looked them over, noted their lack of luggage, and said with a sneer, "I suppose you're married."

Allen spoke indignantly. "Of course we're married. We've been married for three years."

He was not prepared for the reaction. The clerk's face reddened, and he sputtered and waved his hands menacingly. Two more clerks came to his aid. The first clerk pointed a finger. "He says they're married!" he blurted. "The idea—at a first-class hotel, too. Call the police!"

Allen grabbed Ann's arm, and the two of them rushed for the exit. Outside the door, a bellhop caught up with them, scribbled something on a piece of paper, and handed it to Allen.

"Try this place," he said. "It's small, but it isn't a bad hotel, and they aren't so particular. But it's best not to tell them you're married. It doesn't matter what they think, but when you come right out and say it—"

"Thanks," Allen said.

"Don't mention it, fellow. I was married once myself."

The little hotel was clean and primly respectable in its atmosphere. The room clerk snickered when Allen signed the register but said nothing. Allen told him they would be staying one night.

"One double room, fifteen rallods," the clerk said, and turned them over to a cheerful-looking bellhop. They entered a depressor and dropped downward.

"It seems all right," Ann whispered. "So what are you worried about now?"

"I'm trying to figure out how to tip the bellhop," Allen whispered back.

That worthy individual escorted them to their room, took a quick turn around it to see that everything was in order, and as Allen self-consciously turned his back to him, he thrust something into Allen's hand on the way out.

"Of all the insults!" Allen exploded as the door closed. "I didn't make any move to tip him, so he tipped me three rallods!"

Ann took one of the bills. "That's a pretty good picture of Notgnihsaw," she said. "Do you suppose this would buy us a meal?"

"Probably not. Maybe we could have our dinners sent up and added to our room bill. See if there's a menu for room service."

They found the menu and ordered. Their food arrived, accompanied by the same grinning bellhop. Allen cringed in embarrassment at the thought of offering the man his own three rallods as a tip, but the bellhop gave him no opportunity. He deftly slipped some currency onto one tray and hurried out.

"He tipped me again," Allen yelped. "This time it's five rallods."

"Don't complain," Ann said. "Maybe we can work it into enough to pay our hotel bill."

"Nothing doing. Here—I'll put it all on the tray. The least we can do is offer him his money back."

But when the bellhop came for the trays, he carefully removed the money and placed it on the desk. And when Allen picked it up later, the eight rallods had increased to eleven.

The day had been exhausting, and they slept well. It was after nine when they awoke—not quite three, Kroywen time—and they went down and ate breakfast in the hotel dining room to avoid further insults from the bellhop, having the check transferred to their hotel bill. Then Ann returned to their room, and Allen strolled down to the terminal to change some money and arrange their return to Centralia.

The young man at Boolg, Incorporated, was kindly sympathetic and utterly unyielding. "The rules are strict," he said, "and we couldn't possibly permit an exception. Dollars must be changed into rallods at the other end. So I can't help you. The financial basis of our business is extremely complex, you know, since we have to deal in two currencies."

Allen found himself a chair and sat down slowly. The travel agent seemed perplexed at his stricken expression. "If it's as important as all that to get rid of the dollars," he said, "why don't you take another trip and spend them?"

Allen brightened. "Yes. That's the thing to do. How many dollars for two tickets to Centralia?"

"As I told you," the young man said patiently, "foreign currency is handled only by our foreign terminals. Here we deal only in rallods. One thousand rallods for two tickets. When would you like to leave?"

"I'll think about it," Allen said.

Back in the hotel room, Allen and Ann sat staring at each other. "Thanks to the bellhop, I have eleven rallods," Allen said. "Our hotel bill will be fifteen, plus the price of two meals. And we need a thousand to get back. Any ideas?"

She shook her head. "It looks as if we'll have a long stay here. We'll have to work and earn the money."

"We might as well go up and check out and confess to the manager," Allen said. "Maybe he'll give me some help in getting a job."

"Couldn't we just stay here?"

"Too expensive. Over a hundred rallods a week for the room, and that doesn't include meals. And we'll need clothes. I haven't any idea of how much people are able to earn in this crazy society."

Grimly they advanced on the room clerk. "Checking out, I see," he said. "Accounts settled at that window."

A young lady itemized their bill and read off the items. "Room, one day, fifteen rallods. Dinner, by room service, eleven rallods." Allen winced. "Breakfast, three rallods. Total, twenty-nine rallods. Please receipt this bill."

"How was that again?" Allen asked.

Before he quite knew what was happening, his right thumb had been inked, impressed, and wiped clean. Ann contributed her thumbprint, and as Allen was groping for words to explain that he had only eleven rallods, the young lady briskly counted bills across the counter to him. "Twenty, twenty-five, twenty-nine. Thank you very much, sir. I hope you'll stop with us the next time you're in Kroywen."

They staggered away from the window, somehow made their way out of the hotel, and walked half a block before either of them spoke.

"They paid us," Allen said.

Ann said nothing.

"And the bellhop tipped us."

Ann stopped and pointed at a shop. "Women's apparel. I need a change of underwear."

They entered the shop. Ann made a few modest purchases. The clerk paid her six rallods. They went out.

"Another hotel, I suppose," Allen said.

"Yes. We'll get the most expensive room we can find."

"We might ask for the bridal suite."

"You'd shock them. They'd think we were married."

"Isn't there anything more expensive than a hotel suite?" Allen asked. "Supposing we find some kind of rental agent and inquire."

They found a rental agent. He arranged a week's sublease on a luxurious apartment, rent four hundred rallods, paid to them in advance. He also paid them his commission, which was forty rallods. He engaged a maid and a cook for them, and the two servants happily handed their week's wages to Ann when they reported for work.

Allen and Ann treated themselves to an unrestrained shopping tour. They bought luggage, for which they left their thumbprints in receipt and were paid a hundred and fifty rallods. Allen selected a new suit, and the beaming clerk took his thumbprint and paid him ninety-five rallods. They outfitted themselves completely and added more than five hundred rallods to their accumulation.

Then they returned to their apartment. "We have our thousand rallods," Allen said. "So I suppose we can leave any time."

Ann looked about the dazzling living room and gazed pensively at the fountain that bubbled in a far corner. "Yes, I suppose we can."

"We really should be getting back. Doris will have her hands full."

"Yes, I suppose she will."

Allen seized her roughly. "Hang Doris. We never had a proper honeymoon. Let's have it now. Doris can handle things for a week. She won't like it, but she can do it."

"Let's," Ann agreed happily. "Who can say when we'll be able to afford anything like this again?"

Allen embraced her fondly. "Paradise!"

"No," Ann said. "Esidarap."

They made it a week to remember. They flitted lightly from nightclub to nightclub. They ran up staggering bills and exchanged their thumbprints for cash when they left. The waiters tipped them lavishly. They attended the theater and received cash along with their tickets. They shopped, after the initial sensation of awe wore off, only for compact and expensive items that they could carry back with them. They gradually became accustomed to starting a meal with dessert and finishing up with an appetizer. They almost became accustomed to backward-running clocks, a calendar that worked in reverse, and riding down to their forty-fifth floor. It was, indeed, Esidarap.

At the end of the week they were still in a mood of unrestrained happiness but reluctantly ready to return to their normal world and go back to work. And on that fateful seventh day a fist descended rudely upon their door, followed by two heavy-set, official-looking men who brushed their frightened maid aside and stood looking them over coolly.

"IBF," one of them said, flashing his credentials. "We have been reliably informed that you two are unemployed. Is that correct?"

"Yes, we're unemployed," Allen admitted.

"We've come to talk to you about your unemployment compensation."

Ann giggled foolishly, and Allen muttered, "All this and Esidarap too!"

"We are in the process, now, of checking your past record to see if you are paid up to date. But we've established that the compensation is unpaid for the past week, and we intend to collect that now. For the two of you, that amounts to seven thousand rallods. Cash or certified check, please."

Allen choked suddenly on nothing at all and glanced at Ann's white face. He said slowly, "You mean—we owe—"

"Every now and then people try to slip away and beat the government," the IBF agent said. "But they soon find out that it's rather expensive not to work. If you'll take my advice, you'll go back to wherever it is you came from, and go to work, and pay your wages like a good citizen. Right now I want seven thousand rallods."

"My gawd!" Allen exclaimed. "I wonder what the income tax amounts to!"

The agent was momentarily flustered. "If the government owes you income tax, we can, of course, apply that against your unemployment compensation. It would take time to check, though. Better just pay us and take your refund in the usual way."

Allen got out his wallet and counted carefully. "I have four thousand, five hundred and twenty rallods," he said. "Ann?"

She was searching through her purse. "Twenty-one hundred," she said.

"Leaving you three hundred and eighty short," the IBF man said.

"If you'll excuse us a moment, we'll make a couple of quick purchases," Allen told him.

The IBF men accompanied them while they bought a diamond ring for Ann—her third. It brought them four hundred rallods. They paid off the balance they owed and went despondently back to their apartment.

The rental agent was waiting for them. He was a quiet, white-haired, fatherly sort of man, and his face wore a mournful expression that suggested someone near and dear to him had let him down badly. "You two have disappointed me," he said.

"How is that?" Allen asked.

"I'd hoped you would be able to keep this place for the summer. But now—" He shook his head. "Why did you do it?"

"Do what?"

"Live so recklessly. I don't know what sort of wages you pay in your normal occupation, but even if it's above average, you've used up your luxury and entertainment allowances for years. You'd have been stopped if you hadn't done it so fast, but—all in one week! The reports are tabulated, now, and out you go."

"How did you know about it?" Allen demanded.

"My dear young man. Why do you suppose your thumbprint is taken with every purchase? All bills go to central accounting, and a full statement of purchases is compiled as often as the volume requires it. Surely you knew that!"

"Yeah," Allen said. "Surely I knew that."

"So—out you go. You'll be living at a mere subsistence level for a long time. But—" He shrugged. "When you get your credit back, come and see me again. Perhaps I can arrange something just as nice as this—if you promise to conduct your affairs intelligently." He left, calling a reminder over his shoulder that they were to be moved out by noon.

"There goes four hundred rallods a week," Ann said.

"And we're down to twenty, and it's a long way to a thousand. We should have left when we had it."

"I suppose we should have. It has been fun, though."

"So what do we do now?" Allen asked.

The beautifully toned door chimes sounded. It was a detective with a court summons. An hour later they were in court. In another fifteen minutes they were out again, tried, convicted, soundly lectured by the judge, and sentenced.

They were, the judge informed them, a cancerous blight gnawing on the roots of the entire economic system. Their offense was two-fold—first, that they had received more for purchases than they were spending in wages; and second, that they were unemployed and therefore not spending anything in wages.

Allen had an inspiration. "Your Honor," he protested, "I couldn't find a job."

His Honor flushed angrily and shattered his gavel with one vicious stroke. "This court will not tolerate such a fiction!" he shouted. "You know perfectly well that any citizen who is unable to find employment privately can pay wages to the government."

But their sentence did not seem unduly severe. His Honor placed them on probation, banged a fresh gavel, and called for the next case.

A burly police officer led them out of the courtroom and into a small anteroom, where white-robed technicians took charge of them, got them seated at a table, and before they quite knew what was happening had clamped their right thumbs in a small, boxlike device.

Allen protested, "The judge said probation. He didn't say anything about thumb screws."

"Quite a card, aren't you?" a technician sneered.

Allen did not reply. He felt a sudden stab of pain, nothing more. At the same time Ann winced and looked over at him, puzzled.

"All right," the police officer said. "You can go, now." He chuckled. "And don't do it again."

On the steps of the courthouse they stopped to examine their thumbs. Neatly engraved on each was a small P. "I'll be damned," Allen exclaimed. "They've branded us."

They went to the office of their rental agent, and that worthy gentleman greeted them with obvious displeasure. "What do you want now?"

"We'll have to live somewhere," Allen said. "We thought perhaps—"

"I don't handle rentals in your class."

"Could you refer us to someone?"

He sighed and buzzed his secretary. "These people are on probation," he said. "See if you can find them something."

The secretary went out, giving them contemptuous glances over her shoulder.

"This may sound like an odd question," Allen said, holding up his thumb, "but would you mind explaining this probation business?"

"Try buying something," the rental agent said. "You'll understand it immediately. You can't make a purchase without receipting it with your thumbprint. A probation print is not acceptable unless accompanied by a waiver of probation officially certified by the court."

"What do they want to do?" Allen demanded hotly. "Starve us?"

"Oh, you can buy the essentials. The bare essentials. You must register at one store and make all your food purchases there. You can buy clothing, but only such clothing as is necessary for your work, and your employer must furnish a requisition. I don't know the exact amount of your excess, of course, but if you behave yourselves for a few years, the court may take your good behavior into consideration."

"I see. Are there any lending institutions around here?"

"I don't understand."

"Banks, loan companies—"

"Oh. You mean *borrowing* institutions. Of course. Why do you ask?"

"I'd like to borrow a thousand rallods."

"My dear young man! Were you born yesterday? You don't borrow money from those institutions. You lend them money!"

"Why, yes, of course," Allen said. "Naturally."

The secretary returned and handed Allen a slip of paper. "There's the address," she said. "It isn't much. Just a furnished room. The neighborhood is poor, and it's a walkdown, but I don't think you can do any better than that."

"Thank you for everything," Allen said. "Does the government confiscate the things we bought?"

"Certainly not," the rental agent said. "The government merely keeps you from buying more until you have retired the excess."

They attempted to transport their belongings by taxi, and the driver took one look at the "P" that registered neatly in the center of Allen's thumbprint and drove away in disgust. They made four trips by bus and learned later that they had used up their week's quota. Their new landlady was fat, owlish-looking, and hideously suspicious.

"One of those, eh?" she said, studying Allen's thumbprint. "Well —all right. But I'll have you know this is a decent house, and if the police start nosing around here, out you go." She paid him for a week in advance—six rallods.

They got settled in their cramped room, and Allen sat in the lone chair feeling miserable while Ann stretched out on the bed and sobbed.

"I suppose we'd better get something to eat," Allen said finally.

"I'm not hungry."

"We'll have to buy food, whether we eat it or not. If we don't, we won't have any money to pay our wages with, and we can't get jobs. And if we don't go to work, we'll have to pay another seven thousand rallods in unemployment compensation at the end of the week."

Ann got up wearily. "All right. We'll buy some food, but I won't eat it. And I suppose we'd better start looking for jobs."

They registered at a neighborhood grocery store and bought their entire week's allowance of groceries, concentrating on canned goods that would not require cooking. They took their groceries, and seventeen rallods, back to their room, where Allen inventoried their wealth—twenty rallods left from the ring purchase, six from rent, two and a fraction from bus rides, seventeen from groceries.

"Forty-five rallods," he said. "That means we can't afford jobs that cost more than twenty-two and a half. Do you suppose they have such a thing?"

"You take twenty-five," Ann said. "I'll take twenty."

They found an employment agency and went their separate ways for interviews and classification. Allen's interviewer scowled at his blemished thumbprint, scowled at Allen, and said disgustedly, "Hardly worth the trouble, bothering with one like you. Well—I suppose you want the lowest-paying job you can find. Some kind of a sales job, perhaps. You pay a small guaranteed salary and a commission on what you sell. If you don't sell much, you might get along. It better be something that isn't expensive, because selling one large item a week, such as an automobile, would ruin you. This might do it—cemetery lots. Here's the address. And here—" He handed Allen five rallods. "Here is the agency fee. I hope we won't see you again."

Ann was already back at the room when Allen returned that evening. She was lying face down on the bed, and she did not look up when he came in. He sat down wearily and slipped out of his shoes. "I'm a salesman," he said. "I'm selling cemetery lots. They cost a hundred and fifty rallods each. Meaning that the person who buys one is paid a hundred and fifty rallods. I'm on salary and commission. I pay the boss twenty rallods a week, and I pay the customer fifteen rallods of that hundred and fifty for every lot I sell. I don't intend to sell any."

She spoke with her face muffled in the pillow. "I'm a filing clerk. It was the best I could do, and it's thirty-five rallods a week. All I had was the twenty you gave me and five from the employment agency. I have to bring the other ten tomorrow, or I'll be fired. I almost got fired anyway, because using the alphabet backward confuses me. Where can I get ten rallods?"

"Did you try the new-clothes angle?"

She sat up. "What's that?"

"I told my boss this was the only suit I had. He thought it looked pretty good—it ought to, it cost two hundred and fifty rallods—but he agreed that a salesman should have more than one suit. He gave me a requisition, and I bought a new suit for forty rallods. That's the most expensive one they'd let me have. It gives us a little cushion."

"Some cushion. We're getting six rallods a week for this room. We're allowed seventeen for groceries. That's twenty-three. And I have to pay thirty-five in wages and you have to pay twenty." She lay down again and went on tonelessly, "How can we save a thousand rallods if we go in the hole thirty-two every week?"

"You ask your boss for a requisition for clothing, and I'll try to think of some angles. Maybe they'll let me take a prospect to dinner every now and then. I could pick up a few rallods that way. And maybe something will turn up."

Catastrophe struck the next day, when Allen sold a cemetery lot. "The guy practically took the thing away from me," he moaned. "I tried insulting him, and knocking the product, and everything else I could think of, but I couldn't get out of it. So there goes fifteen rallods."

"I tore my dress and gave the boss a hard-luck story," Ann said. "He let me buy forty rallods worth of clothing. So we have our wages for next week, but you'd better not sell any more lots."

"I won't," Allen promised. "I'll turn and run first."

They started the second week with their wages honorably paid and enough surplus to carry them a third week provided that Allen sold nothing. Beyond that lay blank despair.

On the second day of that second week, Allen avoided making a sale with such obvious evasive tactics that the prospective customer complained to his boss. The boss studied Allen's sales record, which was not impressive, and threatened to discharge him. Allen was tired, discouraged, and nauseated at the thought of another cold meal out of cans. He was homesick for a glimpse of blue sky. He lurched through the door and halted in amazement.

Ann had a visitor—a bulky, bald-headed, brownish-red-bearded man who leaned back in the rickety chair and regarded Allen quizzically. It was Mr. Gloob, of the Gloob Travel Agency.

Mr. Gloob pointed an accusing finger. "You shouldn't have done it!"

"You're telling me!"

Ann leaped up excitedly. "We just got here. I saw him on the street, and he almost got away from me. I chased along beside him for two blocks, and he wouldn't pay any attention to me."

"She certainly did," Mr. Gloob said. "I didn't recognize her, so I tried to ignore her. My old mother always warned me about blatantly forward strange women. But you shouldn't have done it. Do you realize the confusion you created in our accounting department? Two return trips, with no outgoing prints to match with them. The directors have held three emergency meetings, and the problem seemed utterly incapable of solution. You'll have to go back, you know. You must promise absolute secrecy and leave at once. I won't have it any other way."

"I won't, either," Ann said fervently.

Gloob was studying the room critically. "Why are you living in such a queer place? I've often wondered what people from your backward world would do in our civilization, but this isn't exactly what I imagined."

"It isn't what we imagined, either," Allen said. He briefly described their week of reckless extravagance and the depths to which they had fallen.

Gloob raised his hands in horror. "My word! But why did you let them put you on probation? Why did you try to live like this? This is terrible! Why didn't you just go back to Centralia?"

"How could we?" Allen demanded. "The IBF men took every bit of our money. We didn't have the thousand rallods for tickets."

Gloob slowly rose to his feet. "My dear friend Allen! Surely you couldn't live in our civilization for more than two weeks and have so little understanding of our ways. You do not pay a thousand rallods for tickets. We pay *you* the thousand rallods!"

"But I thought—" Allen weakly took the chair Gloob had just vacated. "I mean, you charged us at Centralia, and I paid you, so naturally—"

The two of them stared at Gloob, whose face was working convulsively, and suddenly all three of them dissolved in laughter.

"I'll start packing," Ann said.

"I'll help you," Allen told her.

Gloob held up his hand. "Just a moment, now. Not so fast. This thing is more serious than you realize. You could have gone back at any time up until the moment you were put on probation, just by presenting yourselves and thumbprinting a receipt. But now we can't accept your receipt. You've used up your allowance of luxuries, and it will be a long, long time before your thumbprints can be honored by Boolg, Incorporated."

"You mean we're stuck here?"

"That's exactly what I mean. Of course, it wasn't precisely your fault that you didn't understand our economic system and got into trouble. Our citizens have to keep meticulous records of their purchases. If they want some special luxury, like a Boolg, Incorporated, tour, they conserve their allowance ahead of time, or they reduce their luxury expenditures drastically after they return. Conduct such as yours is rare. It's considered a serious crime, which is why the punishment is so severe. I'm sure it was unintentional, but you did commit the crime, and our laws won't permit you to walk away and forget it."

"Do you mean you won't do a thing to get us back?" Allen demanded.

"What can I do? I can't sell a luxury tour to you while you're on probation."

There was a brief silence while Allen glared angrily at Gloob. Then he turned to Ann. "This nonsense has gone on long enough," he said. "We'll go to the authorities the first thing in the morning and tell them how the negligence of Boolg, Incorporated, got us into this mess and ask to be sent home."

"Oh, I say!" Gloob exclaimed. "You can't do that. There'd be all kinds of unfavorable publicity for Boolg, Incorporated. We might lose our franchise. We specifically agreed that our operations would be kept secret in your world."

"Tough," Allen said. "But I'm sure you'll think of some explanation. Now if you'll excuse us, we have our packing to do."

"But you can't! You simply can't! We've just opened new terminals in Europe and South America, and our business is developing splendidly. You have no idea what those tours mean to the citizens of this world. To pay a hotel bill instead of being paid, to pay for transportation, to pay for food or anything else that's purchased, to do a little work and have the employer pay them—why, if the government finds out about you it'll spoil everything. At best we'd have to shut down our United States terminals, and that's the most popular place for tours. Why, it'll be—it'll be—"

"It'll be a dirty shame," Allen agreed. "Now if you'll excuse us—"

Gloob sighed. "All right. I'll manage it some way. Go ahead and pack."

Allen reached for a suitcase. "I don't see why you make such a problem out of it. All you have to do is smuggle us away from here. You don't have to pay us a thousand rallods. What would we do with them?"

"Mmm—yes. Perhaps it can be done without any official record made of it. We'll see."

A heavy fist rattled their door, and the landlady's rancorous voice called, "Phone for Mr. Allen!"

Allen and Ann exchanged startled glances. "Who's calling?" Allen asked.

"Why don't you answer it and find out?" the landlady snarled.

Allen plodded up three flights of stairs and apprehensively approached the telephone. "Hello."

"Mr. Allen?"

"Speaking."

"This is agent Senoj, of the IBF. You'll remember our conversation of a week or so ago concerning your unemployment taxes."

"Not with pleasure," Allen said. "For your information, I now am employed."

"I know. At that time you mentioned that you had some income tax credit coming. We've conducted an investigation, and we find that you have received no income taxes for the past five years. The statute of limitations permits no claim of more than five years to be made against the government, but as long as we've definitely established this five-year delinquency, we would like to make a settlement with you."

"That's—extremely nice of you," Allen murmured.

"We don't know how this could have happened, but it did happen, and I'd like to have you sign the necessary papers and accept a check in full and final settlement."

"How large a check?"

"With penalties and interest it comes to twenty-five thousand rallods."

"You don't say. Give me your office address, and I'll look you up in the morning."

"What's wrong with this evening?" the agent said. There was a note of suspicion in his voice.

"I'm rather busy at the moment. It's mealtime, you know."

"How about an hour from now?"

"Make it two hours." Allen glanced at his watch and counted frantically on his fingers. "Four o'clock."

"That's a little late, but—all right. Expect me at four."

Allen hurried back down the stairway. "IBF," he said. "They want to give us twenty-five thousand rallods in back income taxes."

"Good heavens!" Gloob exclaimed. "You aren't serious!"

"Absolutely. He's coming at four."

"Good heavens! We'll have to get you out of here. If the government gives you that much money, it'll also have to give you jobs to let you spend it, and that means high executive positions. You'll never get away. Here—I'll help you pack."

They left in a frenzied rush, dashing up the stairs and waiting on the stoop while Gloob hurried into the street to hail a taxi. They had loaded in their luggage and were climbing in themselves when the landlady charged into the street after them, screaming vile insults.

"Just what I expected of scum like you," she shrieked. "Trying to sneak out on me. Just what I expected. But I been keeping my eyes open, I have. Here—one week's rent for leaving without notice."

She handed Allen six rallods.

Allen and Ann returned to Centralia, and the Globe Travel Agency, and the rambling, California redwood, ten-room ranch house with a rustic lake view. They never bothered to explain their mysterious absence, and in time their friends tired of asking. And if their friends thought it odd that they named their first son Kroywen, none of them mentioned it within their hearing, not even the boy's godfather, Mr. Gloob.

A warm friendship developed between Mr. Gloob and the Allens, and the two travel agencies achieved a level of co-operation rare for supposedly competitive enterprises. Working together, Gloob and Allen planned tours and applied their ingenuity to the arrangement of colorful itineraries for a mysterious influx of travelers who quickly made Centralia, Ohio—a most unlikely location for one—a tourist's mecca.

Mr. Gloob was a frequent visitor in the Allens' home, and they had delightful conversations concerning all sorts of subjects except the place of Mr. Gloob's origin, which by unspoken common consent none of them mentioned.

One evening, though, when Mr. Gloob sat rocking peacefully, smoking his pipe, and watching his godson kick happily in a playpen, Allen took up the subject of his son's name. "It was Ann's idea," he said. "She insisted on it. And how can the kid ever be a success in life with a backward name like that?"

Merriment flashed in Gloob's eyes, but he spoke firmly. "Kroywen," he said, "is the most forward-sounding name I know."

And there the matter rested.

NO BIZ LIKE SHOW BIZ

Tomorrow and tomorrow and tomorrow
Creeps on this petty pace from day to day
Wace Renoldon Farley, 673 492 479 341 895 to his friends, was
teaching a ballet step to Horace Wangley Whipple. Farley counted
aloud: One, two, one, two, one, two; and sometimes he hummed:
Hmmm ho, hmmm ho, hmmm ho.

And while he worked, his mind wove gossamer funeral shrouds for
fragments of dead beauty.
A stage where every man must play a part
And mine a sad one.
Whipple was learning to dance because one night in a fit of rage
he beat to death his cohabitant, their infant daughter, and his
mother. (He already had learned four card tricks, one magic act, a
comic song, and an inept imitation of an unpopular Director of Public Safety.) He wore a brief ballet skirt and nothing else; sweat glis-
tened on his bulging, hairy stomach as he balanced precariously on
his toes and moved, with unsteady, mincing steps, from one side of
his cage to the other.

He reached the bars, resisted the impulse to grab them, and managed an awkward, stumbling pivot without losing his balance.
Farley's hand relaxed on the punishment button. (Whenever Whipple touched anything to steady himself, Farley gave him an electric
shock.) The hirsute ballerina looked hauntingly like a clumsily waltz-
ing gorilla in a ballet skirt, but the analogy would have been lost on
Farley, who had no personal knowledge of that extinct primate.

They were two atavists adrift in the wrong time and place. Whipple—whose physique should have been magnificent—in a world
where strength and physical skill were meaningless; Farley—whose
keen mind was shaped to the exquisite, dramatic interplay, the iridescent beauties of man and fate contending—in a world that had

abolished both fate and beauty. The one's body met the other's mind only on the simulated musical beat: One, two, one, two.

Now, by two-headed Janus,
Nature hath framed strange fellows in her time.

Farley regarded Whipple with mingled pity and contempt. The slobbering brute's stuttering gyrations were pathetic, but Farley knew that everyone else would find them hilarious, and the successful addition of this ballet number to Whipple's necessarily limited repertoire would add a minimum fifty thousand to his price when he came up for auction.

Farley also knew (this was the fate of one who saw beauty in man's contention with fate) that the enforcement of inhuman indignities on a human being merely because he'd committed a few murders was an outrage. Behind that fear-twisted face and those blankly staring eyes was an indefinable quality of the human condition that the cage and its accompanying gross humiliations were slowly strangling.

These atavistic quirks of Farley's mentality would have deeply disturbed his superiors and his friendly local internal security agents had they so much as suspected them. Farley believed in the human soul, though he did not know what to call it.

*   *   *

Adjacent to the building that housed the Penal Authority were the crematory ovens and the gas chambers of the International Poverty Control Agency (U.S. Branch). On this day ovens and chambers were not in operation, a fact that disappointed those tourists who rode out on the branch conveyor to gape at the exteriors of the infamous extermination and confinement centers.

One of them remarked, "Now that's what I call a job! Work only one day a month!"

*   *   *

Harl Ranno Lyndyl occupied a cage near Whipple's. He sat on the floor, vacantly grinning into the infinite. He did not know where he was, or why, or what Farley was saying to Whipple; but when Farley counted or hummed a dance beat, the regularity of the sound awakened in Lyndyl a flicker of response. Farley counted; almost imperceptibly, Lyndyl nodded his head.

*   *   *

The Penal Authority was located on the edge of a diminishing swamp that once had been a river, and its district, formerly an island, was affectionately referred to as Old Blight, to distinguish it from the various new blights of the districts that surrounded it. It was the leading tourist attraction on the continent, possessing innumerable historic ruins, museums, legendary sites, a vast network of underground conveyors, quaintly ramshackle shops, and two of Earth's three remaining skyscrapers.

Tourists thronged the walkways, and the boldest of them timidly made their way into the Anachron, the world's last surviving public restaurant, the only place on Earth where real food could be bought and consumed. It even had a food store that sold raw and preserved foods for home cooking by those whose apartments were sufficiently anachronistic to still have the means.

In three of its four dining rooms (the small fourth room was reserved for regular local patrons), tourists held their scoops awkwardly and gummed a few mouthfuls of one of the creamy vegetable stews, or the vegetable curries, or the vegetable chowders, or (at an incredible price) the vegetable soufflé before they stole the menus to take home to their disbelieving friends and relatives.

There were tourist rumors that the Anachron would even serve meat, from unmentionable sources, raw or cooked, and at wholly unbelievable prices, but these were based upon the understandable assumption that a place selling any kind of real food would sell anything. The regular customers knew nothing about it, as repeated governmental investigation had proved. (Any kind of a rumor of meat consumption automatically was subjected to investigation by thirty-seven different governmental departments.) The regular customers tended to be morose, solitary individuals, decent enough citizens, eminently law-abiding, who were afflicted with digestive problems or otherwise allergic to wholesome synthetics, and the government was inclined to regard them more with sympathy than suspicion.

In the Anachron's main dining room, Oswald Ossafont Oyner, a tourist, and his family were gazing in stunned disbelief at the steaming bowls that had been placed before them. Oyner gripped his scoop defensively and pointed. "What's that?"

"A piece of carrot," the server answered politely.

"And—that?"

"Tomato."

"And—those?"

"Peas."

Oyner wielded his scoop, slurped the contents distastefully, and swallowed. A moment later his stomach churned, and he clapped his hand to his mouth for a brief but losing struggle with his own physiology. The server resignedly pointed an autocleaner at the mess. It happened a minimum hundred times a day.

* * *

Wace Farley's initial success had emboldened him. He decided to teach Whipple *two* ballet steps, the second to be used to bring the act to a climax. He was counting: *One* two three, *one* two three, *one* two three.

> *Whether 'tis nobler in the mind to suffer*
> *The slings and arrows of outrageous fortune,*
> *Or to take arms against a sea of trouble . . .*

At that moment Georg Donnoho Mallod entered. He took one look at the pirouetting Whipple and dissolved in laughter. "Great act!" he gasped. "Great act!"

The Penal Authority's Resident Administrator daily congratulated himself on his astuteness in rescuing Farley from the inevitable fate of the unemployed, the ovens. The shy young man had seemed intent on suicide, devoting all of his legally allowed training to such an outlandishly unemployable specialty as ancient dramatic arts; but Mallod had a friend in the Poverty Control Agency who made it his hobby to sift out individuals with unusual qualifications and find employment for them. He mentioned Farley's specialty to Mallod, and Mallod had reflected that the ancient dramatic arts were, after all, the primitive ancestors of contemporary public attractions. In sifting the moldy mounds of obsolete information Farley must have turned over a few notions that could be adapted to contemporary use. Mallod hired him.

Farley's immediate, spectacular success already had gained Mallod a promotion that had been five years overdue, and Mallod was generous enough to publicly give Farley some of the credit for it. Mallod was not aware that Farley hated his work, or that he believed in the human soul.

"Dr. Savron is coming," Mallod said.

Farley continued his count. Since he had never heard of Dr. Savron, he doubted that the visit concerned him. *One* two three, *one* two three.

> *How weary, stale, flat, and unprofitable*
> *Seem to me all the uses of the world.*

"He's the director of Rolling Acres. That's the new Public Recreational Center over in District Eleven."

"I've heard of it," Farley said. "I didn't know it had entertainment accommodations." *One* two three, *one* two three.

"It does," Mallod said grimly, "and Savron will have a priority order. He'll want the usual dozen attractions. Why public establishments think they have to compete with private places of entertainment is more than I can understand. I've complained to several legislators about it. Not only is the competition unfair, but it reduces our surpluses. Well—Savron is on the way, and we'll have to make the best of it. I told Karlson to move a dozen attractions with bids under a thousand to the central concourse."

Farley left off his counting. "I have a couple of short-termers I'd be glad to unload. A pickpocket—he's quite good. We got him back when the Happy Hours exhibit failed, and since he only has six months left to serve—"

"Good idea. There won't be any bids, so we might as well let the Rolling Acres budget feed him."

"Also, there's a con woman who has wonderful dexterity. Unfortunately, she's such an ugly old thing that there were no bids, and now she has less than a year to serve."

"Send them down," Mallod said. "I'll unload them if I can."

"I wish we could unload Lyndyl."

"We'll certainly try. I want you to come along and view Karlson's attractions. I think it's mostly his fault we don't get better bids on them."

Farley shrugged and got to his feet. It would be a challenge. Sometimes, if there was a challenge, he forgot that he hated his work.

The two of them left, and the multimurderer Whipple, still painfully balanced on his toes, stared after them.

*   *   *

Even the Anachron's building was anachronistic, a shabby, eight-sided affair with eight doors, and the restaurant's regular customers loved it. Many of them had been eating their daily meal there for years, and the private dining room enabled them to enjoy their food undisturbed by gabbing tourists with unpredictable stomachs.

The regular customers also had their own convenience lounge on the sublevel where stocks of food were stored, and from the convenience lounge, those regular customers who over the years had established themselves as trustworthy followed a labyrinthine path among the pungent-smelling bins to a remote wall. After a meticulous inspection through a secret panel, a secret door opened and they were admitted and for a wholly unconscionable price served a huge, foaming mug of berr, a transaction that would have been investigated by seventy-one outraged governmental departments had it even been suspected.

But the Anachron had performed its own careful, long-term investigation of those regulars who were admitted to the secret sublevel taproom. They were reliable. Some quaffed the forbidden beverage as the only means of rebellion open to them. Others had developed a taste for the berr. If some managed to make a few mugs of berr last through a day or an evening or a night of companionable talk, who was to notice? It was not without forethought that the Anachron had endowed itself with eight entrances—and exits.

On this afternoon Eman Xavion Helpflin was the taproom's only customer. He had been there since morning; much of the time he was alone, because Melisander, the drawer, worked in the storerooms when business was slack.

Helpflin sat in the darkest corner of the room and at lengthening intervals tilted his mug, sipped, and watched the flecks of foam slowly slide back into the berr. He was an employee of the International Poverty Control Agency, and at the most recent E (for Extermination) Day, an employed man and his family went to the ovens because the agency had stupidly snarled its records. This was not Helpflin's fault. The contrary—he received a commendation for his own attempts to straighten out the mess. He did straighten it out, but an accumulation of minor errors of omission elsewhere negated his efforts. He received a commendation; the man and his family nevertheless were dead.

Commendation and merit citations carried automatic grants of leave, and Helpflin was spending his in the dark corner of the Anachron's secret taproom, tilting his berr mug and staring at the foam.

If Wace Farley had been able to articulate his ideas concerning the human soul, Helpflin would not have believed him, but he would have liked to.

*   *   *

Dr. Marnis Murgatroyd Savron carried his lank form at a slight forward tilt, which enabled him to view the world with close suspicion through his bulging pol lenses. Resident Administrator Mallod read him easily: He knew nothing, he had no previous experience with criminal attractions, and he would have preferred to send a subordinate but hadn't dared. He would be far more difficult to deal with than a professional; knowing nothing, he'd be terrified of making a mistake.

Mallod asked, "How many accommodations does Rolling Acres have?"

"Twenty displays," Savron said, sounding apologetic.

"Twenty!" exclaimed Wace Farley, who had been listening quietly while Mallod and Savron exchanged greetings. "Why, no other public exhibit has more than—"

Mallod silenced him with a glance and spoke firmly to Savron. "Absolutely impossible." He opened a folder and inventoried Karlson's list of low-bid attractions. "Six is the very best I can do for you. That's just to get you started, of course—we'll add to them whenever we can until we've filled your displays, but it can't be done quickly. To help tide you over, I can let you have a couple of short-term attractions—a pickpocket and a con woman—in addition to the six."

"I'd hoped for at least two murderers," Savron said, still sounding apologetic.

Mallod shook his head. "There's only one available: Brenda Barris, the cohabitant poisoner."

"Poisoner?" Savron grimaced. "I don't think our public would like that."

"She has a very good act," Mallod assured him. "You'll see her. You'll see all of them."

"I heard that Whipple hasn't been assigned yet."

"He hasn't." Mallod smiled at him. "And the bids have reached half a million."

Dr. Savron's startled, "Oh," was a mixture of incredulity and disappointment.

"We're the only branch of government that shows a profit," Mallod said, still smiling. "We turn millions back to the treasury annually, and those millions support many worthwhile projects—such as the Rolling Acres Recreational Center. We're sympathetic to free public exhibits in parks and recreational centers and community malls, but the directors much understand that merely because the attractions are transferred from one branch of government to another doesn't mean that they're without cost. They cost whatever we would have been able to lease them for to private exhibitors. If we turned our really valuable attractions over to public exhibits, the budget wouldn't balance and there'd be an investigation. Did you by chance get the written approval of the Penal Commission before you built the twenty displays? No? The code limits you to twelve, you know."

Savron said uncertainly, "Well, the funds were available, and the people seem to enjoy the displays, so we thought—"

Mallod was nodding grimly. "I'll do the best I can for you. If you'll promise not to complain, I'll promise not to call anyone's attention to the twenty displays. Fair enough?"

"Well—I suppose."

Mallod patted his shoulder familiarly. "Come along. You can pick out your six."

* * *

Melisander, the Anachron's taproom drawer, was becoming deeply concerned about Eman Helpflin. The man had stretched three mugs of berr over most of a day, which did not seem excessive, but he had been staring into his mug for so long that Melisander knew he either was intoxicated or hypnotized.

"Don't you think you ought to eat something?" he asked.

Melisander's suggestions were the taproom's only code of law. Helpflin knew he wouldn't get a refill until he had eaten, so he pushed his empty mug aside and went up to the Anachron's private dining room. An hour later he was back in the taproom, slowly sipping berr and staring at the foam.

* * *

Karlson was waiting in the central concourse when Savron, Mallod, and Farley arrived. A garrulous, middle-aged man of limited intelligence, he had been maneuvered into his job by a prominent politician relative to save him from extermination, and he ploddingly attempted to use the same tired entertainment ideas over and over. Farley, who felt sorry for him, helped him out whenever he could, but persuading him to drop a bad idea in favor of a good one was not easy—Karlson couldn't tell the difference.

With a smug little smile Karlson led them to the Brenda Barris display; probably he expected her to charm Savron into accepting the rest of his badly trained riffraff. He sounded the warning buzzer; the stage lights came on; the curving panels became transparent.

Brenda Barris was a faded, bulgy, graying woman whose cohabitant had wanted to leave her for obvious reasons. Karlson attempted to make sirens out of all of his female criminals, and he had attired Barris in trousers cut so short they were almost nonexistent and a transparent shirt. She wearily went through the motions of setting a table, making cafron, adding simulated poison to one cup, and then seating herself to wait for her doomed cohabitant.

Savron was shaking his head disgustedly. He knew he was inexperienced, but he resented being considered stupid. Mallod said to Farley, "Tell Karlson what's wrong."

"The casting," Farley said. "An ugly old woman doesn't become an attractive young woman merely because she's committed murder. Make Barris a surrogate mother. Dress her conservatively and teach her to smile. And when she's made the drink, she ought to pretend she's inviting someone in the audience to share it with her."

"Get working on it now," Mallod ordered. "We'll make the rounds without you. By the time we're back here, I want to see a good act."

"Yes, sir," Karlson muttered and turned away.

"Give her a bigger bottle for the poison, with a warning label large enough for the audience to read," Farley called after him.

They took Savron, still savoring his disappointment, to see Farley's short-term pickpocket; but the pickpocket was in fact very good. He did dexterity tricks and juggling, and during the act he picked his own pockets. Savron accepted him eagerly.

"I think I'm beginning to understand this," he said. "You need a few sensational attractions to pull the people in, and once they're in it's good solid acts like this one that keep them entertained."

"That's true enough for the private exhibitor," Mallod said. "He charges admission, and he has to have sensational attractions to make people buy tickets. Free exhibitions pull crowds regardless."

Savron did not seem convinced. He grudgingly accepted the short-term con woman while complaining about her ugliness, and Mallod said tartly, "All kinds of people commit crimes, and we have to do the best we can with what's available. If Barris were young and pretty she'd fetch a high price without any act."

Karlson's next offering was a half-witted burglar he'd tried to make funny by having him tiptoe about in a dim setting knocking things over. While Savron was gloomily contemplating this, Mallod took Farley aside.

"We've got to give him one really good attraction," he said.

"How about letting him market-test an arsonist for us?" Farley suggested. "I've worked out a new act for our twelve-year-old."

"Good idea."

Mallod drew Savron away from the burglar's dreary performance. "That's no act at all," he said apologetically, "but we have to give every one of them a chance. I know you'll like the next one. An arsonist."

Savron was doubtful, but his attitude quickly became rapturous. The pink-cheeked youngster artfully spread combustibles through the display and ignited them. And as the display went up in flames, the youngster broke into a frenzied, elated dance, his body trembling, his mouth drooling, his face twitching spasmodically, his eyes wildly flashing excitement.

Savron's enthusiasm so mellowed him that they took him back to Barris and got his grudging approval on her act as a kindly, poisoning surrogate mother.

"But I wish I had another murderer," he said.

"How about an ax murderer?" Mallod suggested.

"Really? You'd let me have one? That's wonderful! Who is it?"

He had never heard of Harl Ranno Lyndyl, and when he saw the cherubic little man seated on the floor of his cage and smiling vacantly, he refused to believe it. Lyndyl did in fact look like the most congenial of toenail curlers, which he had been before he took an ax to a patron.

Unfortunately—from the Penal Authority's point of view—he bungled the job. The patron was on his tenth heart transplant and hadn't long to live anyway, and his heirs managed to dampen the publicity. When the patron finally died there was doubt as to whether Lyndyl really killed him. Not only did that make Lyndyl an unknown, unsuccessful murderer, but he had no talent of any kind for entertaining. Farley worked out several acts for him, but all Lyndyl would do was sit in his cage and smile.

They abandoned Lyndyl. Savron indifferently accepted an attraction where two criminals convicted of thuggery pounded each other with gloves too padded to do harm, and he was delighted with a con man who had worked up a monologue in which he tried to sell the audience the continent of Brazil. In the end Savron had put together six nicely varied attractions plus the two short-term acts—a good beginning even though he had nothing sensational. He arranged to take immediate delivery, and Mallod escorted him out past the checkpoints.

When he returned, he said sternly to Farley, "We've got to do something about Lyndyl, or we'll have him on our hands for life. Anyway, we have so few murderers that we can't afford to waste one."

"It's hard to train a man who won't do anything but sit and smile," Farley pointed out.

"Put him in punishment," Mallod said. "Make him understand he's going to stay there until he has an act worth viewing. If that doesn't work, I'll see if we can get him released temporarily on some pretext."

"But he's certified a dangerous homicidal maniac!" Farley protested.

"Right. By the time we'd get him back, he ought to have a reputation that'd make him worth a quarter of a million, at least."

*   *   *

"The maximum?" the punishment attendant asked hopefully. He was one Penal Authority employee who enjoyed his work. Farley told him to start Lyndyl with five per cent and give him a daily increase.

They chose the electrical regimen. There was one neutral spot in the punishment cage, which changed with each cycle, and until the criminal found it everything he touched shocked him painfully. Lyndyl hopped wildly about the cage, a pathetic, whimpering, slobbering animal. When finally he located the neutral spot, he had to stand on one foot while the charge built up around him. Once he lost his balance and landed screaming on the floor. At the end of the cycle, at the moment prescribed in Lyndyl's medical chart, the neutral spot delivered one massive shock that knocked him unconscious. On a five per cent electrical regimen, this happened once every twenty hours.

Farley visited the punishment cages only when he had to, but the sight of a criminal being privately and scientifically punished affected him far less than the sight of one being publicly humiliated in an entertainment exhibit. Those who committed crimes merited punishment. No one merited humiliation; which was, Farley thought, why he hated his work.

*   *   *

The Anachron's taproom was crowded that evening when Wace Farley arrived. Farley had been a regular customer since his student days, and Melisander, the drawer, gave him a friendly grin as he passed him a brimming mug of berr. Farley noticed an apparently empty table in a dark corner and started toward it, but before he reached it he saw that it was occupied. He was looking about him again when Eman Helpflin glanced up and motioned Farley to join him. For a time the two of them sipped berr together and contemplated the foam.

Helpflin, without knowing it, was intoxicated. He didn't know it because he'd never been intoxicated before. Very few living men ever had been intoxicated. One hundred seventy-two governmental departments would indulge in a frenzy of investigation if Helpflin's condition became public knowledge.

Helpflin said, speaking slowly and distinctly, "I killed a man."

Farley eyed him skeptically. He associated with all sorts of criminals during his working hours, and it took more than a confession of murder to ruffle his equanimity. "So why aren't you in a cage?" Farley demanded.

"Cage?" Helpflin echoed.

"Murderers get put in cages. All criminals get put in cages."

"Never thought about that. Anyway, it wasn't my fault."

"That's irrelevant," said Farley, wise to the ways of the law. "Most criminals didn't mean to do it. You should be in a cage." He chuckled. "Heard a funny one today. Promoter found he couldn't afford new criminal attractions. He'd read somewhere that people used to pay money to see animals in cages, so he decided to add some animal attractions. Turned out it's against the law!"

"Do you mean to say," Helpflin asked slowly, "that it's illegal to exhibit animals, but it isn't illegal to exhibit people?"

"Right. Animals can't be subjected to inhumane treatment. Humans can."

"But only under the proper circumstances," Helpflin pointed out. "That is, only if they're criminals."

"Wrong." Farley leaned forward and lowered his voice. "They can if there's money in it. Government makes huge amounts of money leasing criminals for exhibitions. Government wouldn't make any money if animals were exhibited."

"Is it illegal to kill animals?" Helpflin asked.

"I suppose."

"But it's perfectly legal to kill people. They do it every E Day."

"But only under the proper circumstances," Farley pointed out. "That is, only if the people are unemployed."

"Meaning that there's money in it," Helpflin said quietly. "In this case, money to be saved."

"True. Fellow can't find work, he draws unemployment for two years, still no job, zip." Farley drained his mug, excused himself, went for a refill, and returned licking the foam from the top of the mug.

They spoke of other things, the mugs were refilled again, and the evening wore on pleasantly. "Getting put in cages," Farley said suddenly, "is worse than dying."

"Why do you say that?" Helpflin asked.

"Two years, no job, zip. But go beat an old woman to death or something worse, and they put you in a cage. Doesn't that prove being caged is worse than dying? Otherwise, they'd put the guy that can't find a job in a cage, and they'd exterminate the murderer."

"That way there wouldn't be any money in it."

The taproom temporarily had changed drawers. Melisander had become suspicious about the two quietly talking figures in the corner, both of whom had been drinking far too long. His substitute was unaware of this; he cheerfully refilled their mugs. There now were two intoxicated men in the room, and if the hundred seventy-two governmental departments found it out there would be a hundred seventy-two cases of departmental apoplexy.

"I still think it's inhumane putting people in cages," Farley said half a mug later.

"Let 'em out," Helpflin suggested.

Farley stared at him.

"Then they'd be unemployed, and the government would exterminate them!" Helpflin guffawed.

"Never thought of that," Farley admitted. "Can't let 'em all out. Too many checkpoints. Might let Lyndyl out, though. They're torturing him with electric shocks."

"They shouldn't ought to do that," Helpflin observed. "It sounds inhumane."

"Naw—it's just punishment. He's a murderer, he should be punished, but they're not punishing him for that. They're punishing him because he won't learn an act and perform in public in a cage, and *that's* inhumane."

"Why don't you let him out, then?"

"I will. It'll take planning, though. Will you help?"

"Of course. I'm good at helping people. They die anyway, but I'm good at helping. I have a commendation."

The two of them moved their heads closer together and continued to talk.

*   *   *

They loomed up out of a chill night and rang the Penal Authority's gong. Farley was wearing an outlandish, enveloping cloak; Helpflin was similarly attired and also wore a disguise Farley had selected from his collection of props for criminal attractions: false nose and teeth. In addition, Helpflin had stopped off at the Poverty Control Agency and manufactured a complete identity kit.

The door guard gazed at them curiously. "This is Dr. Berr," Farley said. "I have to get medical approval for Lyndyl's new act."

The guard sourly signed him in and waved them along. All the security checks were casual. No one ever had escaped from the Penal

Authority, or even tried to. How could the prisoners escape, when all of them were in cages?

Farley hurried Helpflin past the three interior checkpoints, each superintended by a watchman who nodded sleepily from his enclosure. The punishment night attendant was asleep. Farley did not hesitate—he released Lyndyl, attired him in his own concealing cloak, giving it a fold that hid the face, and watched Helpflin lead him away. Surreptitiously he saw them past the first checkpoint, and then he went to an upstairs window and watched until they safely emerged from the building.

With a feeling of immense satisfaction he staggered drunkenly back down to the punishment ward, entered Lyndyl's cage, and closed the door.

* * *

"I appreciate the loyalty," Mallod said, "but you shouldn't have done it."

Farley had never seen his boss so flustered, but because of a gigantic headache he was having difficulty in concentrating. He could only stare at him.

"I didn't mean that seriously about getting Lyndyl released," Mallod explained. "But it worked. He'll be worth half a million to us now."

Comprehension came slowly to Farley. "You mean—Lyndyl has committed another crime?"

"Another murder," Mallod said, with deep satisfaction. "Now he's a double murderer, and also the only criminal escapee in two generations, and he won't have to have an act. He can sit there smiling and make the audience shudder."

"Who did he murder?" Farley asked, aghast.

"Who'd you expect? That Dr. Berr you brought to see him. We found his cloak and identification, but Lyndyl won't tell us what he did with the body. If he shoved it into a commercial disposer, and he had the opportunity, we'll never find a trace of it. Which is neither here nor there. You shouldn't have done it. The Authority doctor is of the opinion that you were of unsound mind due to a food poisoning he can't identify, and that's your best line of defense. Stick to it, and don't mention what I said about getting Lyndyl out, and I'll do everything I can for you."

* * *

"Life imprisonment," the arbiter said, "with mandatory punishment at a minimum fifty per cent level. I'm prohibiting your lease to any public or private exhibition—though why one would want the author of such a sordid crime I couldn't comprehend."

Farley said bewilderedly, "But I didn't do any murder!"

"You helped to free a homicidal maniac, so you were responsible for what he did—which is beside the point. I wouldn't give you mandatory punishment for that. Murder is a crime against one person. In conspiring to release a legally confined criminal, you committed a horrendous offense against your government—in other words, against half a billion people. Get him out of here before I make it punishment at the hundred per cent level!"

*　　*　　*

A wretched soul, bruised with adversity . . .

Twelve times each day—once every two hours—Farley felt the preliminary tingle that signaled the beginning of the next punishment cycle. Wearily he began to search for the neutral spot. His few attempts to defy punishment failed; he was physically incapable of standing the shocks, and eventually he would be forced to search desperately for the neutral spot with the same pathetic, groveling whimpers that had so revolted him when he witnessed the punishment of others. He looked forward to the final shock that brought unconsciousness; it was the only rest he had.

> *There's some ill planet reigns:*
> *I must be patient till the heavens look*
> *With an aspect more favorable.*

He nevertheless had cause for thanks. He had committed a crime; he deserved punishment. At least he had escaped the humiliation of public exhibition.

*　　*　　*

He suffered eight days of continuous fifty per cent punishment; then, regaining consciousness after a punishment cycle, he found himself caged in the Penal Authority 'copter used to transfer criminals. It landed, and he was brusquely removed and thrust into another cage.

A beaming Dr. Savron looked in on him. "Welcome to Rolling Acres!"

Farley regarded him incredulously.

"Mallod and I arranged this," Savron said. "Officially, someone made a mistake and brought you instead of the criminal we contracted for. It'll take time to straighten out the mixup, and you'll have a few days of rest from punishment."

"Thank you," Farley said. "That's very kind of you."

"Not at all. I'd like to have you here permanently, to help with the attractions. But since you're an enemy of the government, under a sentence of mandatory punishment with exhibition prohibited, naturally that's out of the question."

"Naturally," Farley agreed, with a faint smile.

"Unless," Savron went on, "you're able to perform an act yourself."

"I'm a student of history, not a performer."

"Exactly. But if you were to come up with something extremely popular, and it would have to be sensational, then we could put pressure on the arbiter to let us keep you. Mallod thinks you can do it. You created so many great acts for others—surely you can do one for yourself. That's the real reason we arranged this. Mallod says to tell you he's doing the best he can for you, but it may be a long time before you'll have another opportunity like this one."

"Thanks," Farley said, "but I prefer punishment to public humiliation."

"Exactly. But we have some distinguished visitors in addition to the usual afternoon audience. The entire Board of Commissioners is here, and if they see something they like they'll certainly persuade the arbiter to let us keep it. It's the chance of a lifetime for you, and you may never have another one like it. But the act will have to be exceptional. Good luck—you're on in half an hour!"

His face vanished. Farley stared after him contemptuously. "I haven't got an act!" he shouted. "I don't want an act! I won't do an act!"

There was no response; Savron had left, and the panel was closed. Farley dropped into a chair and looked about him. The exhibit's stage was set to resemble an ordinary room: chairs, a table, a rack of book tapes (but no player), cheap ornaments, and knickknacks. Idly he wondered what preposterous stupidity of an act had been planned for such a setting, but it was no concern of his. The one dignity left to him was the right to refuse the indignity of performing publicly in a cage. When Savron returned he would tell him so, emphatically.

But he was not ungrateful for the respite from punishment. He was exhausted, and certainly it would be a long time before he again enjoyed the luxury of uninterrupted sleep. He stretched out in the chair and dozed off immediately.

What hath this day deserved? What hath it done
That it in golden letters should be set
Among the high tides in the calendar?

*   *   *

The warning buzzer awakened Farley. For a moment he could not
think what it was, or where he was. Then he shouted, "I haven't got
an act! I won't do an act!"

The stage lights came on, the panels went transparent, and he
found himself glaring furiously at his audience.

He had never seen an audience before. In the past, he always had
been *in* the audience, listening to its reaction but concentrating intensely on what the performer did. Now, for the first time, he saw
the faces.

The leering, the coarse, the mocking faces. From the front, small
boys were shouting taunts at him. Girls were tittering, women
giggling, men grinning. Only the commissioners, unmistakable in
their flamboyant uniforms, looked on solemnly.

Farley leaped to his feet. At one side, staring at him, was his al-
leged friend from the Anachron, the supposedly murdered phony
Dr. Berr, whose real name Farley had not learned. "You told me to
do it!" Farley screamed. He pointed a quivering finger. "You! It's
your fault!"

The crowd dissolved in hilarity. An explosion of laughter smote
Farley; a hideously cackling mouth gaped at him from every dis-
torted face. Only Dr. Berr was not laughing. He was staring in consternation.

"You!" Farley shouted.

Dr. Berr turned and fled.

Fury overwhelmed Farley. He picked up his chair and sent it
crashing against the panels. "You!" he screamed again.

Another chair. Crash.

A table. Crash.

"You!" Farley screamed. "You told me to do it!"

Cushions. The book tapes. The ornaments and knickknacks. Anything he could lift, and his strength was prodigious. He dashed into
the adjacent sleeping quarters, returned with a chest, and flung that.
From the convenience lounge he brought tumblers of water at a
panting run and splashed them at the audience.

Then he hurled himself against the panels and futilely beat on
them with his fists.

His anger began to fade, and he stared dully at the packed faces before him.

They were convulsed with laughter. The children were rolling on the ground, the adults were helplessly clutching their sides, even the dignified commissioners were howling.

Again his wrath overwhelmed him. He screamed insults, he hurled every loose object in his cage, and when the stage lights faded and the panels again became translucent, he lay on the floor at the front of the cage, kicking with impotent rage and futilely hammering the panels with bloody hands.

Slowly he got to his feet. For a long, stunned moment he contemplated the debris that lay scattered in the wake of his anger, and then, defeated, humiliated beyond any hope of atonement, he sank to the floor and wept for the cool dimness of his punishment cage, for the honest torment of the electrical regimen's unsullied pulsations.

"Farley!"

He looked up uncomprehendingly. Dr. Savron was beaming at him. "Great act! Absolutely great! Sensational! You did it! You're the best attraction we have! I'll get statements from all of the commissioners and see to your permanent transfer in the morning. I'll also tell the stage man to get you some cheap props so you can put on a show without breaking up good furniture. We won't exhibit you again until it's ready."

His face disappeared. The stage man entered a moment later, wiping his eyes. "Never laughed so hard in my life," he said. "Great act. I'll find some cheap props for you."

He removed the debris from the cage and returned with an inflated chair. "Just to give you something to sit on while we rummage the prop room," he said. "You can throw this one as much as you like."

He left, and Farley dropped into the chair and closed his eyes.

He was caged. It was illegal to cage animals for display, but it was not illegal to cage Wace Renoldon Farley, 673 492 479 341 895, and train him under the threat of dire punishment if he learned slowly, and make him perform ten times daily for a leering audience of inhumane humans.

Never before had he thought of an audience in terms of *faces*, but now he had seen them: the hideously flushed, twisted, coarse, cackling, screaming, howling puffs of animate flesh. He had not imagined that anything could be so repulsive, and he was caged and helpless and fated to look out on them ten times daily.

But he had not lost, not yet. They could not force him to perform. Punishment was his lawful destiny, and it held no terror for him.

He opened his eyes and looked about him. The Rolling Acres accommodations were the most lavish he had seen. He got to his feet and made a hasty inspection. Behind the stage was a comfortably sized bedroom and the private convenience lounge with bath. The stage was oversized and could serve as living quarters and study when he wasn't performing. The apartment he'd been able to afford on his Penal Authority salary seemed cramped by comparison. Probably they would let him have his library if he claimed to be studying Shakespeare in search of ideas for a new act.

They could not force him. There was no possible way they could compel him to perform.

He sat down again. If his demented violence had brought howls of laughter, what would a real act do—an act with pacing, and continuity, and motivation, and climaxes, and a finish with a genuine punch to it?

They could not force him.

But if they'd let him have a water tap in full view of the audience, he could fill a container with water and throw that. He'd need two containers. He'd fill one and splash the panels, and they'd be convulsed. Then he'd fill it again.

Somehow he'd have to arrange for the panels to slide aside at precisely the right moment. Then he could pick up a container and dash toward the audience, the panels would open, and the audience would think this notorious criminal was loose and about to drench it with water. But he would be carrying the second container, and as the spectators tried to scatter in panic, he'd dump a cloud of paper confetti over them.

It would slay them.

He leaned back in profound satisfaction. Wace Renoldon Farley, notorious enemy of the government and the people, Wace Farley would kill his audiences dead.

With a gentle smile on his face he fell asleep.

His glassy essence, like an angry ape . . .
Condemned into everlasting redemption . . .

WHAT HATH GOD WROUGHT!

The monthly National Lottery drawing was being held in the 100,000 car parking lot of Yosemite Valley. Searchlights dissected the night sky, and on the dim rostrum a young lady in spangled, iridescent tights stood postured beside a fountain of tossing, luminous globes, her long-handled net poised to strike. In the foreground, heavily pulsing music contested with the incessant, grinding purr of the fountain; in the background hung the rumbling murmur of the waiting thousands. In every direction, as far as the ubiquitous infrared TV cameras penetrated, the valley was a tossing blur of tense faces.

The net swooped. With practiced deftness the young lady flipped the captured globe into a launcher's yawning mouth. The TV scene switched to a night view of the valley from Glacier Point, and cameras followed the fiery arch of the globe's path until it exploded spectacularly into a gleaming number six that hung suspended over the valley and slowly began to blur into a luminous cloud.

On the rostrum below, on marquees at L Headquarters across the nation where millions thronged the streets and stared upward, on the L Specials from the nation's TV stations, the A Boards flashed the number six; and on the drawing rostrum, the spangled young lady was poised to fish for another globe.

Benjamin Franklin went to the bar to fix himself a drink. Although diligent and expensive research had uncovered no family connection with the famed historical figure, Franklin liked to hint that there was. If pressed, he would concede that he had followed a famous ancestor's bent for electrical research. Franklin was chairman of the board of one of the nation's largest energy conglomerates.

With his present associates, Franklin liked to pretend that the relationship was ironic. The historical Benjamin Franklin had once sponsored a lottery to finance the purchase of cannon for the defense of Philadelphia. The later-day Franklin was masterminding a conspiracy to destroy the National Lottery, and he'd put up half of a million-dollar fund dedicated to that purpose.

On the wall-sized TV screen, the spangled young lady had captured and launched another globe, and the gleaming number three was slowly dissipating. Franklin said, raising his glass, "The state of Georgia once ran a lottery to raise five thousand dollars for a school. That was back when a dollar was worth fifty. The cost of the lottery exceeded three hundred thousand dollars, and that didn't include the prizes. Even so, when compared with our National Lottery's management—"

Edmund Cahill, president of the nation's largest brokerage firm, drained his own glass, set it down, and remarked pompously, "Well, we've got to do something. We've got to re-educate the public. When a man buys a bad stock, at least he has something to show for it. Very few bad stocks are completely worthless, and a bad stock can improve. But what is a nonwinning lottery ticket worth after the drawing?"

Charles Jaffner, an insurance executive and notorious statistic dropper, announced, "According to the latest economic projection, the National Lottery will drain off thirty per cent of the national income this year, and the proceeds returned to the government will have dropped to one per cent of the original projection. Thirty per cent of our national income—buying nothing! The Lottery Governors answer complaints of mismanagement by adding a few more piddling prizes, and the people give them resounding votes of confidence. We've got to do something, but I'm not sure that fixing the Lottery—"

Franklin grinned good-naturedly. "Don't try to run out on me now. We agreed at the last meeting that this was the only way. We've got to make the public see how ridiculous the Lottery is. Unfortunately, most of the Lottery categories are invulnerable. People overlook silly results like teen-aged girls taking lunar safaris and little old ladies going bankrupt trying to manage the businesses they win. The fact is that on most of the category boards a winning ticket is the dream of a lifetime come true, and the dream of a lifetime can't be ridiculed. There's no point in exposing the hideous waste if people approve of the result."

"I'm still not convinced that the PR Board is any more vulnerable than the others," Jaffner said. "*Be anything you like*—what's wrong with that? Most people would like to be something other than what they are."

"That's why it's so popular," Franklin said. "Do you know anything at all about what the winners are asking? And getting?"

"That's confidential," Cahill said.

"Of course. It's got to be. The winner doesn't want the world to know that his success is due to a clever public-relations firm backed by unlimited funds from the National Lottery. The current mayor of Kansas City is a PR Board winner. Just another little clerk that always wanted to be a bigshot. Prockly and Brannot—that's the Lottery's PR firm—built him up, gave him tutors in political science and public speaking, wrote his speeches, and organized his campaign. Funny thing is, he's made a pretty good mayor."

"So how can we ridicule that?" Jaffner demanded.

"What would happen if a PR winner decided he wanted to be President? Do the American people want their high officials selected by a lottery by way of a public-relations firm?"

"Isn't that what happens now?" Cahill asked dryly.

"Consider the other winners. There's a well-known author who's never written a word. PR winner, didn't want to write, just wanted to be a famous author. Prockly and Brannot paid a real author—paid him very well—to ghost three novels for the PR winner. Same thing has happened with two would-be artists who won the PR Board. Prockly and Brannot got them the best in private instruction. That didn't work—neither would-be artist had much talent. So Prockly and Brannot commissioned paintings to be made in their names. As a result, two well-known modern artists never did a stroke of work on the paintings they're admired for. There was a pig of an amateur soprano who wanted to be a prima donna at Bayreuth. No amount of training would have helped her—she had no talent at all—so Prockly and Brannot hired the auditorium, the orchestra, and the rest of the cast, and even paid audiences to listen and act properly enthused. For an entire Wagner *Ring* cycle. The audiences earned their money."

"How'd you find out?" Jaffner asked.

Franklin grinned. "It's confidential, but Prockly and Brannot aren't above confidentially letting a prospective client know how effective they are in making PR winners anything they'd like to be. I'm compiling a file."

"Well, we've certainly got to do something," Cahill said. "People not only squander their savings on lottery tickets, but now they're going into debt to buy them. Did you see that loan company's ad? The company will loan you money to buy your lottery tickets. It'll also scientifically select a spread of tickets for you to invest your borrowed money in. If a rigged PR Board will bring people to their senses, then—by the way, who holds the winning ticket?"

"Man named Alton Smith. Character I've known for years. He was janitor in the old building in St. Louis where I had my first office. He's retired, now. Has a lifelong hatred for gambling, and lotteries are gambling. Wrecking the National Lottery would be the glorious climax of his life. He'll co-operate fully."

The others were regarding Franklin apprehensively. Any leak, any hint of a suspicion that three business and financial leaders were conspiring to wreck the Lottery could ruin them. A mob actually had lynched the chairman of an antilottery group in Rhode Island. Jaffner asked, "Does he know about us?"

"No," Franklin said. "Neither does his contact. We're covered perfectly. Smith will wait a couple of weeks before he claims his prize—just for effect. Then he'll pretend he thought he was buying a ticket on the VR Board and doesn't want the PR prize. It'll scare the Lottery people witless. When he finally breaks down and asks for something, they'll jump at it—and that'll be the beginning of the end for the National Lottery."

The A Board now bore the numbers 63 74 28, and the spangled young lady was fishing for another globe. Edmund Cahill said slowly, "You have things rigged to make this Alton Smith the PR Board winner, which gives him the prize of being anything he wants to be, and that'll wreck the National Lottery?"

Franklin nodded confidently. The young lady dipped a globe, fed it into the launcher, and the number one floated over Yosemite Valley.

"So what'll he want to be?" Cahill asked.

Franklin smiled. "God."

Walner Frayne was one of four Prockly and Brannot employees who held the post of Senior Lottery Consultant. They alternated in planning and supervising campaigns to make the monthly PR Board winners what they wanted to be—whatever they wanted to be.

Frayne was a valued Prockly and Brannot employee, highly respected and well paid for his skill with Lottery winners. He thought the job idiotic, and he hated it, and several times a year—when confronted with new PR Board winners demanding the impossible—he found himself on the verge of resigning. Then he considered his salary, fringe benefits, expense accounts, seniority, and retirement status, and he desisted.

With this particular drawing, the idiocy had taken on a new guise. A week had passed, and every board except the PR Board had win-

ning names posted under the winning numbers, from the 63 74 28 19
25 of the A Board (own your own apartment building, enjoy a super
income for life) to the 21 91 56 38 40 of the Z Board (the zillion-
dollar board, the grand sweepstakes, with numbers from all of the
boards eligible except those already drawn). This was normal; since
names of PR Board winners were protected by an elaborate security
system, they could not be posted. As a result, only the Lottery
officials and Prockly and Brannot employees knew that the PR
Board prize hadn't been claimed.

Frayne and his two assistants, Ron Harnon and Naida Ainsley,
had kept packed bags with them since the night of the drawing. The
moment the PR Board winner checked in, they had to go to him, obtain his signature on a contract that guaranteed Prockly and Brannot's services in making him whatever he wanted to be (subject to
the conditions stated in the Lottery rules), and put their campaign
in motion.

Wherever he was. Lottery winners had checked in from as far
away as Bombay and Brisbane.

But a week's delay was unheard of.

F. Pierpont Prockly, exuding essence of lavender and lime ciga-
rette smoke, waddled into the office where Frayne and his assistants
sat regarding each other glumly. "Nothing yet?"

Frayne shook his head. "We've been listing the possibilities." He
picked up a memo pad. "He's lost his ticket. He's in some hospital
in a coma. He bought two tickets, and they're stuck together with
the winner underneath. He's on a meditation retreat in the Amazon
jungles—he claimed his prize immediately, but the carrier pigeon was
blown off course by a hurricane."

Prockly glared at them. Unheard-of situations had to be blamed
on someone, and he had the air of a man looking for a candidate.
"When the Lottery Governors hear about this—" Gloomily he
turned on his heel and left them.

"There are times," Frayne announced, "when I wish I was working the T Board."

Ron Harnon, who had a youthful unconcern for seniority because
he possessed so little of it, said with a grin, "You think it's easy
dealing with elderly women who want to climb Mount Everest?"

"Nothing to it," Frayne told him. "I have a friend who works the
T Board, he's with Transworld Travel, and he tells me all you have
to do is pick a steep hill near the woman's home and tell her she'll
have to climb it twice a day for practice. After the third day it's a
cinch to switch her to a trip around the world with a stop at the
Everest Hilton on the way to Tahiti."

"Have any of the boards ever had an unclaimed prize?" Naida Ainsley asked.

Neither of them knew, and it was the wrong moment to be making inquiries on that particular subject.

Another two weeks passed, and they were helpless to do anything but wait. Had the missing winner been on any other board, the Lottery Governors would have launched a worldwide publicity campaign to locate him. With the PR Board this was impossible.

Finally, on the twenty-fifth day, one Alton Smith timidly presented himself at St. Louis L Headquarters. Frayne left at once for St. Louis, with his two assistants.

The little house was shabby but scrupulously clean, and so was its owner. Alton Smith was a small, elderly man with thinning white hair, a wistful face, and an oversized Adam's apple. His bulging contacts occasionally gave his eyes a glint of humor, but more often he seemed to be gazing into the infinite. His voice had the pathetic squeakiness of the aged. He was so obviously a gentle, kindly soul, and he radiated such innocent friendliness, that Frayne liked him at sight—until he remembered why he was there.

Then he regarded him with horror. This was the winner of the PR Board lottery prize. He had won the right to be whatever he wanted to be, and no one would ever make of Alton Smith anything other than what he was.

Smith said wistfully, "I don't suppose there's any money."

It was not a question. Obviously he knew there wasn't any money. Frayne said firmly, "No. No money. Haven't you read the rules?"

"I don't need it myself," Smith said apologetically, "but it would be nice to be able to help my daughters."

"What would you like to be?" Frayne asked him.

"Nothing, I guess."

Frayne stared at him. "You've won the PR lottery and you don't want to be anything? Then why'd you buy the ticket?"

"I thought the agent said VR," Smith said. His manner was that of a first-time offender confessing a crime. "I thought it would be nice to own a little vacation resort. When my number wasn't drawn, I threw the ticket away. One of my grandchildren found it, and yesterday she was playing lottery with it, checking it against the winning numbers, and when she saw it was the same as one of them she asked her mother what she'd won. So I filed just in case there might be a little money. I wouldn't have bought it if I'd known it was PR."

"Come, now," Frayne said, radiating a confidence he did not feel.

"A winning PR ticket is a lot better than money or owning a vacation resort. You can be anything you like."

"I'm too old."

"Nonsense. What's your occupation?"

"I used to be a floor manager."

Harnon caught Frayne's blank reaction and leaned over to whisper, "He was a building custodian. He was in charge of keeping floors clean."

"How about a promotion?" Frayne suggested. "Wouldn't you like to be head floor manager?"

Smith shook his head. "It was a small building, and I was the only one. Anyway, I'm retired."

"Or a change in rating?" Frayne persisted. "We could send you to school or get tutors for you."

"You could get an engineer's rating," Harnon put in. "Operate heating and air-conditioning units. Lots of small buildings hire part-time engineers. The money you earned would supplement your pension."

Smith shook his head. "I don't learn too good. Anyway, I'd rather just be retired."

"That doesn't keep you from being what you'd like," Frayne said desperately. "Politics? Represent your precinct on the neighborhood council?"

"I wouldn't like that. I mostly just like to take it easy and do a little gardening. I guess there's nothing. I told my daughter there wouldn't be."

Frayne felt himself teetering on the brink of an unthinkable disaster: A PR Board winner refusing his prize! "There's got to be something!" he exclaimed.

Smith shook his head. "No. I really don't want to be anything. I could have used a little money, though."

Frayne sent appealing side glances at his assistants and received only blank looks in return. When the silence became embarrassing, he said lamely, "We'll look into your problem and see what we can work out for you."

They got to their feet, and Smith followed them to the door. His manner remained apologetic; he seemed to sense their distress and in his kindly way feel sorry for them. He said, "Maybe—"

They turned eagerly, but he thought for a moment, shook his head, gestured absently. When the three of them reached the tiny front porch, they turned again. Smith said, "Well—" and they waited expectantly until again he shook his head.

"I'm sure there'll be something," Frayne said. "We'll get up a list of suggestions and call on you tomorrow."

Smith's eyes were focused on infinity. He said softly, "I used to think it'd be nice to have my own religion, but I don't suppose—"

Frayne paused. He was not too panicky to examine a straw with care before grasping it. "Your own religion. Do you mean you'd like to be a priest? Or a minister?"

Smith shook his head. "A priest has to learn ways to do things, and theology, and things like that. He even has to learn what to say. I'm too old to do very much of that, and anyway, I wouldn't want people telling me what to say and do."

"Your . . . own . . . religion," Frayne mused. He studied Smith perplexedly. "A church of your own? There are ministers or priests who establish independent churches. Some of them even devise their own doctrine and ritual. Just what do you mean by your own religion?"

"So I could decide things myself," Smith said.

"What sort of religion?"

"Any kind I want."

"Some variant of Christianity?"

"Any kind I want. Like the Pope, only with everything mine. Like —well—God."

Frayne winced. He said slowly, "Then you want to be the head of a new religion with a doctrine and ritual of your own devising."

"I guess so."

"We couldn't contract to make you God," Frayne said, smiling faintly, "but I don't see why we couldn't establish a religion for you." Suddenly he grinned. "It might even be fun. Anyway, you won the Lottery, and our commitment is to make you whatever you want to be. I'll draw up a contract."

It wasn't until Frayne faced F. Pierpont Prockly that he experienced misgivings, but Prockly received the news noncommittally. "If that's what he wants, that's what we'll give him."

"He's going to wind up his affairs, rent his house, and tell his neighbors he's going to live with a married daughter in Vancouver," Frayne said. "He'll come East as soon as he can get away. I figured we might as well locate his church where I can draw on the staff whenever I need it. We've started surveying religions and religious leaders, but what we've found isn't very helpful. Founders of religions always have their careers prophesied before their births, they're born of virgin mothers, they're mature philosophers at the age of six, they perform miracles, and so on."

Prockly waved a hand. "That's only a mess of mythology concocted by their followers after their deaths. Or maybe it's theological speculation, but theologians are notorious liars. How much of that mishmash was known or believed during their lifetimes?"

"Maybe some of the miracles."

"We'll have miracles," Prockly said confidently. "Problem is to get people to believe. Once they start believing, they'll believe anything. Look at the testimonials a worthless nostrum can inspire. Mountain spring water or chicken soup can have curative properties if people want to believe it. Make Smith's religion impressive, make the doctrine make sense, train him to perform the rites effectively, and he'll develop a following that will experience all kinds of miracles." Prockly tilted back and folded his hands over his ample paunch. "You're wasting your time analyzing myths. What you've got to do is run a computer analysis on the established religions. Find out what each one has that's universally appealing. If you combine those elements, you'll have a universal religion that'll appeal to everyone."

Naida Ainsley and Ron Harnon gazed at Frayne blankly. "How was that again?" Harnon asked.

"Boss's instructions," Frayne told them. "We take each of the established religions and peel away its encrusted traditions. When we get down to the skeleton we'll find something in its doctrine or ritual that's universally appealing. That's what we use to build our religion."

Harnon said doubtfully, "You mean—we're to analyze priests' costumes and borrow a robe pattern from the Buddhists, and a hat or something from—what's his name—the Chinaman—"

Naida Ainsley said frostily, "Confucianism isn't a religion."

"That doesn't matter," Harnon said. "It passes for one. If it's got anything with universal appeal, let's use it."

"I don't agree," Frayne said. "My own hunch is that the success of any religion must be due more to its uniqueness than its universality. The measure of its success is the number of people the uniqueness appeals to. Otherwise, one religion would have crowded out all the others long ago."

"But wouldn't it be possible to base a religion on sound psychological principles?" Harnon asked.

"Sound psychological principles and theological universals," Frayne suggested. Harnon nodded eagerly. "Then suppose you tell me what they are."

"I guess maybe we'd better get started with that computer analysis," Harnon said.

"You do that," Frayne told him. "We'll also need Smith's ideas on religious doctrine. Whatever we decide will have to please him. Naida—can you go to St. Louis today and talk with him?"

Benjamin Franklin had called a special meeting. He led Cahill and Jaffner into his sumptuous private office and got them seated. "I want you to hear something," he said.

"What's gone wrong?" Cahill demanded gloomily.

"Everything is going perfectly. That's why I want you to hear it. Smith is recording his Prockly and Brannot contacts for us. They sent one of their employees, name of Naida Ainsley, to interview him and find out his ideas about theology and doctrine and ritual and so on so they can give him the kind of religion he wants. Here's the interview."

Franklin placed a pockette on the cube beside him and touched a button.

Naida Ainsley's voice: "I understand that, Mr. Smith. But most of the great religious leaders came to us as prophets—for gods, or a god, or for some religious principle or other. It was only much later that their followers made them gods. Will your religion have a god?"

Alton Smith's voice: "I don't understand."

Naida Ainsley: "God. G-O-D. God. The creator of all things. The ruler of the universe. The supreme being. Most religions have at least one. Doesn't your religion have one?"

Smith: "I—I guess so."

Naida Ainsley (demonstrating magnificent patience): "What is the nature of your god?"

Smith (his squeaky voice throbbing with perplexity): "Nature?"

Naida Ainsley: "What sort of a being is he? What does he look like? He doesn't have to have an appearance at all—he might be totally invisible—but you must have some definite ideas about him. He might have the form of an animal, though I'm afraid that'd be rather difficult to put across these days. He might have an abstract form, or he might be represented by an abstract symbol. Some religions have worshiped the sun. Some consider their god to be an exalted creature in human form. In other words, when their god wants to, he can look like a man. Many people in the Judaic and the Christian religions think of their god as an old man with a beard."

Smith (light exploding through his perplexity): "Ah! An old man with a beard."

Naida Ainsley: "Then you're going to follow the Judaic and the Christian traditions?"

Smith (immensely pleased and enthused): "An old man with a beard." There was a long pause. "A fat old man with a beard, and he wears a red suit. And at Christmas he brings everyone presents."

Franklin touched off the pockette. His two coconspirators were convulsed with laughter.

Naida Ainsley touched off her own pockette, and Walner Frayne sat with his face buried in his hands. "God!" he muttered. Then he looked at the others apologetically. "It could be worse, I suppose. It could have been the Easter bunny. Does this monstrosity of Smith's have a name?"

"I didn't think to ask him about that," Naida said.

"What's wrong with 'god'?" Harnon demanded.

"Every Tom, Dick, and Harry of a religion has a god," Frayne said. He reached for a synonym dictionary. "The Deity, the All Wise, the All Mighty, the All Holy, the All Merciful—"

"Why not just call him the All?" Harnon suggested.

"We could make up a name if we had to," Naida said. "Just plain 'god' has a lot of things going for it, though. For one thing, everyone knows what it means."

"Everyone knows what 'cracker' means," Frayne said, "but manufacturers go right on calling them krispy krax or crackly crisps or some such stupidity. You've got to have a striking and distinctive name to sell the product." He closed the synonym dictionary and pushed it aside. "I suppose I'll have to put someone to work on a name for god."

In the art studio, a staff artist named Al Koten was designing ecclesiastical costumes. As he worked, he glumly contemplated a photo of Alton Smith, and as he demonstrated to Frayne, no matter what he surrounded that head with, conventional vestments, or wild folds of costume, or unabashed frills, the head continued to look ridiculous.

"The only thing that'll work is swimming trunks," he announced. "Maybe it's not an appropriate religious costume, but the way to keep this guy from looking silly is to put him in a tank of water with face mask and snorkel. That Adam's apple—"

"Never mind," Frayne said. "Put it aside until the makeup people have their crack at him. The right wig, for example—"

Koten shook his head despondently. "A wig isn't enough. He needs a mask."

Frayne returned to his office and forced himself to run, for the fourteenth time, a pathetic five-minute sound motion picture of

Alton Smith. Smith was reading from the Bible, stammering his way
through the simplest passages, mispronouncing words, losing his
place, and making fumbling repetitions. Watching it, Frayne asked
himself why he hadn't tried to talk the little man into being something easy, like a professional football player.

The launching of a new religion was proving far more complicated
than Frayne had expected. Smith would arrive at the end of the
week, and nothing had been settled. Nothing at all.

Ron Harnon reluctantly accepted the designation as Smith's
official nurse. He got the little man settled in a modest hotel and
delivered him at the Prockly and Brannot offices each morning. The
makeup department was given first crack at him, and two days later
he emerged in a splendid aura of dignity, his wig moderately long
and touched distinguishedly with gray, his stylishly trimmed beard
concealing his weak chin. Special shoes compensated somewhat for
his diminutive stature. A new set of teeth did wonders for his mouth,
but nothing at all seemed to help his squeaky voice.

Frayne took new courage, and Koten began to sketch costumes
with some effect. "The mysticism of the East," he announced,
"blended with the medievalism of the West." He produced a
striking robe, with a high collar that concealed Smith's bulging
Adam's apple.

While Harnon shepherded Smith from department to department, and—when he wasn't needed—took him sightseeing to keep
him out of their way, Frayne and Naida Ainsley grimly made a con-
certed attack on the doctrine problem. Frayne had posted a Buddhist
motto on his wall: "From good must come good; from evil must
come evil. This is the law of life." The two of them studied it until
they were bleary-eyed.

"He's a wonderful old man," Naida said suddenly.

"Smith?" Frayne asked, mildly surprised.

"He is. Actually, he's never had the slightest interest in religion.
He hasn't attended any kind of a church in years. He's a highly
moral old guy—you should hear him go on about gambling!—but he
certainly isn't religious. Would you like to know why he said he
wanted his own religion?"

Frayne was regarding her dumfoundedly.

"From our reactions, he sensed that we were in trouble because he
didn't want to be anything. So he said something he thought would
please us. That's the sort of old fellow he is. Whatever we decide
will be all right with him—he wouldn't know what to do with a religion if he had one."

"Well—he's going to have one," Frayne said grimly. "And it doesn't matter that he'll accept anything we suggest. This project also has to be accepted by the boss and the Lottery Governors, and they won't."

"But Smith will agree with anything we say and do his best at anything we ask," Naida persisted. "In the meantime, he's having a nice vacation, so he's getting something out of winning the Lottery. So let's just plan on pleasing the boss and the Governors."

"All right," Frayne said. "Let's just plan on that."

The two of them stared at the motto.

For a week they struggled to evolve the perfect religious doctrine, accompanied by a profundity of ritual, all of it aimed at pleasing Prockly and the Lottery Governors, and everything they devised seemed fatuous. Finally Naida said, crumbling a stack of paper, "It's no good. Let's forget the boss and the Governors and try to please Smith."

Frayne said irritably, "I thought you said anything at all would please him."

"It would. And if he's pleased, and insists it's what he wants, the boss and the Governors will have to go along, won't they?"

"I suppose they will, if it isn't too outrageous."

"Remember that interview I taped in St. Louis?" she asked. "The one where he described god as Santa Claus?"

"I've been trying to forget it."

"I've been reviewing all of our tapes, and that one started me thinking. Do you know how many giveaway shows the networks are offering these days? I counted them last night. Twenty-seven. Twenty-seven shows each week where people play stupid games or supply stupid answers to stupid questions or let a stupid MC play stupid practical jokes on them. In return, they receive fabulous rewards. The shows have huge audiences. Surely it isn't the games, or the questions, or the jokes that attract people. It's the pleasure of watching someone get those fabulous prizes."

"What's that got to do with religion?" Frayne asked.

"The point is this: Those contestants don't deserve prizes. They deserve appropriately placed kicks for allowing the networks to make fools of them. What if we were to put on a show and reward people who actually deserve it—in the name of religion?"

Frayne was gazing at the sign on his wall: *From good must come good; from evil must come evil.* "Maybe you have something there," he mused. "Santa Claus rewards good children with gifts and punishes bad children with no gifts. The Christian God rewards good people with heaven and punishes bad people with hell. A religion based on the Santa Claus mystique should be perfectly sound. It might even be popular, since Santa Claus gives gifts here and now instead of making his deserving followers die in order to be rewarded."

"It'd be a hell of a popular religion as long as the gifts lasted. How long are we prepared to make them last?"

"I'd have to ask the boss."

"There is one problem," Naida said thoughtfully. "We can use the Santa Claus mystique, but we can't use Santa Claus, no matter what Smith wants. No one will accept a god with a belly that shivers and shakes like a bowl full of jelly. The image doesn't command the respect a god has to have."

"We'll disguise him. He'll be the all merciful and the all bountiful. The ultimate giver of all things because he is the creator of all things. And instead of rewards in an uncertain hereafter, very conveniently impossible of verification, *this* god returns good for good *now*."

"As long as the gifts last, it'll sweep the country," Naida said.

Frayne nodded. "But we'll have to forget the evil for evil part. We'd be sued."

"It'd spoil the show anyway. The TV way of dealing with a murderer would be to dump a pail of water on him and make the audience laugh. Then it'd give him a prize. No, this religion will accentuate the positive. It'll concentrate on returning good for good."

"We can threaten evil for evil," Frayne said. "The bad people won't complain if we don't deliver. As for the TV show approach—do we actually give merchandise?"

"Certainly. That's the appeal of the thing. The MC says, 'Mrs. Homer Popalwitz, here is your reward for devoting twenty-seven years of your life to caring for your dying mother.' And the curtain goes up dramatically on a three-day vacation in Rio."

"I like it. We can give cash when appropriate, but we'll concentrate on merchandise or package vacations or whatever reward seems most suitable. We'll have to have Smith's approval before we go any further."

"He'll love it," Naida said. "He's such a nice old man."

Smith loved it. Frayne told him, "We've worked out a religion for you. You're going to give people presents for being good—not just at Christmas, but all through the year. Is that what you want?"

Smith nodded happily.

Prockly was horrified. "It'll cost a fortune!"

"No, sir, it won't," Frayne told him. "A TV giveaway show doesn't pay off the entire studio audience—just three or four contestants. A giveaway religion wouldn't have to reward the entire congregation—just a few meritorious members at each meeting. Also, some of the rewards can be quite minor—a new pair of eye lenses, a pair of orthopedic shoes—and such relatively inexpensive things can be splendid rewards to a deserving person genuinely in need of them. And we can select our recipients so the rewards won't exceed a reasonable weekly budget."

Prockly thought for a moment. "Well—he *is* the PR Board winner, and if this is what he wants—get up an estimate of the capital outlay required to get the thing started, plus a weekly budget, and I'll ask the Governors how long they're willing to keep it going."

"We can count on a little income from the religion," Frayne said.

"How?" Prockly demanded.

"An offering usually is taken at a religious service."

"Well—maybe. But let's not count on very much."

Frayne went back to his office and brooded over his next problem, which was Alton Smith. With his revamped appearance, and in the robes Koten designed for him, Smith was a genuinely impressive religious figure—until he opened his mouth. Neither elocutionists nor a throat doctor had been able to do anything about his squeaky voice.

Frayne called in Harnon. "Smith has got to talk," he told him. "This religion will be his personal property, and it would spoil all his fun if he had to stand around and watch someone else perform. We can hire an assistant minister to do the sermons and keep the service going, but at an absolute minimum Smith should hand out the gifts himself and bless the congregation personally. Take a throat mike, and have him whisper, or purr, or murmur, or speak softly, or anything else you can think of, until he comes up with something that can be amplified into a respectable voice."

Charles Jaffner exclaimed, "They're really going to base the religion on Santa Claus?"

"Santa Claus and TV giveaway shows," Benjamin Franklin said. "When do we blow the whistle?"

"Not until they get established and make suckers of a lot of people."

Edmund Cahill nodded wisely. "It's called, 'giving them enough rope.'"

Frayne found a dilapidated, unused theater in a rundown, virtually abandoned shopping center—a victim of FHD, the Free Home Delivery craze.

He took Smith to see it. "The available churches are much too small," he said. "This can seat a thousand, which is too many, but at least you can grow without having to move. You won't get any limousine traffic in this neighborhood. There isn't even a landing area, though we could convert part of the parking lot if there was a need for one, but not many of your followers will be flying in. You'll get them from that housing development across the way, and those apartments and condominiums—even the high-rises, which probably have a lot of welfare cases. Satisfactory?"

Smith said softly, "Oh, yes. Very satisfactory." He spoke without squeaks. Harnon had taught him to speak softly into a microphone, and now he used his microphone voice all the time. When amplified it sounded odd but strangely impressive.

Prockly drew the line at buying the theater for Smith, but they were able to arrange a lease with very favorable options for long-term renewal or purchase. The owners knew that no one else was likely to want it.

"We'll pay the lease out," Prockly said. "That gives Smith's religion a rent-free headquarters for a year, and you can include living quarters for him in the remodeling. In addition, we'll furnish enough money for overhead, including a reasonable allowance for those gifts, for three months. After that he's on his own. That's the Governors' final decision."

"What about the choir?" Frayne asked. "And an organist? And an assistant minister to read the ritual and sermons?"

"They're included in the overhead. Three months—but the allowance is for ordinary church singers, not imports from Old Lincoln Center. Any money that comes in as an offering is Smith's. He can use it to run a fancier show, or for overhead beyond the three months, or he can call it his salary. Does this sound satisfactory?"

"I'm sure he'll have an enjoyable three months," Frayne said.

They hired an assistant minister, a middle-aged, out-of-work actor named Harvey Borne, who had a beautifully resonant speaking voice. With Smith looking on in his usual gentle, friendly fashion, the four of them—Frayne, Harnon, Naida Ainsley, and Borne—set about working out the practical application of the new religion's doctrine. The first thing they did was throw out the survey on new names for god and tie their doctrine firmly to the Christian Bible.

"Why should we go to all the trouble of making up sermons," Borne asked, "when the Bible has a million sermons ready to use?"

They seemed to be making progress at last, so Frayne returned to the problem of budget estimates. When next he looked in on them, he found them gathered about a massive photo of the old theater's crumbling marquee. The sign, TABERNACLE OF THE

BLESSED, had been painted into the photograph across the top of both faces of the marquee, and Harnon was fitting biblical texts into the remaining space. *Come, ye blessed of my Father, inherit the kingdom prepared for you from the foundation of the world.*

Frayne said distastefully, "A church with a marquee?"

"If a theater can have a marquee, a church can have a marquee," Harnon said cheerfully. "They're both offering an evening's entertainment. And doesn't the Bible say something about not hiding your light under a bushel?" He added another text, *The righteous shall inherit the earth.* And, below it, *He shall reward every man according to his works.*

"The architect's plans call for tearing it off," Frayne said. "It'll be replaced with a Gothic-type entrance. Something with dignity."

"There's been a change," Harnon said. "Smith likes it this way, so they're going to repair it and leave it on. Anyway, with Santa Claus and TV shows for a model, we couldn't be dignified if we wanted to. This religion's going to be exuberant and happy, and the hell with dignity. Right, Altie?"

Smith beamed at him. "Right, Ronnie." He proclaimed in his new, hushed voice, "Happy—that's the way we want it. People enjoying getting presents."

The new assistant minister gave Smith a grin and a wink. Borne was a hearty man, generously proportioned—Frayne suspected that he was out of work because of the limited availability of roles for fat men—and he possessed an infectious, booming laugh. "Right on, Altie. Make it a happy show with lots of action, and we'll have a record run."

"Audience-participation action," Harnon put in.

"Right on," Borne said. "This stuff sends me—takes me back to my childhood. Mother made me go to Sunday school, and I hated it. Now the stuff sends me." He picked up a sheet of paper and read oracularly. " 'I was hungry, and you gave me meat. I was thirsty, and you gave me drink. I was a stranger, and you took me in.' Solid! I never thought of it that way when I was a kid, but it's a promise. Churches been making that promise for centuries, and when anyone wonders why they don't pay off, they make noises about what a wonderful thing death is. Well—life is much more wonderful, and a religion that rewards its followers in life has got to be a sensation." He read again, " 'Whatsoever good things any man doeth, the same shall he receive of the Lord.' See? Nothing there about being dead. It says you do good, you have good done to you, period. A religion that won't pay off until you die is like a policy in a life insurance company that may or may not be bankrupt—and you can't find out which it is until your claim is filed." He leaned over and patted Smith on the back. "You've got a great idea there, Altie, and we'll make it a great show."

Smith beamed happily.

"Better save your sermons for the congregation," Frayne said.

Frayne put Naida Ainsley to work on a public-relations campaign. She hired a dozen college students who thought they were taking a public-opinion survey, but their questions were artfully designed to publicize Smith's church. "Have you heard about the new church in the Golden Glow Shopping Center, the Tabernacle of the Blessed? Its doctrine is that God will reward people in this life for the good they do in this life. What do you think of that? Do you know a really good person who's down on his luck and deserves to be rewarded now?" And so on, through a long list of questions.

While the students were publicizing the church, Naida screened the names of the unfortunates that they collected and had them discreetly investigated. At the proper time the most deserving of them could be enticed to church and rewarded.

"Things seem to be going well," Frayne told his staff. "As soon as the remodeling is finished, I think we can—as our new assistant minister likes to put it—get this show on the road."

Prockly overheard him. "And about time," he said.

Outside the converted theater, a special electric sign was in use for the first time. It flashed on and off, SERVICE TONIGHT. Inside, the theater was three-quarters filled—a respectable attendance for the first night of a new religion and a tribute to Naida Ainsley's publicity efforts.

A massive, double-tiered altar had been constructed at the back of the theater's stage, where the motion-picture screen had been. Harvey Borne held forth on the lower level, flanked by choir and organ. On the upper level, Alton Smith performed his ritual, proclaimed his blessings, and inserted an occasional pronouncement that the amplifier caught with marvelous effect. Under the lower altar, at stage level, was a row of curtained compartments where the blessings of a Just God could be kept until their dramatic unveiling.

Harvey Borne's resonant twang filled the theater with the stirring sermon Harnon had written for him. *The Lord will not suffer the soul of the righteous to famish.* And *Love ye your enemies and do good, and lend, hoping for nothing again; and your reward shall be great.* Smith, on his high rostrum, was a kindly, reverential figure, yet awesome in his striking robes, and he rose to underscore Borne's most telling points with murmured contrapuntal commentary.

Then came the climax: The Procession of the Blessed. A stairway unfolded at Smith's feet, and he slowly descended to the stage, proclaiming as he went, "Blessed are the deserving among you, for they shall be rewarded. Blessed are those of you who pray to be deserving, and doubly blessed are those whose prayers are answered. For the Time of the Just God is fulfilled, and He will reward good and punish evil."

The congregation bewilderedly allowed itself to be coaxed into the aisles, where each member was handed a lighted candle.

"For the light of the righteous rejoiceth," Smith proclaimed, "but the candle of the wicked shall be put out."

The members of the congregation, grappling awkwardly with their symbols of righteousness, filled the outer aisles and began to slowly circle the sanctuary, passing below the stage and the massive, sculptured cornucopia at its center that represented an unsubtle embodiment of the Just God's beneficence. Occasionally one of the righteous—a member of the Prockly and Brannot staff planted in the audience to help establish the new church's ritual—mounted to the stage and crossed it, and at the center knelt to receive Smith's blessing.

The balcony was closed to the public for this service, and Frayne and Prockly sat there with two of the Lottery Governors and a sprinkling of Lottery officials and Prockly and Brannot employees. With earphones they were able to monitor the instructions Harnon radioed to Smith. "The small boy with the crutch. He's coming up the outer aisle on your right. That's Timothy Allen. Start your prayer now."

Smith intoned, "O Just God, have you directed here tonight any whose goodness has gone unrewarded? I pray that you have, and that you will guide me to them to bestow on them the blessings that await them here, in the Tabernacle of the Blessed. Where are the unjustly persecuted? Where are the virtuous who have been slandered? Where are the honest who have been victimized? Where are those who labored to help others only to be abandoned in their own time of need? Guide my hand, O God of Justice, so that I can dispense a mite of this Earth's plenty to the unrewarded righteous."

He raised both hands. "Stop!"

The procession came to an uneasy halt. Smith made his way back along the line of curious but bewildered righteous, seemed to hesitate, to peer here and there, and then, under the Just God's guidance, he pounced. He took the candle from a small boy with a crutch and held it aloft.

"Timothy Allen," Smith proclaimed. "The hour of your reward is at hand. On your lame leg have you run errands for those weaker than yourself, you have helped others whenever you could, you have suffered without complaint, you have cheerfully accepted cruel taunts of those more fortunate, you have brightened one small corner of this dark world with your own pure sunshine. *The Lord maketh poor, and maketh rich; he bringeth low, and lifteth up; to the righteous good shall be repaid; According to their deeds, accordingly He will repay; He shall reward every man according to his works.* And to you, Timothy Allen, the most deserving of the righteous, here is the beginning of your good fortune."

Still carrying the candle aloft, Smith helped the crippled child up to the stage and led him to the row of curtained compartments. He paused dramatically, and then he gestured one of the curtains aside. An assistant was at his elbow to wheel out a gleaming autocycle with sidecar. In the future, Timothy Allen would perform his good deeds in style.

The congregation's first stunned reaction was silence. Then—many of those present were poor people from the neighborhood who knew Timothy—it burst into thunderous applause. Smith placed Timothy's candle on a ledge below the altar while two assistants lowered the autocycle from the stage. Wet-faced, tears flowing freely, Timothy started to limp away supported by the cycle, but Harvey Borne, bluff, grinning, was there with a microphone to congratulate him.

"How did he know me?" Timothy's high-pitched voice blurted, and he pointed at Smith, who smiled down on them benignly from the stage.

"A Just God knows you," Borne said, patting him on the head.

A moment later Smith, prompted by Harnon's radio signals, began another blessing.

As the row of candles left by the rewarded righteous lengthened, the congregation became increasingly excited. Some of the gifts were trivial: An old man who scraped together what he could from his pension money to feed birds during cold weather received a fifty-gallon can of birdseed and a pair of binoculars so he could observe his feathered friends more closely, and he left the stage shedding tears of happiness. An elderly couple received hearing aids; another received a television set. A Mrs. Schobetz, who had kept her family of five children together after her husband deserted her and who always had time for a neighbor in need, received a freezer full of food. For a bright teen-aged girl whose hands were paralyzed, there was a voicewriter. A housewife with a large family and a solvent allergy received a portable dishwasher.

The end came on a climax that matched the beginning: Smith, guided by Harnon's radio signals, pounced on a man in a worn pink suit—a man with one arm missing. "Jefferson Calder," Smith murmured. But this time the magic curtain opened on an apparently empty compartment—empty except for a certificate entitling Calder to be fitted with an artificial limb. He left the stage to an avalanche of applause and embraced with his one arm a tearful wife and children. Like Timothy Allen, most of these people knew him: a good man who'd had a tough break but never whined; a man who helped others when he could.

The services concluded triumphantly with the choir rendering a hymn of thanksgiving to the Just God for creating this bountiful Earth.

"Pray," Borne's resonant voice proclaimed, "but ask not for yourself. Ask that the righteous be blessed, whoever and wherever they are, and if you pray for yourself, ask only that God give you the strength to be righteous."

Finally Smith pronounced the benediction and invited everyone to join them on the following night.

The Governors were delighted. Prockly, beaming his satisfaction, came over to congratulate Frayne, but Frayne ignored him. He had grabbed a microphone, and he snarled into it, "What's going on? Services are supposed to be two nights a week—Sunday and Wednesday. Period. That's all the budget allows."

"Smith wants daily services," Harnon's voice answered.

"You should have stopped him."

"How?" Harnon asked. "It's his church. He can hold services whenever he likes."

"He's not getting a penny more than what's allocated, and that covers two services a week."

"We figure that we can spread the money out, now that we're started. Tomorrow's giveaways will be a lot less expensive."

Frayne shrugged. "If that's what Smith wants—what'd the offering amount to?"

"About a thousand bucks."

Frayne whistled. "No wonder he wants daily services!"

Harnon resigned from Prockly and Brannot the next morning. He thought the Tabernacle of the Blessed had a future, and he chose to remain with Smith. Frayne accepted the news indifferently. His part in the launching of Smith's religion was finished. Prockly and Brannot's part was finished except for twelve more weekly checks to cover the estimated overhead. Frayne was assigned to the next lottery drawing, and he found himself looking forward to it. As far as he was concerned, the next PR Board winner could want to be anything at all, as long as it wasn't God.

Edmund Cahill said indignantly, "You mean—Smith refuses to co-operate?"

"He rather enjoys being head of a religion," Franklin said.

"You mean—after all of our work and expense—"

Franklin chuckled. "We have a complete record of everything that's happened, which is all the evidence we need. There's nothing more he can tell us, and if he won't co-operate, that just might make the exposure more effective."

Walner Frayne drew the easiest PR Board assignment of his career: A man who had everything but public recognition. Frayne laid out a campaign that would bring him, one at a time, all of those voluntary jobs fraught with recognition and civic achievement that no one else wanted. It took less than a week to get his subject appointed chairman of the local Community Fund Drive. In a month his campaign was rolling, his subject had received reams of local publicity, and they were ready to move on the state and regional levels.

Then Prockly's formidable visaphone presence summoned Frayne. "Get back here immediately," Prockly said. "We've got a problem. Blake will take over for you."

A chilling premonition smote Frayne. "Smith?"

Prockly nodded. "Smith. You've never seen a problem like this problem is a problem. Meeting this afternoon."

There were four men in the room, and all of them were strangers to Frayne. Prockly introduced them in turn: a plump, florid-looking person with the unlikely name of Benjamin Franklin; Edmund Cahill, a slender, elderly man with a matinee profile; Charles Jaffner, a tall, husky individual and the only one of the group who offered to shake hands; and an anonymous-looking character named John Ferguson.

"This is Walner Frayne," Prockly said. He added sadistically, "He's the one that did it." Once again Prockly had the air of looking for a scapegoat. He turned to Ferguson. "Tell him about it."

Ferguson took an envelope from an inside pocket, opened it, and took out some currency: twenty- and fifty-dollar bills. "Forty-eight thousand, seven hundred and fifty dollars' worth of this stuff has turned up," he said. "We have no idea how much of it is in circulation. We've traced most of the forty-eight grand to this Tabernacle

of the Blessed. Some was given away in cash, but most of it was used
to buy the merchandise they give away."

"*Counterfeit?*" Frayne exclaimed.

Ferguson handed the bills to him, and Frayne examined them and
handed them back, shaking his head. "They look genuine to me."

"They are genuine," Ferguson said. "The paper is genuine, the ink
is genuine, the engraving is genuine, and no expert in the world
could find a thing wrong with these bills if it wasn't for one thing."

"What?" Frayne asked feebly.

"The serial numbers. The only thing wrong with these bills is that
they haven't been printed yet."

Frayne goggled at him. Prockly took Frayne's arm and led him
over to the man named Benjamin Franklin. "Tell him about it,"
Prockly said.

"Using the Lottery to establish a phony religion was our idea,"
Franklin said. "We put Smith up to it—rigged the Lottery so he'd
be the PR Board winner. We thought the Lottery was ruining our
economy and we could destroy it by making it look ridiculous. We're
looking ridiculous. Smith's church is ten times the danger to the
economy that the Lottery is. Know how much Smith gave away last
week in money and merchandise?"

Frayne goggled again.

"Just slightly under a million dollars," Franklin said. "He's holding services in shifts, early morning until late at night. He's taken
over the surrounding buildings in that old shopping center and he's
going to use them as extensions to his church. We've exerted every
possible influence and pressure to keep him out of the newscasts, but
word is spreading anyway. I understand he's had people come from
as far away as Maine and Indiana to attend his services. Relatives
wrote to them about him. If he continues to expand at his present
rate, by the end of the year he'll be holding services in a hundred-
thousand-seat stadium and his giveaways will top the national
budget. We've got to stop him."

"But where does he get the money?" Frayne demanded.

"That's what the Secret Service would like to know," Prockly said.
"Smith says a Just God will provide. Harnon is the treasurer, and he
says he doesn't know. Smith tells him what's needed in presents for
the next day, and Harnon says they don't have enough money, and
Smith tells him to use the offering. And the offering always has
enough. People toss it into that big cornucopia while they're walking
around with candles, and Harnon wants us to think that they tossed
in almost a million dollars last week. That moth-eaten crowd

wouldn't have a million spare dollars in a hundred thousand years and wouldn't give it away if it did."

"I don't know about Just Gods," Ferguson said grimly, from the other side of the room, "but if one ever shows up, I'm betting he won't come as a counterfeiter."

"Harnon says he thought of that," Prockly said. "He was worried because there were so many new bills in the offering, but the bank assured him that they were genuine. Smith says a Just God's money has to be genuine."

"Except for serial numbers," Ferguson muttered.

The door opened, and Ron Harnon entered. "Smith and Borne are on their way," he said. "I hurried ahead of them because there's something I want you to know."

"Good," Prockly said. "There are several things we'd like to know. I've been telling Frayne how a Just God rewards his faithful with counterfeit money."

"Listen." Harnon's face was pale, his manner intensely serious. "We had a system for the giveaways. We found out about deserving people and got them to church. They'd be pointed out to me, and I'd keep an eye on them, and when one approached the altar during the procession I'd tip Smith off and describe the person, and Smith would go into his spiel, and the Just God would guide him to the righteous. That went on for a couple of weeks. No slipups. Then one evening Smith walked right past the woman we'd picked for a washing machine and gave it to someone else. I thought we'd blown the show until it turned out that the woman he picked was more deserving. It went on that way—most of the time he passed up the people we'd investigated and made his own choices, and his choices always were better. When we asked him, he'd say a Just God was guiding him to the righteous. So we stopped the investigations. Now Smith tells us what to buy for the next day—he knows who's going to be there and what he wants to give them. And the money for what he wants us to buy is always in the offering. If a Just God isn't responsible, who is?"

Franklin muttered, "It's a slicker operation than we thought. Someone's tipping him off."

"It couldn't be done without my knowing about it," Harnon said fervently. Then he smiled. "Unless, of course, a Just God *is* telling him what to do."

Prockly roared, "Do you mean to tell me you believe—"

Alton Smith entered, followed by Harvey Borne.

"Peace, brothers," Borne said, smiling benignly.

Frayne was staring at Alton Smith. He was not the same little man whom Prockly and Brannot had costumed, bewigged, and chased to dentist and elocutionist. He had grown in confidence and inner stature. He had a sense of purpose and the aura of leadership. When he smiled, he was no longer the nonentity trying to be agreeable. He had the smile of a man confident that others would agree with him.

As he positioned himself in the center of the room with a swirl of robes, Prockly demanded, "Where are you getting the money?"

Smith smiled and did not answer.

Borne planted himself beside Smith, towering over him protectively. "Look here, you," he said to Prockly. "Man has been worshiping the One God of Judaism and Christianity for thousands of years, and the more he proclaims his beliefs, the less faith he has in them. Without the essential inner faith, he believes and expects nothing, and God gives him nothing. But the Bible proclaims the message, over and over, for any man who has the faith to believe: *The righteous shall inherit the earth. The desire of the righteous shall be granted. To the righteous, good shall be repaid. He that putteth his trust in the Lord shall be made fat. Whatsoever good things any man doeth, the same shall he receive of the Lord."*

Borne smacked his hands together. "Over and over the Bible brings that message. And what have our hypocritical churches talked about down through the centuries? Purgatory and indulgences and heaven and rewards after death. They have not had the inner faith that enables them to believe what the Word of God clearly tells them—that He is a Just God, and He will reward the righteous— now! But God also said, 'Cast not away therefore your confidence, which hath great recompense of reward.' And He said, 'Ye have need of patience, that, after ye have done the will of God, ye might receive the promise.' At the Tabernacle of the Blessed, my brethren, we have the faith in a Just God, the inner faith. And after all these squandered centuries, the Just God is so pleased to find a community with faith and confidence that He rewards our righteousness lavishly and does not deign to test our patience. Join us, my brethren. Join us in good faith, and if you possess righteousness, it will be rewarded."

Smith gestured with a dramatic sweep of his robes. Borne broke off and turned to him respectfully.

Smith's soft voice sounded thunderous in that hushed room. "There is one Just God, and Alton Smith is His prophet."

He strode toward the exit, an erect, awesome figure, and Borne and Harnon followed him.

Franklin turned angrily on Ferguson. "Haven't you got enough to arrest him?"

"To arrest him, maybe, but we'd never get a conviction. A minister can't be held responsible if someone puts counterfeit money in the offering. And he can't be held responsible for spending it if his bank tells him it isn't counterfeit."

"We've got to close him down," Franklin said. "If nothing else, he's certainly a public nuisance. Let's get down there right now. I'll bring the police commissioner with me. We'll find something to base a charge on."

The four of them—Ferguson, Franklin, Cahill, and Jaffner—rushed away. Prockly dropped into a chair and sat there for a moment, lost in thought. "What do you think?" he asked finally.

"I don't know what to think," Frayne said.

"Pretty obvious, isn't it? Those three were going to use Smith to wreck the Lottery by making it look ridiculous. The Lottery Governors found out, and they used Smith to make Franklin and his friends look ridiculous. There've been some pointed questions about what happens to all the Lottery money. A lot of it probably went into a nice nest egg for emergencies like this."

"That's possible," Frayne agreed, "but the Governors wouldn't have that nest egg in bills that haven't been printed yet."

"All they'd have to do is buy a few people at the mint."

They faced each other doubtfully. "This doesn't concern us," Prockly said, after a moment's thought. "Prockly and Brannot had a contract, and the Governors approved everything we did. All the same, I think we ought to go down there and see what happens. And I think we ought to notify the Governors. If they're backing Smith, it'll show them we're on our toes. If they aren't, they'll certainly want to know what's going on."

The milling overflow of Smith's congregation completely surrounded the Tabernacle of the Blessed, and Prockly and Frayne could not get near the place. As they stood looking helplessly at the patiently churning mass of humanity, Harnon appeared beside them. "Smith said you'd be coming," he told them and matter-of-factly turned them over to a pair of burly attendants, who elbowed a way through the crowd for them. At the entrance, an usher greeted them by name and showed them to reserved seats. Franklin, Ferguson, and associates already were seated, along with the police commissioner. Looking about him, Frayne recognized two of the Lottery Governors. The service had begun.

Smith stood in his high pulpit, arms outstretched. They had altered the lighting, or perhaps it was Frayne's imagination that a misty cloud of brightness encircled him. Borne's resonant voice made

G 35

timeless music of the Bible's eternal message: *Thus saith the Lord God, I will even deal with thee as thou hast done. I shall reward every man according to his works. Whatever good things any man doeth, the same shall he receive of the Lord.*

And then, as Smith slowly descended to the stage, the Procession of the Blessed began. *The light of the righteous rejoiceth: but the lamp of the wicked shall be put out.*

The congregation eagerly pressed toward the outer aisles, where attendants were passing out the candles. Watching, Frayne felt strangely moved. A Just God—

He blinked his amazement, for Franklin, Ferguson, the police commissioner, Cahill, Jaffner—even the two Lottery Governors—all of them were meekly moving in the procession, heads bowed, nursing their flickering candles as though their lives depended on keeping them lit. Frayne turned to point them out to Prockly, but Prockly already was on his way to the aisle.

Frayne took another look at Alton Smith, the luminous prophet of the Just God, and then he moved toward the aisle himself, hurrying to catch up with the procession.